FLIERS

Book 1

Laura Mae

Fliers by Laura Mae

Edited by Sarah Jane Day

Cover by Angie Alaya

www.lauramaeauthor.com

This is a work of fiction. Names, characters, businesses, places, events, locales, and incidents are either the products of the author's imagination or used in a fictitious manner. Any resemblance to actual persons, living or dead, or actual events is purely coincidental

First Edition

ISBN: 9781645162230

I am dedicating this book to my family, because family
is the most important thing in the world.
Marti, Larry, Summah Lummah and Scooter.

Love you guys.

Chapter One

With no control of anything going on, Sydona Wilder watched from the closet as men in white coats entered her home. The look on her parents' faces burned into her memory. Her mother offered them coffee, but only as a standard gesture. One of the white coats sat stiffly on the couch with a blank expression while the other poked around the house. Her father grew impatient because he knew why they were there. Her father and the men had only said two things to each other before the men grabbed him. Sydona shook at the scene happening before her eyes. As she covered her wet, red eyes with her hair, her mother pulled her out of the closet.

"Grab Raoul. Now." Her mother kissed her forehead and pushed her out the back-patio door. Sydona stumbled but kept going, wiping her tears as she ran across the backyard. Approaching the oak tree, she called for her fairy, Raoul, who appeared within seconds. Evelyn joined them shortly after and shoved a green tote bag into Sydona's arms.

"Take him and run. Run as far as you can, Syd! Don't worry about us; we'll be fine. I need you to remember this. Don't trust anyone. Raoul is the only one you can trust now. Don't let them take you. You're my special girl..." Evelyn choked back tears. She grabbed Sydona's face with both hands, and Sydona memorized her mother's eyes, fearing that she may never see them again.

A rooster call forced Sydona's purple eyes to open, relieving her of the painful reoccurring dream. Trying her best not to dwell, she stretched her arms up high and let out a big yawn. She looked out the window as the sun peeked above the nearby treetops. A loud snore from a tiny, red-winged fairy asleep on the windowsill disrupted the peaceful scene, but it just made her smile. She then grabbed a golden frame on her night stand that pictured a young couple in a black and white photo from the early thirties. The man held the woman around the waist, and she had a hand on her extended, round belly. Sydona outlined her young mother's face with her index finger and gave the photo a quick peck before setting it back down.

Going about her normal morning, she headed down the creaky stairwell to the kitchen, grabbed her wicker basket, and strolled out the back door to her luscious garden. It was ripe with carrots, cucumbers, radishes, broccoli, and cauliflower. She set her basket down next to the carrots and radishes and bent down to start digging them up. Reaching to her side, she pulled out a sharp, small blade with inscriptions that read *Borba i amor bez strah,* and it made her smile. Written in the ancient language of the fairies, it would always have a special meaning in her heart.

Once she finished in the garden, she headed behind her great blue, two story home. Bright green vines decorated the white columns that held up the wrap around porch and even covered some of the windows on the second floor. Popping inside a small wooden shed on the west side of the house, she scooped up some chicken feed from a large plastic container and opened the gate to greet six hens and one mighty rooster. Using one hand to hold the food and the other to fan it out amongst the clutter of chickens, she did her best not to step on any of them as they always seemed to get under her feet. Soon, a fleet of fairies that lived in the giant oak tree a few feet away from the garden came to her aid. One of the fairies, sporting red see-through wings a smidge smaller than his sixteen centimeter self, was Sydona's best friend, Raoul. He wouldn't help feed the chickens so much as jokingly boss his family members around and sit to chat with Sydona. Raoul was very proud of his thick brown hair that he always styled with a bit of tree sap and was afraid running around with the chickens would mess it up too much. As the fairies finished feeding the birds, she took the opportunity to gather up the eggs from the coop that she handmade for them.

Sydona wiped her hands off on her worn blue jeans, grabbed her basket full of vegetables along with the eggs, and went back inside the house to wash up. She set the food down on a small space she cleared off on the counter and began to store everything in containers to put in the fridge. While washing her hands, she looked outside and realized it was around 8 a.m. With help from the fairies over the years, she learned to keep in touch with nature and rarely looked at the clock. She yelled out Raoul's name, and he joined her in the kitchen while she gathered up a worn green tote bag. Strapping it across her body, she then grabbed her keys from the table by the front door. She locked her house up tight with a couple extra pushes on the handle. She squinted at the morning sun on her way over to her red Jeep and placed sunglasses on top of her head.

With a sputter from the engine and a heavy sigh, she backed down the long dirt driveway that wound for a quarter of a mile before meeting the paved country road to the city. The drive was long, but she always had the company of Raoul and her favorite radio station that played classical music. She always dreaded getting to the city because of all the traffic and the constant honking of horns in every direction. Only five minutes in standing traffic and Sydona's eyes would flash green with frustration, but it always made Raoul laugh.

"Might be a good time to wear your sunglasses, Syd," Raoul said, snickering in the passenger's seat with his legs sprawled out.

Sydona agreed and tried not to laugh as she placed the dark concealing glasses on her pale face. Once the traffic finally let up, she drove down a less congested part of town and found a parking spot on the side of the road. Throwing her bag back over her shoulder, Sydona opened a gap in the top, and Raoul routinely dove inside. Walking down the familiar sidewalk, she nodded her head toward a large man sitting on a stool in front of a modest newspaper stand.

"Ey there Syd, how we doin' today?" the man asked.

Sydona smiled. "I'm great Jim, how about you?" she asked as she read the front pages of some magazines full of celebrities she had never heard of.

"Still here, ain't I?" he chuckled, "What's you gettin' today?"

"Oh, I think just this one." She handed him a newspaper called the *Chicago Tribune* and grabbed some change out of her pocket.

"Thank yous. You have a good day, miss Sydona, a'ight?"

"You too, Jimmy. Stay cool," Sydona said and waved her hand as she moved along.

Walking her normal path to the local farmers market a few blocks away, she observed the city scene. She held her head high and tried to focus on more familiar sounds like birds and the wind blowing through the trees stuck in the concrete sidewalk instead of the car honks, beepers, and people yelling at each other. She did enjoy looking in store windows that had clothes she could only dream of owning, though they weren't practical like her jeans that needed to have pockets for supplies or boots to support her ankles for running. Peering down at her own steel-toed brown boots she put on that morning, she grinned with satisfaction. Catching her reflection, she got a second look at her simple white tank-top that fitted her perfectly. Loose clothes could be grabbed. This theory failed when it came to her dirty blonde hair, however, as it reached down past the middle of her back. She noticed she had dirt on her fair white-skinned cheek. She wiped it away swiftly and continued on her way.

Finally, she arrived in a quieter part of the city filled with local farmers lined up on either side with hand painted signs. She always stopped at a fruit stand with some usual faces smiling from behind the wooden frame with mangos, limes, and cantaloupes hanging in baskets.

"Hey, Syd!" a kid yelled from behind the stand as she approached. He ran up to her and gave her a big hug, squeezing the tote that Raoul was in. Sydona heard Raoul make a grunting sound and quickly removed the kid off her tote.

Sydona grabbed his shoulders. "Joseph! How are ya, buddy?"

A boy about seven years old with shaggy short brown hair and little freckles on his face beamed up at her. "Goood… How are you doing?"

"I'm wonderful! How's school going?" Sydona asked Joseph while looking up at a dark brunette woman with her hair pulled back in a messy ponytail. She smiled brightly and rolled up her sleeves.

"Good. I got lotsa homework though," Joseph said.

"Oh," Sydona laughed, "I do not miss those days!" She glanced up at his mother, Annie, who laughed with her and nodded in agreement.

"So, how's the garden doing?" Annie asked.

"It's good. You know, water, dig, water, dig," she said while examining the fruit for spots.

Annie nodded. "Well, you know, I'm still recovering from that storm we had last week. How did you recover so quickly?" she asked.

Sydona paused for a second. When the storm hit, the fairies helped clean up and get everything back in order. What took days for most only took mere hours with the help of her fairy friends. Of course, no one could know about the fairies, and Sydona hated to arouse suspicion. She quickly came up with an excuse. "Oh, I uh, had help. Had some family in town at the time," she answered while avoiding eye contact and inspecting her items.

"Oh," Annie said, "Well, I would've come and helped you out."

"Aw, thank you, but it's fine now," she said, grabbing her last kiwi. "I appreciate it, though."

Annie placed Sydona's kiwis in a bag. "Yeah, not a problem." She changed the subject. "You know, I've always wondered something. How come you can grow vegetables, but you always come here to buy fruit? Why don't you just grow fruit trees?"

"Well..." she confessed. "I'm pretty sure I have bugs or something. I've tried everything to get rid of them, but it seems like nothing works." The real reason was because her fairies were fruit fanatics, and when the fruit became ripe, by morning it would all be devoured.

Raoul blurted out a muffled laugh inside her bag that she hoped she could only hear.

"Alright, it's gonna be five fifty," Annie said, and Sydona handed over the cash.

"Well, I'll see you in a few days," Sydona said to Annie and peered over at Joseph. "You behave now, and stay out of trouble, okay?" She grabbed his shoulder and grinned.

"I will..." Joseph answered, swaying back and forth bashfully on the balls of his feet. "You too!"

Sydona laughed as she left the stand. She continued to stroll down the street to another sidewalk full of businessmen and people who always seemed to be in a hurry. She walked past a wall that a had a huge graffiti symbol of a wing outline surrounded by a circle. She walked this street frequently and had never seen it before. Thinking it might be fresh, she furrowed her brow in curiousness but continued on her way to the car.

They finally returned home, and the sunset never looked more beautiful to her as it burst through her kitchen windows. She grabbed her bag full of fruit, walked into her messy kitchen, and spread it out on the countertop. Wandering over to the living room, she opened up an old recipe book with a fruit cake on the front cover. She then began to cut the apples, mangos, pineapples and kiwis into little pieces and put them into a cake mix. She prepared to bake the dessert, placed it in the oven, and set the kitchen timer.

Once she completed her baking, she boxed the cake up and headed outside where the fireflies began to shine. The insects made the backyard sparkle as the sun dove behind the trees. Sydona helped the countless number of fairies to build a bonfire that reached easily ten feet high. She took a seat on a wooden stump among the fairies, and they all patiently waited for something to begin. Soon, a fairy with a large headdress and robes joined the rest of the party, and everyone hushed.

"Welcome, welcome, welcome one and all!" He had a much deeper voice than other male fairies. He floated proudly in front of the fairy tree that was decorated in white lights and shiny objects as he addressed the crowd. "Tonight! Tonight is a big night for one of our little fairies, Jubilee! On this day, four years ago, she was birthed onto this great planet. The spirits have blessed me, Shaman Faro, to grant this beautiful young darling her dust to make her fly! This tradition as most of you know has come to be known as our Vila Prah, or--VIP as some youngsters have modernized it. However, the acronym deems valid as

Jubilee is a very important person tonight. At this time, please donate some of your own dust to her pedestal in which she will sleep on tonight. Your donations are very helpful, and the more of you who donate, the more the Spirits will bless us in great ways! Alright, enough chit chat! Let's all do what we do best before the ceremony. Let's party!"

Four fairies flew out from behind the tree carrying a little fairy with yellow wings and made their way to the center. Jubilee wore a lace pink dress made by her grandmother and a flower hat made by her mother. Music started up, followed by cheering and dancing. Sydona opened up her box to reveal the fruit cake, and it was the hit of the night. It always surprised her how much an average fairy could consume. VIP was her favorite day to look forward to because it was her way of rewarding everyone for their hard work in helping her with the chickens and storms. It was also a chance for her to socialize and get to know more of Raoul's family. They were always growing, and it was hard for her to keep up sometimes. Seeing young fairies get their 'wings' was moving for her, and she loved seeing the looks on their faces when they could finally fly. Jubilee had been gabbing on about it for the past month to Raoul, and Sydona could tell he was getting sick of it.

After a few hours, the party came to an end, and it was time for the Vila Prah to commence. Everyone waved at Jubilee as she entered a hole in the tree that had her wooden pedestal covered in fairy dust. Shaman Faro closed off the area with a sheet as he performed his ritual. Sydona took her box of cake crumbs and headed back to the house, but not before searching for Raoul. She found him surrounded by three giggly fairies.

"I'm heading to bed. Are you coming?" Sydona asked with a yawn.

Raoul kissed a fair skinned, blue-winged fairy on her dainty hand as she blushed tomato red. "In a minute, Syd."

Sydona sighed and headed up the stairs to get ready for bed. Raoul flew up shortly after to his own little bed on the windowsill that overlooked the backyard to search for the fairy he kissed goodnight.

"Hey, that was a great party, Raoul! I'm happy for Jubilee. She'll be able to follow you anywhere now!" Sydona said sarcastically.

Raoul ignored her tone and had a silly grin on his face from the blue-winged fairy. "Yes, it was…"

"Goodnight, buddy," she said as she turned off the lantern sitting on her side table and pulled a handmade quilt over herself.

"Sweet dreams, Syd," Raoul answered as he slipped into his tiny bed.

The next morning, the trusty rooster called out again, and the sun blinded her barely opened eyes. She threw her feather pillow over her head and tried to get a few more minutes of sleep from a late night of partying. After a few more calls from the rooster, she finally got out of bed. She began her day with brushing her teeth while trying to get dressed at the same time. She rummaged through her messy closet for a white tank top and her favorite one shouldered red top. Struggling to fit her shirt over her toothbrush, she got toothpaste residue on her hair, forcing her to put it up in a ponytail. Once she got situated with dressing herself, she headed to the shed to feed the chickens. As she reached down to scoop out the corn, she found it was almost empty, and she frowned. Shaking her head in confusion, she went to look for Raoul. Hiking back up through the chicken pen as they pecked at her feet, she apologized and closed the gate. As she entered the back door, she spotted Raoul on the counter munching on a mango like a ravenous hyena.

"Morning," Raoul said with his mouth full.

"Wasting no time eating, I see," she said, grabbing an orange and digging her nail into the peel.

"It was just staring at me." He wiped his mouth of mango juices.

She smirked. "I'm sure it was, Raoul," she said and popped an orange slice in her mouth. "Oh, are you coming to the city with me today?" Sydona threw her peels away.

"We just went yesterday! What do we need to go back for?" Raoul paused his eating.

"I'm glad you asked! On my way out to the chicken coop this morning I could have sworn there was more feed in there, and now, there's barely a handful."

Raoul blushed and turned away from her with eyes darting in every direction.

"Do you know anything about this?" Sydona asked and crossed her arms with a stern but not entirely serious face.

"Noooo…"

Sydona tapped her boot quickly without saying a word.

Raoul threw his hands up. "Fine! A bunch of us were a little buzzed on fermented fruit and got into the chicken coop…"

"What--did you eat it?"

"Ew no!" Raoul made a sour face and stuck his tongue out. "We… got the idea if we took enough corn and planted it, you could grow corn! We were trying to help!"

Sydona's face lightened, and she burst out laughing. "Whose brilliant idea was this?"

Raoul slumped over with his wings low. "Mine…"

"Well, congrats! Now we need to go back into town and get more," Sydona said and gathered up her things for the trip back to the city.

Raoul put down the rest of mango and lazily flew to the table at the front door, waiting for Sydona.

"Bye, chick chicks! We'll have some more food for you when we get back!" Sydona yelled throughout the house, not caring that she was talking to chickens or that they couldn't hear her at all.

"Alright, ready bud?" she asked Raoul as they hopped inside the Jeep.

"I guess," Raoul said and flopped his head on the back of the seat with a sigh.

"I know you hate getting in my bag when we go to town, but maybe you should've thought about that before you stole all the chickens' food," Sydona said while she started backing down the driveway.

"We were trying to help!" Raoul argued and slumped his head down.

"No, you were showing off to that blue-winged girl!" Sydona spat back and laughed.

Raoul didn't respond, but his face was suddenly pink, which made her laugh harder.

As they arrived to town and got through the traffic, she was able to park down the same street as they normally did. They went through their normal routine of Raoul hiding in her bag and Sydona wearing her sunglasses as she stepped out of her Jeep. She headed straight to the farmers market and bought a twenty-pound bag of feed that she lunged over her shoulder. As she looked around the rest of the stands, she didn't see Annie or Joseph there. Normally, she never went to the city two days in a row because of the drive. She assumed maybe they were never there during the weekend. Strolling back to the car, Sydona decided to stop by the newspaper stand to see Jim and get the paper.

"Hey Sydona, how you doin' this mornin'? And 'ey, wasn't you just here yestaday?" Jim asked before taking a sip of coffee.

"Hey, yeah," Sydona laughed, "I ran out of food for my chickens."

"I can see that! You need help with that? Looks heavy!" Jim offered instantly.

Sydona grinned. "No, thank you. I got it."

"Suit yaself!" Jim said and shrugged, moving back over to his stool. He grabbed a paper from a stack on the ground. "Hey, you seen this yet? Some crazy shit, eh?"

"Oh yeah, what happened?" she asked distractedly as she read headlines of pop magazines.

As Jim handed her the *Chicago Tribune*, she dropped the feed on the concrete, almost bursting the seams as she read the headline article of the paper:

New Scientific Camps Set Up For 'Fliers'

OREGON - Scientists from the National Fliers Association (NFA) have started new studies on the human-like species of fliers. They say they have reached a breakthrough in replicating the gene that gives fliers the ability to fly and can soon start modifying it for human use.

"It's really very exciting," said Dr. John Malik, lead scientist of the NFA. "We can soon apply this ability to everyone so that we can further improve life for human and flier alike."

While controversial, Dr. Malik assures the public that the research is for prosperity. "We're not playing God, as some groups would have you believe. With this ability, we can begin to do things never thought possible. Building infrastructure, accessing places previously inaccessible–the possibilities are endless."

Because fliers are rare, the NFA has encouraged fliers around the world to come forward to be a part of the study and will be compensated for their contribution. Dr. Malik also encourages friends and neighbors of fliers to contact the NFA. "That way, we can personally pay them a visit to inform them of this exciting opportunity to be a part of something bigger..."

Sydona stopped reading. Her palms sweat, her heart raced, and she found it hard to breathe. She mumbled to herself, *"It's happening again...."*

Chapter Two

"Yo' Syd, you okay?" Jim asked.

Her hands shook like a leaf, and she couldn't find any words.

"Sydona? What's wrong?" Jim asked again.

All reality as she knew it seemed fictional now. She looked at Jim as nothing more than a stranger. Could he be part of the NFA? Does he know about her? Jim kept speaking to her, but for some reason, she couldn't hear anything he said. Her heart was beating out of her chest, and she suddenly felt suffocated, like more people had populated around her from out of nowhere. Whispers from all the people clogged up her thoughts, she felt trapped, and the Earth felt like it rotated at an accelerated speed. She rolled the paper up, heaved the food over her shoulder, and took off running without saying a word.

Jim yelled after her, but she was so far gone, she couldn't hear him anymore.

She hurled the feed in the backseat of her car and then did the same with her tote bag, unaware that Raoul was still inside. He yelled as it hit the seat.

"Sorry, Raoul..." she apologized and rubbed her face nervously, hoping the motion would turn back time. Or if she rubbed her head long enough, she would somehow erase the article from her mind.

Raoul shimmied out of her bag, smoothed out his shirt and hair, and grabbed the paper she had thrown on the seat.

"What's this?" He used his whole body to flatten it out and read it to himself. His eyes widened and flew straight up in shock.

"This can't be true! It has to be one of those fake newspapers, you know, where they say that a monkey went into space! Like that could *ever* happen," he laughed loudly. "I wouldn't worry about it, Syd."

Sydona stared ahead, ignoring his joke. "No--" she said blankly, "this isn't a fake paper. It's very real."

She gripped the top of the steering wheel and dropped her head on top of her hands. Raoul's wings laid flat to his body, and he flopped down on top of the paper, staring at the name 'John Malik'. Silence overcame the car.

She sat back up with a red face and watery, bloodshot eyes and spoke softly. "I can't believe this is happening again..."

Sydona blinked her eyes clear of tears and wiped her face of sweat. She had to clear her head and think of a plan, but first she needed to go home. Taking a deep breath, she started up her car and drove out of the city as fast as she could. She left the radio off, unable to listen to music with so many thoughts flying through her head. They both sat reserved the entire thirty-minute drive home. Anger began to pulse through her veins and stepping on the gas pedal more seemed to help. It felt like she was in limbo between wanting to speed and get anger out and the fear of getting pulled over. Then, she would really be in trouble. There were a few times Raoul wanted to interject when she went over ninety miles per hour, but he was smart to stay quiet.

The arrival home felt less than happy and more like entering a trap. She felt if she stayed there, it would only be a matter of time before they found her. A sudden image of men in white coats popped in her head, and she imagined them invading her home. It was enough to turn her eyes green, and she slammed her fists on the steering wheel. The camp wasn't as innocent as they were making people think, and she knew it. It needed to be shut down and now.

Shutting the car off that she parked on the lawn, she quickly hauled the bag of feed over her shoulder and over to the hungry chickens. Raoul zipped over to the great oak tree and informed everyone of the news. Once Sydona had quickly fed her birds, she listened in on the fairy tree. Most of them were there the day it happened last time, and the tree filled with cries. The elder fairies whispered amongst each other, trying not to upset the little ones. Raoul simply informed them of what the article said, not what happened years ago. It was hard to hide the panic in some of the fairies' voices and actions, and it still upset some of the newborns. Sydona couldn't listen to the heartache anymore and darted inside her house. She grabbed her tote and a black backpack and filled it with clothes, food, and medicine.

"Where are we going, Syd?" Raoul asked immediately as he flew in the back door. Sydona couldn't answer that question right away and was afraid that if she opened her mouth, emotions would take over. She found it easier to keep her lips pursed and focus on grabbing essentials for the long journey ahead.

Raoul floated in one spot in the middle of the kitchen while Sydona continued to grab things. "I can't leave my family. What are they supposed to do?" he yelled as loud as he could.

Sydona blinked, trying to disperse the water that wanted to break free. It blurred her vision, making her double check the items she was grabbing. Her shaky hands didn't help either.

"Sydona?" Raoul asked with a worried tone.

She stopped and took a breath. "I wish I could tell you. I couldn't hear them anymore. It was--too hard."

"Are you making me choose? Between you and my family?" Raoul whispered.

His words made her stomach twist because she thought that she was part of his family. "No, I'm not..."

"So what do I do?" Raoul asked.

Sydona hung her head low. "That's something you need to ask yourself." She paused. "But I'm going to Eagle Lake. And I would love for you to accompany me. But I'm not going to make you come if you don't want to."

It was obvious that Raoul wanted to get angry, but he was so conflicted that he sat and clenched his fists, making his knuckles turn white.

Sydona continued, "I need to do something, Raoul. I mean, do you not realize what this is? It's the same shit they pulled all those years ago. I was--powerless to stop it then. I was just a child. But maybe now that I'm older... I can maybe have a chance."

"Chance to do what?" Raoul asked with anger lingering in his voice.

"Stop it? I don't know. I just know that I need to try. And maybe... Maybe they're there, too," Sydona said.

"You don't really think? Syd, that was... Sixty years ago. They can't be--"

"Why can't they? They're strong. Strongest people I ever knew. They have to be there."

"They would be well into their hundreds now, kid," Raoul whispered, leaning in closer to Sydona.

The two sat reminiscing in the kitchen for several silent moments.

She lowered her voice, "I never knew you to be the pessimistic one, Raoul."

Raoul fluttered his wings. "I'm not... I guess you're right. I bet they are there..." Raoul smiled but then frowned. "I just can't up and leave with my family here."

Sydona lifted her nose and wiped her reddening eyes. "I don't want to make you choose, but I don't think I can do this without you. And I need to think about my family, too."

Just as she gave up on things to say, a certain phrase popped into her head.

"Borba i amor bez strah," Sydona whispered.

Raoul perked up at the familiar phrase he seemed to have forgotten but then sunk his head with even more conflict. Feeling defeated, Sydona picked up her black backpack she filled with things she couldn't fit in the tote and threw them both over her shoulders. Raoul sat looking like a sopping wet butterfly on the countertop, and her stomach twisted. He glanced at her for a second with jaded brown eyes and then back down to the tiled floor. It was the only look she needed to know that he wasn't leaving, and her eyes changed from purple to auburn.

She moped through the house, walking slowly and hoping that Raoul would eventually fly over. Opening the door, she waited for a few minutes and peeked back through the kitchen, but he never came. A heavy sigh left her lungs, and she locked her door shut.

As she sat in her car, stalling on starting it up, she stared at the house. It was eerily quiet. Almost like the birds and creatures felt the tension of the news, too. Sydona eventually started up the Jeep and with a heavy heart, backed down the excruciatingly long driveway. Her heart beat faster with every full rotation of the tires.

"What am I doing?" she said to herself. Nothing about this felt right. Raoul had been with her every minute of her life and leaving him behind weighed heavily on her. Should she have given him more time? It was too big of a decision to make in such a short amount of time. She stopped right at the edge of the driveway, still wavering on leaving alone. With a shake of her head, she grabbed the gearshift and began to put it back in drive

when Raoul came flying up to the car. Her face lit up, and her eyes turned back to normal as he hugged her shoulder.

"You changed your mind?" Sydona grinned.

"I didn't have it decided one way or another. But as I sat there, I thought about you as a child and the look on your face when you had to tell Evelyn goodbye. You had that same look just now, and I couldn't do that to you again," Raoul said.

Sydona smiled from ear to ear, touched by how genuinely nice he was being without being sarcastic.

"Besides, Jubilee would have been driving me bonkers, and I wouldn't be able to escape with you gone," Raoul said.

There he was. She backed the car up and took one last look at her beautiful house before they took off. The lighthearted reunion soon turned quiet as the real reason they were leaving sunk in, and Sydona no longer smiled. Raoul dragged the newspaper back out and read it over again.

"It says here the camp is at Eagle Lake. In Oregon. Do you know how far that is?" Raoul read on the other page where the article continued. He did his best to keep the pages from flying away by stepping on it and forcing it down with his tiny arms.

"Yeah, I think it's about a two day drive..." Sydona answered while maneuvering her head to keep her hair from whipping her in the face. She hoped that her old car would be up for the challenge. She only drove it a couple times a week, and even then, she never had much faith in it. She tried fixing little things herself with manuals she took from the library. She was no professional, but it did the job.

They sat quietly in the vehicle listening to the radio, switching it every time they heard anything about fliers or the NFA. Sydona eventually turned it off. Even the station she listened to her classical music on was constantly interrupted by the new story.

Raoul finally spoke up in the silence. "So, why don't we just fly there? You know we would get there in like a third of the time."

"Don't be silly. You know we can't do that. If anything, right now would be the worst time to fly. It's been decades since I've flown..." She shook her head. "I wish we could, though. I hate this stupid Jeep."

And as if she jinxed herself, the car started to sputter and shake more than she was used to. She groaned and hit the steering wheel before pulling off to the side of the road. Frantically, she seized her backpack from the floor and dug around. After throwing things out and making the car even messier, she found a rag and tools she thought might help. Walking to the front of the Jeep, she propped open the hood and, after examining it for a few minutes, decided nothing seemed wrong with it. The sun beat down on her hard as she wiped her forehead of sweat and then heard a whistle from inside the car. She peered around the hood and saw Raoul standing on top of the steering wheel.

"Did you fix it?" Raoul yelled, his arm shading his face from the unyielding sun.

"No," Sydona said. "I think it's the transmission--not a cheap or quick fix."

She slammed the hood down, went back to the driver's seat, and threw the items onto the passenger's side floor. Sydona didn't know what to do. Finding a car mechanic out there would be nearly impossible and fixing it would cost more money than she could afford. The mechanic would probably find fifteen other problems with it, too, as it had not been serviced in several years.

Sydona waited for a sign, for anything, but there was nothing. Not even a single vehicle drove by in the twenty minutes they sat in the car. Sydona reached over and opened the glove compartment to rummage around for a map. Spreading it out over the seat, she saw that they had been going in the right direction, which was good, but now they needed a way to get there. Hitchhiking was absolutely not in the cards at all, driving was apparently out of the question, and she thought if she stayed in the sun any longer she would melt.

"I guess we're walking…" she announced to Raoul who was using a scrap of paper to fan himself. It was the best option and a less risky one, too. She thought about going somewhere to get gas, but if the car didn't break down here, it would only be a matter of time before it did. Unsure of where they would get faster transportation, she tried staying positive that something would come along. Then, Raoul mentioned they could just fly all the way there.

"Stop it." She sighed, sluggishly grabbed her bags and keys, and began to walk. Raoul flew to her and landed on her shoulder, where he usually went when he was too lazy to fly alongside her.

"Come on, Syd! We're gonna die in this heat! At least if we fly, we can have wind in our faces to dry up the sweat," Raoul said and tugged on a chunk of her ponytail.

Sydona looked around cautiously. They *were* in the middle of nowhere with nothing but abandoned corn fields surrounding them, and not a single car had passed by.

"You need to be my lookout though. If you see a car or a person or plane or a bird! Tell me, okay?" Sydona asked.

"A bird?" Raoul laughed.

Sydona threw her hands up. "I'm just being thorough!"

Raoul had already flown above her head to look out and said to himself, "You're being paranoid--"

"What?" Sydona called up to the little fairy several feet above her.

"Coast is clear!" Raoul held up two tiny thumbs up and flew back down to her.

Her heart and stomach fluttered at the idea that she would be flying again. Her face flushed as she tried to remember what to do, but she still couldn't help smiling. It had been at least thirty years since the last time she flew and could barely remember the last time she did. She laughed thinking about it, wondering if it was when she ran from the cops. Raoul grew impatient as he waited on Sydona to stop spacing off.

She began by sprinting for several feet and, once she picked up a good speed, kicked her left foot off the ground. Soon, she was two, ten, fifteen feet ascended into the sky above the wheat fields. Angling her body slightly forward, she was able to fly faster, and when she leaned back, she went higher into the air. The Jeep no longer looked like a car but a red blur as she soared high above the treetops. Raoul joined her as he trailed red-orange dust behind him. As the wind blew her hair, she closed her eyes, and she thought of the first time that she learned how to fly.

Sydona ran out of the house with a spring in every step and a smile on her face. "Come on mom! Let's go!" she yelled. She took in a big whiff of the autumn leaves littering the yard and exhaled dramatically. The sun was just coming up, but Sydona didn't care. This was the day she looked forward to since she could talk. Her mother walked towards her while putting her dirty blonde hair up in a bun.

"Okay, sweetie. Now stand over there and watch me first," her mother said.

"I already know what to do, mooom!" Sydona whined as she bounced up and down on her feet, looking like she was about to explode. She then noticed a neighborhood kid curiously watching them from his backyard. Sydona waved at him, although she had never met him before.

Her father then joined them, sitting at the patio table with a cup of coffee. "Now Syd, listen to your mother. She'll tell you how to start."

Evelyn began to run across the giant unfenced backyard, kicked her feet, and soon, she was high in the sky. Watching her fly back toward the house and then away again made Sydona's heart swell. After twisting and rolling and doing tricks in the air, Evelyn finally straightened back up and floated back down to earth like a feather.

"Me next!" Sydona ran up to her before she barely had two feet on the ground.

"Okay, come on. I'll hold onto you," her mother giggled.

She grabbed Sydona's hand tightly, and they sprinted off together. Her mom kicked off the ground along with Sydona, and Sydona shut her eyes quickly. When she opened them and looked down at her dad, he looked no bigger than her pinkie finger. Looking down at the neighborhood around them, she saw the kid next door. He pointed in awe at her. She waved back to him again and couldn't contain her laughter. It was nothing she had ever imagined feeling. As light as a feather, she felt she could literally do anything. She had no bounds.

"I'm going to let you go. Are you ready?" her mother asked.

Sydona nodded her head, and Evelyn let go gently but kept her arm outstretched in case she needed to grab her daughter again. But Sydona was on her own and flying perfectly. She tried doing the same tricks as her mother but wasn't very good yet. Her new fairy friend, Raoul, soon joined the fun and flew in circles around her.

"Hey buddy! Look at me! I'm just like you now!" she laughed. They ventured over treetops, houses, buildings, and flew down the street. Sydona waved at anyone she saw, and all they could do was stare and watch her fly away. Some people waved back and some smiled, but most were awestruck. A car came rolling down the street, and Sydona got a bit too close, making the car veer off and hit a fire hydrant. Her mother made her come straight home after that, but Raoul and Sydona couldn't stop laughing about it. The look on the driver's face was priceless.

She wasn't allowed to fly for a while after that, but the experience was worth every second, and she knew she would not soon forget it.

Opening her eyes to the vast scene in front of her, her face wrinkled from a smile she couldn't subdue. She let her hair down from the ponytail and let it play in the wind. The sun did not seem so cruel now but rather warmed the goosebumps that appeared on her arms and legs. She glanced at Raoul who did rolls and used his hands to do a 'wave' motion. She laughed and felt like an innocent kid again, flying for the first time.

Raoul perked up, flew way in front of her, and yelled back, "There's a sign up ahead! Mayfield is ten miles away!"

Chapter Three

It wasn't long until they began to see houses coming into view right outside the small town. Edging closer and closer to the ground, Sydona took an upright position and landed on her two feet. Adjusting her bags more securely on her person, she reached into her tote bag and put her sunglasses back on. Mayfield was a quaint town with the main road looking about the majority of the city with little stores lined up alongside it, all touching each other. There were a few people walking around, but for the most part, it was pretty quiet. It had been a while since Sydona had visited a new town, so she was a bit on edge, although the news of what was going on didn't help. She tiptoed along until she found a lovely little diner that looked fairly empty. Raoul crawled in her green tote to stay out of sight.

A bell rang as she entered. It was littered with red tables and blue booth seats, reminding her of the restaurants she and her parents used to visit. Windows stretched along the entire wall and were painted with flowers and butterflies. She noticed a few people scattered throughout the restaurant, including three men smoking cigarettes at the bar and a young girl in the corner with her nose in a book.

A lady came right up to her with a menu in her hands. "Just you today, darlin'?" she asked in a sweet, high-pitched voice.

"Yep," Sydona said and adjusted her glasses with hands shaking a bit.

The waitress led her to a table near a window and sat her in a seat that was way too large for one person. Sydona ordered a glass of water, and the waitress left the table. Sydona carefully placed her bags to the inner side of the seat and leaned the tote bag so that Raoul wouldn't be suffocated. She made herself comfy on the bouncy blue cushions and caught her breath after the long trip. As she read over the menu, she glanced up occasionally at the other people around. They were all really invested in conversation, and she became less nervous as she realized that no one really cared she was there. She especially liked watching a baby, rejecting all the food his parents gave him and then laughing about it. The young girl alone in the corner reminded her a lot of herself, as she was nose deep in a thick book with her knees up in a booth on the far side of the restaurant. She reminded Sydona of the times where she would sit by herself in diners with a book at that age, usually in the the corner.

A small wall-mounted television resided on the end of the counter and was barely audible. She glanced over at it as she listened to the reporter on the news mention fliers.

'...*the NFA are reporting that many folks are having questions on how to identify these humans. They don't imagine that you would see them flying around your hometown, so here's some helpful tips to help you spot one. Fliers have lavender colored eyes that most of them like to cover up, usually with sunglasses. Look for humans that wear them indoors or in darker public areas. Please be aware that your and their contribution will be greatly rewarded...*"

Her ears tuned out the rest of the story as she veered her eyes down to the small bar. Three gentlemen were also watching it, and one of them stretched his neck over his shoulder and stared intently at her. The man nudged his friend, and then, all three men had their attention on her. Sydona's hands began to shake again, and she redirected her attention back to the menu.

Her heart sank and eyes turned auburn underneath the dark frames. A man walked up to her table wearing a baseball cap, cowboy boots, and tattered clothes. He scratched his scruffy beard and put his dirty hands down next to her. "You s'posed to be someone famous or somethin'?" he asked.

Sydona instantly looked out the window to the right of her and pretended to look at her menu. Her heart slowly began to beat faster as she chose to ignore him.

He leaned in closer to her and flicked his hat up. "You hear me? Why else you be wearin' sunglasses in here?"

Her fists start to wrinkle the edges of the menu, and her eyes grew emerald green as she stayed silent.

"What? Are you deaf or somethin'?" the man yelled, making everyone in the restaurant turn their heads toward her. His friends at the bar were all laughing to each other as their buddy did his best to make a fool of her. Sydona stayed strong, facing the window and ignoring him the best she could. After a long agonizing three minutes of this stranger berating her, he finally removed his hands from the table, and she held the menu normally again. She kept her back turned from the rowdy group as he went back to them but not without hearing some whispers. Eventually turning back around in the booth, Sydona made an effort to watch them out of the corner of her eye. They were all staring at her now and laughing, making the families around them uncomfortable.

After a while, the diner fell silent, and she heard the swing of the door from behind her. Out of the corner of her eye, she saw one of the men at the counter stick his foot out just as the waitress passed by with an oversized tray. It happened so fast that Sydona had zero time to react.

With a gasp from the waitress, the tray slammed into Sydona and knocked the sunglasses right off her face. The dishes crashed to the floor in a brilliant display of coffee, egg yolk, and gravy swirl splattered all over the tiled floor. As she watched them fly off, she glanced up for a quick second to see the man smiling with his yellow and black teeth and looking directly into her eyes. Instantly, Sydona looked away, slammed her eyelids shut, and reached her hand out to grab the sunglasses, unaware of where they landed. But it was too late. Sydona could only stare at the ground under the booth where she saw a hand reaching toward a pair of sunglasses. The thought of looking back up at the man who grabbed them made her eyes turn green, but she dare not look at him for another second. Timidly extending her arm back out to grab the glasses, Sydona continued to focus on the ground.

The man holding the glasses spoke up, "I knew it. Yer a Flier, ain't ya?" He looked her up and down as if he was trying to memorize her face.

Sydona's eyes grew even brighter, and her hand became a tight fist ready for anything he might throw at her.

He leaned in closer to her. "Where ya headed, baby girl?"

When Sydona stared him down without response, he continued. "I know yer not from around here. Small town, Mayfield."

"May I please have my glasses back?" Sydona grumbled.

The man laughed and twirled her glasses around, teasing her like a small child. After a few taunting moments, to her surprise, he dropped the glasses down on the table right in front of her. Without hesitation, she immediately grabbed them and placed them back on her face. The waitress began cleaning up the mess she made while Sydona grabbed her bags, stepped over her, and bolted out of the diner.

"See ya around, baby doll!" She heard him one last time as the swinging door closed.

Fiercely walking away from the diner, she made her way a couple businesses down and hid in the first alley she came to.

She was as paranoid as a fly in a web, noticing every little thing that moved from the wind. But after several minutes of no one walking by on the street, she sat down and let Raoul out.

"What was that all about?" Raoul asked as he climbed out of the tote bag.

"Wish I knew." Sydona leaned her head back to hit the brick wall behind her.

"Did I hear him say he knew you were a flier?" Raoul asked as he landed on Sydona's curled up knees.

"Yeah.. it's like it was set up. He knocked my glasses off only to hand them back to me? I don't understand it," Sydona said as she pushed her hair back between her fingers.

Raoul shook his head, wondering the same thing. "This place isn't safe."

"We need a car. There's no way in hell we can fly anymore. It's too risky," Sydona stated confidently but honestly felt very unsure. They could steal a car like she did when she was in her twenties, but that didn't end up very well. The friends she had were people living under bridges and half-houses. To say the very least, she was easily influenced, and stealing cars was just the tip of the iceberg. She had to admit, she was better off living with chickens and fairies.

"I agree, but where are we going to find one?" Raoul asked, fluttering off Sydona's knee as she stood back up. She didn't answer as she wandered back behind the buildings and began forming a plan in her head. She couldn't risk being seen by that unpredictable man. Walking down the dirty street and thinking of a plan, she faintly heard a noise from behind her. Not footsteps but more like a muttering. Sydona kept her guard up as she tried to keep her normal walking pace and avoided looking over her shoulder too obviously. From the corner of her eye she noticed a bright pink color, and this made her curious. Raoul was flying in front of her, so Sydona made a sound and head gesture to guide the fairy back into her bag.

Running would only make her more suspicious, especially after what just happened. Avoiding any kind of trouble in this town seemed impossible. She secured a hand on the dagger at her hip and cautiously turned her head to see the person following her. A young teenager with light brown skin and jet black hair froze in her tracks and stopped mumbling. The pink color Sydona saw was the girl's jacket, and it suddenly looked familiar; she was from the diner.

"Why are you following me?" Sydona approached the timid girl.

"Oh. Uh..." She stood straight up in shock, unable to form words.

The response the girl gave her was surprising. If the girl was following her, why did she suddenly stop?

"Well?" Sydona asked again.

"Ug, sorry. I... was going over what I was going to say to you. You messed me up." The girl blushed and gripped her yellow backpack.

Sydona kept her shield up. If she was sent by the NFA, she sure was terrible at her job. But then again, why would they have someone so young in that line of work?

"So say it," Sydona pressed.

"Well, I was gonna, but you're interrupting me," the girl said with a bit more confidence.

Sydona smirked slightly. "Go ahead then."

The girl gave Sydona a glare and then took a deep breath. "I saw you in the diner. Rather--I saw your eyes."

Sydona's heart jumped, and her grip tightened on her knife.

"I wanted to meet you. I've never met anyone else like me," the girl said.

Even standing twenty feet apart from each other, Sydona could tell the girls eyes were not that of a flier. This only perplexed her further.

"Is this a joke?" Sydona widened her stance into a fighting position.

"No!" The girl waved her hands side to side. "Look!"

The girl carefully inserted a finger into one of her eyes as if she was taking something out of it. Her hands blocked Sydona's view of what exactly she was doing, and Sydona backed up slightly in confusion. Soon, the girl looked over at Sydona with two different colored eyes. One was the brown color she saw originally, and the other one was purple. Sydona squinted her eyes in order to make sense of what she was seeing. Stepping closer to see it better, she was now only five feet in front of her with her mouth agape.

"How'd you do that?"

The girl smiled. "It's a colored contact lens."

"Really?" Sydona inspected the palm of her hand, and there sat a brown reflective concave circle. It hid the purple underneath. It was ingenious and a much better way to hide from humans than wearing sunglasses all the time. Sydona fought with herself on how to acquire a pair, thinking it would be the best way to get into the camp. Even though she didn't have a plan yet, this was a start.

"I--" Sydona started but was startled by a metal door swinging open and a man with an apron carrying large trash bags. The man seemed to be intent on getting them disposed of quickly, but both girls were looking at him. He turned his attention to Sydona as he threw the bags in a large green container.

"I have to go," Sydona said.

She grabbed her sunglasses to make sure they were secure before marching hastily down the alley, leaving the young girl dumbfounded.

"Wait!" the girl yelled after her.

Sydona slowed down after she felt a comfortable enough distance from the onlooker.

"What?" Sydona quickly turned around, making the girl almost fall into her.

"Oh... uh... Where are you going? I would like to sit down and talk with you more if that's okay?" The girl smiled a pretty smile.

"I can't. I need to be somewhere." Sydona kept walking, but the girl stayed close beside her.

"I understand. I was just hoping that maybe I could pick your brain a little bit? I mean, you're the first flier I've ever come across before and--"

"Shh!" Sydona grabbed her mouth. "Are you trying to get us caught?" She looked around in a panic. Nothing but tall brick buildings surrounded them and maybe some mice and pigeons.

The wide-eyed girl shook her head nervously. Sydona glared deep into the girl's eyes, seeing nothing but innocence mixed with ignorance. Feeling sympathy, she removed her hand, and the girl stayed quiet for a minute.

"Are you in trouble?" she whispered.

Sydona laughed. "I guess you could say that. But then that would mean you're in trouble, too."

"What did you do?"

"It's not what I did. It's what we are." Sydona stepped away from her and continued walking.

The girl lagged behind, trying to process her vagueness. "That's why that man did that, wasn't it? He wanted to see what you were."

Sydona pointed her index finger up.

The girl ran and caught up to her again. "I think I can help you."

Sydona paused and released a brief grin.

"Come on. I have more at my house." The girl motioned her head.

Sydona hesitated. This girl was the first flier she has met in several years, and the contacts could help her blend in. She was young and a little naive, but Sydona couldn't help but listen to her gut. Eventually, she gave in and followed her out of the alleyway and onto the street.

"I'm Gia, by the way. Giovonna, actually. But almost no one calls me that." She grinned back at Sydona and walked with a skip in her step.

"Sydona," she answered back.

"I like that! Hey, is it okay if I pick your brain a little bit on the way?"

"I'd rather not. I don't want people to overhear us." Sydona clenched her bag as they walk by people on the sidewalk.

"Why don't you want people to overhear?"

"Again. Not the place for this conversation."

Giovonna quickly got the message and calmed herself.

Sydona took the long walk to observe the town. They had left the small downtown area and were now in neighborhoods lined with what Sydona thought of as cookie cutter homes. They were all made from the same sheet. Even as a child, she never lived in neighborhoods like that. She never understood how people found their houses every day.

Giovonna ran up to the front door and put her hand in her pocket to get her key.

"I'll be right back. Uh, you can just hang out down here," she said as she ran up the flight of stairs.

Sydona looked after her, wanting to say something, but Giovonna was gone. Standing inside the cookie house, she compared it to one of the houses she had seen on the cover of home and garden magazines. It was like a house only made to take pictures of and not to actually live in. She walked around and noticed pictures of Giovonna's family all over the walls and table tops, fake house plants, an alarm system by the door, and a bowl of artificial fruit on the glass kitchen table.

"Raoul, check this out!" she whispered to her tote bag.

He popped out to see Sydona tapping a banana on the counter and making a loud noise.

"Where in the devil are we?!" he gasped, clasping his hands over his mouth. Sydona found it more amusing than shocking, and she placed the perfect banana back in its pristine spot.

The house was spotlessly clean and smelled like many different flowers mixed with cleaning chemicals that gave her a slight headache. She walked into the living room and noticed a huge television sitting in the corner, taking up almost the entire wall. There was not a thing out of place. Everything was perfectly symmetrical and straight, completely opposite of how she lived at home. She walked back into the brightly lit kitchen and opened the stainless steel fridge to see if there was anything she could take. She grabbed some cheese, a colored drink, and veggies. Then, she heard someone opening the front door and chatter slipping into the house. She shoved all the food in her bag quickly, forcing Raoul to fly out angrily.

"Sydona! You do realize I'm in here, right?!" Raoul scolded.

"Shhh!" she said as she grabbed him from the air and put him back in her bag as fast as possible. She slammed the refrigerator door shut, causing a loud noise and making the chattering stop. Sydona stood in the doorway like a deer in headlights.

"What's this? Who are you?" a dark skinned man with angry brown eyes asked Sydona.

"I uh, I…"

Giovonna ran downstairs, sounding like a herd of elephants. "Mom, Dad!"

Her father was a large man with several frown lines creasing his face. Sydona noticed his big hands curling up and turning white as he gazed at her. He then looked at Giovonna for an explanation. "Gia, who is this?! Why is she in our house?"

"She's my teacher. She came over to help me grab my homework," Giovonna quickly fibbed.

Her mother, a much smaller version of her father but with a face of innocence spoke up. "Your teacher? Why have we never seen her before?"

Giovonna looked at Sydona and hesitated. "She's a sub. She has a teaching method to come to her student's houses on the weekend and then… go to the library!"

She grabbed Sydona's hand. "I'm learning a lot!" She hugged her mom with one arm as they headed out the front door. "Bye!"

She slammed the door shut and left both her parents speechless.

Chapter Four

The house faded further and further from their sight, and Sydona couldn't help but notice Giovonna looking back and smiling like a weight had been lifted. Sydona didn't blame her if she seemed happy to be out of that house; they were feeding her plastic fruit. A boxy designed car drove by them, and Sydona scoffed. "You would think for being 1996, they would have better looking cars by now. They're just so ugly."

Giovonna looked at her with a perplexed smile. "Don't you have a car?"

"I did," she sighed heavily. "But a lot of good it did me. I would fly everywhere if I could. It's so much cheaper."

"Ha-ha! Right?!"

Sydona looked over at her. "So, where are we going? The library?"

"Yerp. I'm there almost every day. Better than being at my house," Giovonna said.

"Your parents seemed nice. Frightened and alarmed, but nice," Sydona said, trying to make small talk; it was something she had never really been good at. It was a strange feeling to find herself wanting to willingly talk to a stranger. She assumed it was because Giovonna was like her, and they had one rare similarity. It was like she found a needle in a haystack and wasn't about to throw it aside.

"Yeah, I guess," Giovonna said.

Quickly dropping the topic, Sydona walked beside her in silence, but Giovonna was busy waving to folks across the street and greeting everyone. They all seemed to know her name and smiled back at her. After walking down the streets for a while, she found them approaching a decrepit, brick building that looked as if it was around before Sydona's parents were born. Giovonna led her up a flight of white stairs that were severely chipped and cracked and up to a heavy wooden door that creaked when it opened. The smell of old books and dust rushed past her face as they entered the darkened library that appeared much larger on the inside than the outside. The building seemed empty, much emptier than when she used to visit her library thirty-some years ago. Giovonna's face lit up as she walked through the familiar place and led Sydona up a flight of stairs in the middle of the building. Wearing sunglasses in such a dark building made her feel as though she was being watched.

"Where are we going?" Sydona whispered.

Giovonna shushed her. "Just follow my lead." She wandered up to a desk where an older woman with bright, gray hair sat.

"Well hello there, Giovonna," the woman said and then glanced at Sydona with a confused look. Sydona was used to that reaction though, so she flashed her a quick, fake smile.

Giovonna leaned over on the desk. "Hi, Ms. Oliver. This is my math tutor, Mrs. Sydona, and I was wondering if you could possibly give us a private room. No disturbances; I need to be in complete concentration," she said with a stone-cold expression. Sydona was thoroughly impressed and crossed her arms to be witness to this brilliant act. It was almost as if she had done this before.

Ms. Oliver nodded. "Well of course, hun. Here, I know just the place." She led them to a door in the back, unlocked it, and even held it open for them.

Giovonna curtsied. "This is perfect. I appreciate you doing this for us."

The woman replied with a slight head bow and walked back over to her tiny desk. The room was set up like a classroom with a few tables and chairs lined up in rows. A couple of outdated computers sat next to the walls with a layer of thick dust covering them. These got Sydona's attention almost immediately.

Giovonna sat her backpack down carefully on one of the tables and started taking things out one by one. She dug through her clothes and snacks until she found some little containers labeled 'B', 'Br', 'G', and 'H'. Sydona got bored with the computers as soon as she found out none of the buttons she pushed worked and wandered back to look at what Giovonna had set out. The girl unscrewed the containers to reveal colored circles in each.

"Incredible." Sydona put her finger in the one with the H (Hazel). The contact stuck perfectly to the tip of her finger, and she examined it from every angle, squinting her eyes to get a better look, trying to understand it more. Giovonna smiled giddily and intertwined her fingers like a mad scientist before grabbing a tiny bottle.

"What's that?" Sydona asked as she put the contact back in the container.

"We need to put this in your eyes first. It will make your eyes not *freak out* when you put them in. Sit, please." Giovonna pulled a wooden chair over for her.

Sydona followed her instructions and eyed the bottle intently. "Is it going to hurt?"

Giovonna unscrewed the cap as she shook her head. "Just don't move."

"Wait," Sydona swallowed. "I'll do it."

"What? Are you sure?" Giovonna stepped back.

Sydona grabbed the bottle from her hand and read the instructions over completely. She didn't want to admit she didn't know any of the medical words on it but acted as if she knew what it was already. Testing it out, she squirted some of it on her hand to see if it did anything. After nothing happened, she held it above her eye. With a shaky hand and her eyes resisting the urge to close, she finally let a drop out, and it hit her naked eyeball.

Sydona stood up instantly and laughed at the feeling of a thick watery substance on her eye, but it didn't affect her vision at all.

"Fascinating," she whispered with amazement and closed her eyes tightly. Pacing back and forth while shaking her hands, she patiently waited for the feeling to subside. Finally opening her eyes again, she sat back down ready for the next one. Sydona then dropped the solution into the right eye and had the same reaction again.

"Alright, now we have to wait a little while till we can put the contacts in," Giovonna informed her as she took the bottle back.

"How long?"

"Oh, a few minutes or so," Giovonna answered while she searched in her bag for something.

Sydona looked around the room, avoiding any kind of conversation. Taking a closer look at Giovonna's apparel, she noticed a band name, ACDC, on her t-shirt under the pink jacket. She thought about asking her what the letters meant but just stayed quiet.

"Time to put your contacts in." Giovonna said.

Picking up the hazel colored contact piece, she readied herself to put it in. Giovonna grabbed a mirror so that she would be able to see her eye better. Steadying her hand, her finger came closer and closer to her eye, and just like a suction cup, it was on. Her left eye was now hazel while her other was its usual lavender. Blinking a few times to adjust to the change, she was surprised how little she noticed it. She then placed the second one in and took a good look at herself in the mirror, hardly able to recognize the person staring back.

"I look just like *them*…"

Raoul fluttered out of her bag to see what she looked like with dust trailing behind him. He gazed at Sydona and her new colored eyes with a grin on his face. "Oh wow, Syd! No one could ever tell the difference now!"

Giovanna's eyes widened at the sight of Raoul. "Oh my gosh… You-you're a..."

Raoul turned to her with a smile. "Fairy."

Giovonna squeaked as her eyes rolled back, and she fainted to the floor.

Sydona heard the thud and quickly turned to see the girl on the floor. "What did you do, Raoul?"

"Me? I didn't do anything! Maybe I'm getting better looking with age." He stroked his hair back.

Sydona scoffed as she helped Giovonna off the floor and sat her in a nearby chair. She grabbed a piece of paper from the girl's backpack and fanned her off. Giovonna slowly came to, but as she saw Raoul, her eyes widened again.

"You okay?" Sydona asked.

"Are you real?" Giovonna asked with disbelief and reached her hand out to touch him.

"Of course I'm real!" Raoul bellowed.

"I don't think she has seen a fairy before, Raoul. She didn't mean offence," Sydona said.

Giovonna continued staring at him like he was a specimen in a lab. "No. I've never seen one of you before. I'm sorry if I offended you." She released a smile once she took in his presence and knew he was not a dream.

Sydona went back to looking at herself in the hand-held mirror. She couldn't get over seeing herself this way; she looked like a human. Her eyes were the one thing she loved about herself because she knew no one had eyes like hers. She set the mirror upside-down on the table, unable to look anymore.

Raoul focused his attention on Sydona. "What's wrong?"

"It's like I'm human now…" Sydona said only above a whisper.

Raoul planted himself on her knee. "But that's good, isn't it? It's the best way to hide."

Giovonna got over her fascination with the little fairy and chimed in. "You'll blend right in now. No need to wear sunglasses anymore!"

"Yeah, I guess you're right. It'll be the only way to get in," Sydona said.

Giovonna cocked her head curiously. "What do you mean? Get in?"

"Oh, nowhere. Just somewhere I have to go." Sydona stood up and motioned for Raoul to hide back in her bag. He sighed heavily.

"Wait, you're leaving?" Giovonna asked. "Just like that?"

"Yeah, we need to be somewhere." Sydona put her bag over her shoulder. "Thank you though, for everything," Sydona put her hand on Giovonna's shoulder. "I wish you the best." Sydona smiled and turned towards the door.

"Wait!" Giovonna ran back to her backpack and frantically shoved all her things back in. "I'm coming with you!"

Sydona grabbed the doorknob, hung her head, and sighed. "No, Giovonna. You're too young. Actually, how old are you? Are you even in high school?" Sydona turned to face her.

Giovonna threw her backpack over her shoulders. "I'm fourteen, and I am not too young! I'm really sick of people telling me I can't do things."

"Gia… You don't understand," Sydona began to explain.

"Please." Giovonna gave her a look of such desperation that it gave Sydona a twist in her stomach.

"We're going to Eagle Lake, up in Oregon. Do you know why?" Sydona crossed her arms, dreading the fact she had to explain it.

"No. What's there?"

"A camp. They are keeping fliers there… for experiments."

"What?"

Sydona searched through her bag and showed her the article.

"We think it's the same thing they were doing back in the 40's," Raoul said. "When they took--"

"Raoul, enough," Sydona blurted before he could say more.

The room fell silent, and Giovonna read the article over and over.

"What do you plan on doing?" Giovonna asked as she handed the paper back.

"I'm not sure yet. Right now I just want to find it. And I'll think of something closer to the time."

"Okay," Giovonna nodded.

"What?"

"I'm coming with you. Along with my contacts," Giovonna said.

Sydona sighed heavily.

"I have never met anyone like me before. I'm not going to be aware of this… situation… and not try to do anything to stop it. I don't know what happened fifty years ago, but if you are going all the way to Oregon from here, I'm under the impression it's pretty serious. Either you take me with you, or I will follow you. You're not gonna get rid of me that easily." Giovonna glared at her with determination.

Sydona scratched her head and looked at Raoul who shrugged his shoulders.

"What about your parents?"

"They'll be fine," Giovonna said shortly.

"Gia. This is not something I want you doing without your parents' knowledge. Especially if I am the last person they saw you with. Where we are going might be dangerous, and I would hate for them to worry," Sydona said.

Giovonna rolled her eyes and headed toward a phone in the corner of the room. She sat by it for a few moments with a thoughtful expression. Finally dialing, she waited on the phone until a voice answered.

"Hi, it's me," Giovonna started with a mumble.

"Gia."

"It's going fine. Can I talk to mom?"

"Because."

Giovonna rolled her eyes, waiting for her mother to get on the phone.

"Hey, mom. So I ran into Suzanna here, and she had the idea of having a study weekend. You know with the finals coming up, it would be beneficial for both of us."

"Yes."

"She has clothes I can wear. We're like the same size."

"She has toothbrushes, mom," she snapped.

"Come on, please?"

"No, her parents aren't out of town. What, we're not gonna have, like a party, or something."

"Come on, you guys never let me stay at friends' houses anymore!" She stomped her foot.

"Please, I'll do twice as many chores when I get home.
I promise!"

She stood silently, swaying her body back and forth
impatiently.

"Thanks, mom."

"Mkay, bye."

She slammed the phone down.

"Problem solved!" Giovonna grinned as she hung up
the phone and headed back toward Sydona and Raoul.

Sydona nodded her head approvingly. "How do you
know they won't call your friend's house to check up on you?"

"Because Suzanna's family hates my parents, so they
won't answer the phone for them anymore. They screwed up
their taxes one year, and it's never been the same. I had to really
convince my mom to let me stay." Giovonna grabbed her
backpack. "Are we ready?"

"Why do you want to come with me so badly? I'm a
total stranger. What if I am lying about everything?" Sydona still
couldn't understand why she wanted to tag along so badly.

"I don't know. I guess I trust my gut. And I don't think
you're very good at lying. I lie a lot, so I can tell." Giovonna
winked.

Sydona nodded. "Alright. Let's get going then."
Giovonna muttered 'yes' under her breath, and Sydona smirked.
They were stuck with a teenage girl.

Chapter Five

The girls left the library at one in the afternoon after checking out a couple books for their travels. Sydona made a point to find something quickly as Raoul had to stay in her bag the whole time. Giovonna could only fit a few since she had school books in her bag, including, chemistry, physics and calculus. Sydona didn't know much about this girl yet, but the books made her seem intelligent. Mainly because Sydona sneaked a peek of a paper sticking out of the calculus book and saw a red A+ in the corner. Sydona was never really good at math, but in her defense, she hadn't gone to school since she was nine. Everything she knew was either self-taught, read in books she stole, or learned by trial and error.

As they walked down the stairs of the library and onto the main street, Sydona felt naked. Without her sunglasses, she felt like her entire body was on display for everyone to see. She hated feeling vulnerable, but this time was different. The few people who did walk past barely noticed her and never looked at her twice. Feeling out of her element, she kept her head low and tried to think of something else to focus on.

"So I'm guessing since you're only fourteen, driving is out of the question, huh?" Sydona spoke up after only a block down the road.

"We have a bus station. It's only a couple miles from here," Giovonna suggested.

A bus was not on the top of Sydona's list of transportation because that meant being trapped in a small space surrounded by humans. This was turning out to be more complicated than she had anticipated.

"I don't think going on a bus is the best idea," Sydona weighed.

"But you look like a regular person now. No one will notice," Giovonna said.

"I'm not staying in this bag for fifteen hours while you guys sit on a bus!" The bag muffled Raoul's voice.

Just then, a red van honked a couple times and pulled to the side of the street, stopping right next to them. A single meter reader and mailbox stood between them and the mysterious car. Backing up with uncertainty, Sydona squinted at the car with tinted windows, unable to see who was inside. As she reached for her knife hiding under her shirt, the driver rolled the window down and waved.

"Hey, Sydona!" Annie from the farmers market smiled brightly. Sydona relaxed and retracted her hand.

"Oh. Hi, Annie! How are you?" Sydona walked up to the side of her car and saw Joseph in the back seat. "Hi, Joey."

"Hi Syd!" He waved excitedly.

"We're good." Annie relaxed her arm on the side of the car.

"What are you doing way out here?" Sydona asked.

"We were visiting family. His cousins live out here. What about you? Weird we're both here at the same time, huh?" Annie laughed.

"Yeah, I came out here for family, too."

"Oh. Is this--" Annie pointed to Giovonna who stood shyly behind Sydona.

Sydona and Giovonna both looked at one another, trying to somehow communicate without saying anything. Sydona hoped Giovonna didn't say something idiotic like where they were headed.

"Hi, I'm Gia. I'm Syd's cousin," Giovonna said slowly.

"You're here for cousins, too? How strange... And she lives only one town over. How come you've never mentioned her to me before?" Annie asked.

Sydona hesitated, trying to think of a good, believable lie. "Because she just moved here."

"Yes. From--Albuquerque," Giovonna spun off her tongue.

"Oh wow. Well, Michigan is quite a change then, isn't it?"

Annie then looked more closely at Sydona, into her eyes. "You know Syd, I don't think I've ever seen you without your sunglasses on. You sure do have some pretty hazel eyes," she said.

Sydona looked away bashfully, not comfortable with people looking into her eyes and more so, saying something about them. But she smiled and thanked her quietly. With a quick glance through the passenger's side window, Sydona's fists clenched at the sight of the man from the diner. Ducking quickly behind the door, her heart began to pound. Annie watched her with a worried face.

"What's going on?" She peered down at Sydona, clinging to the side of the car. Giovonna ducked down beside her. Sydona ignored her while she listened to her own heart pound in her ears.

"Who is that?" Annie asked.

"Trouble," Sydona whispered.

"What do you mean?"

"I'm sorry, we have to go," Sydona said. But as she looked around, she couldn't find a way to avoid being spotted.

"They'll see us," Giovonna said.

"Syd, would you please tell me what's going on?" Annie asked assertively.

Bouncing on her feet, Sydona reeled over if she should tell her friend what she really was. It was boggling to her that only yesterday she would trust Annie enough to tell her anything. Anything except that she's a flier, but that went for anyone. But this woman had been in her life for several years. This was her only chance to prove if Annie was a real friend. There didn't seem to be any other choice except maybe to hide behind the car until the man left, but she didn't know how long that would be.

"What's he doing now?" Sydona asked as she was too afraid to peek over the window.

Annie glanced over. "He's uh... Standing around talking to some guys."

Sydona raised her eyebrows. "He didn't see me, then?"

"I don't know. You won't tell me what's going on," Annie said impatiently.

Sydona sighed deeply as she decided not to beat around the bush anymore. "I'm a flier," she admitted as quietly as she could.

"A what?" Annie said in disbelief.

"And that guy, with the hat... He saw me."

"What does he want with you?" Annie asked much more calmly than Sydona anticipated.

"He saw me in the diner up the street. But then let me go," Sydona said, hesitating on looking up and over the window. Not knowing or seeing where he was at all times was killing her, though. She chewed on her fingernails nervously.

"He let you go? Then you're okay now, right?" Annie said while she kept an eye on them from across the street.

"No. Not exactly..." Sydona said. The unknowing was too much for her, and she had to look. Had to see where he was. She peeked over the hood of the car and saw the man was still with his friends from the diner. Her eyes narrowed as she tried to figure out what they were doing and what they could be talking about. One of the guys looked in her direction and pointed at her. She hid back behind Annie's car as quick as she could.

"Shit!" Sydona panicked. Sydona heard voices coming closer, mentioning a blonde woman, and she knew she was seen clearly enough.

"We have to go," Sydona told Giovonna.

"They're gonna see us!" Giovonna argued.

"I don't think we have a choice," Sydona said bluntly as she looked over her shoulder.

Annie sat listening to them bicker and spoke up. "Do you guys want a ride then?"

"No. We couldn't put you in the middle of this," Sydona said but then kicked herself for denying the offer. It was the ride she needed, and it would get them to where they needed to go. But her friend and her son would be going across the country with, essentially, two fugitives and a fairy. The moment was too intense to explain where they were going and why, and she came back to her original comment. It would be too dangerous and not something Sydona wanted to be held responsible for.

Annie nodded with understanding, and Sydona could tell that she came up with the same conclusion. She wondered if Annie had read the article like most people and knew where they were headed. Her offer was simply a friendly suggestion, and she was probably relieved that Sydona turned her down.

"You guys go on ahead; I'll distract them." Annie looked at both Sydona and Giovonna with respect, making Sydona relax more.

"What are you going to do?" Sydona stood up but still hunched over behind her car.

"Don't worry about it. Just leave." Annie winked and put her car into drive.

The men made a B-line for Sydona and Giovonna. The girls began to run in the opposite direction, and Sydona saw they made a run for their truck instead. Annie took off and blocked the roadway, so they couldn't pass. The sound of crunching metal, honking horns, and shouting filled the town.

Their feet carried them all the way out of town to a large apple orchard. The trees stood at the perfect height for them to hide in easily. Ducking in and out of the trees full of white flowers, the girls stopped running once they were deep inside. Sydona took a moment to look at her surroundings as it was almost like a fairy tale. Long rows of bright green grass contrasted the enchanting white flowers that hung off the trees and powdered the space below like sugar. The smell was intoxicating as she buried her nose in a bushel of buds. It was so surreal, she almost forgot why they were running.

A cough from Giovonna brought her back to reality. Sydona stood up straight and glanced down the deserted trail.

"You know how to fly, right?" Sydona asked.

"What?!" asked Giovonna who was hunched over with her hands on her knees.

"...I'll take that as a no." Sydona adjusted her bag to let Raoul out.

"I mean, I've read about flying, but no. I've never actually done it," Giovonna said and tightened the straps on her yellow backpack.

"Welp, best way to learn is by doing!" Sydona smirked.

"Are you serious?"

Sydona stood next to Giovonna with her feet spread apart vertically and leaned over a bit. Giovonna followed her instructions and mimicked Sydona's stance. Raoul floated next to Sydona and lined up with the girls.

Sydona spoke up, "Okay, when I say, you have to kick off the ground with your dominant foot, and you will start to go up in the air. Lean forward to go faster and stand upright to slow back down. You will feel your body get lighter like your bones are hollow."

She gave a nod to Sydona to let her know she was ready, and they were off. Sprinting as fast as their legs could go, Sydona gave Giovonna the signal, and they kicked off the ground. The higher into the air they went, the bigger Giovonna's smile grew and the wider her smile became to take in all the magnificent scenery.

"How do you feel?" Sydona yelled.

"Amazing! Why have I waited so long to do this?!"

Sydona couldn't help but notice Giovonna's face lit up like a Christmas tree. She wondered if that was what she looked like the first time she flew. But Giovonna was fourteen, well past the age most fliers first learned the skill. The feeling Sydona felt when flying must have been intensified by a thousand to the new flier. She would have given anything to feel that joy herself.

Her slight jealousy didn't last long as Raoul warned her that the men were following them in their truck and watching with binoculars. Sydona looked down on the dirt road where she saw a truck that she recognized from Mayfield filled with the men from the diner. She spotted one man in the back of it with a big gun that he aimed towards them. Sydona grabbed Giovonna's arm tightly, leaning forward more to pick up more speed. It was almost too much for Giovonna to handle, and her smile disappeared. Several darts whizzed by them, and a couple of them almost hit Sydona's leg, causing her to weave dramatically. Adrenaline pumped through her veins a she maneuvered the best she could while holding another person. Up ahead, she saw the edge of a large forest filled with pines and oaks. It looked dark and dense, and Sydona thought it would be the best place to get away from them. Speeding up as much as she could, they entered through the widest opening in the trees, and the darts stopped.

Flying into the depths of the woods, they spotted a sunny clearing, and Sydona leaned upright to land with Giovonna copying her actions. She stopped for a moment to listen for any sign of the men, but all she could hear was the rustling of leaves in the trees, birds, and a woodpecker knocking on tree bark.

Raoul flew over to Sydona and lay down on a low hanging tree branch next to her. Giovonna lay sprawled out on the forest floor, her chest heaving up and down. Sydona's mind wandered back to what happened in Mayfield and what Annie did for them.

"I wish I could thank her," Sydona said. "Can't imagine how much worse that could've been if she didn't try to stop them."

"You can't think about that," Raoul said.

"I saw the look on that guy's face. Like he knew who I was. What I was... And wanted to hurt me. Maybe worse..." Sydona whispered as she relived the event over and over again.

"What's wrong Syd?" Giovonna asked and sat next to her on a fallen tree.

"Nothing," Sydona murmured and took a deep breath. She sat silently next to Giovonna who was still breathing hard. Digging around in her tote bag, she found her wrinkled map. Mayfield was such a small town that it was barely noticeable among the highways and byways, but to the north of the town, she saw the forest they probably flew into. A line, indicating a road, did go through it, but it was so far out of the way, she didn't worry much about it. Memorizing the layout for the next several miles, she locked in which way they needed to go. She folded the map back up and put it back inside her bag.

"I believe we need to head this way," she said, using the sun as a lead way.

The three began walking even deeper into the woods until they could only hear themselves and the sound of crickets slowly coming into ears reach. The sun began to set, but there was still enough daylight to see the ground in front of them. As much as she enjoyed flying, taking a break by walking was a nice change. After she landed, she didn't feel light anymore for some reason, and it was like landing with a sandbag. The smell of the trees and dirt was soothing and refreshing. She always imagined she was a squirrel or beaver in her past life as much as she enjoyed wooded areas. The silence was pleasant, and she took in a deep breath to enjoy the moment.

"How old are you?" Giovonna asked, shattering her peacefulness.

Sydona grinned. "Older than you."

"Gimme a range. Cause I know we live a lot longer than humans. I think like over a hundred years or something?"

"She's six--" Raoul began.

"Hey!" Sydona shouted, refusing to let him finish the number.

"Sixty?!" Giovonna blurted loud enough to almost hear it echo through the trees.

"I am not sixty! Raoul doesn't know what he's talking about," Sydona huffed.

All Raoul could do was block his mouth to keep from laughing too loudly.

"You don't look that old. I would peg you for about mid-thirties?" Giovonna said, studying Sydona's face. "I see some wrinkles on your forehead. So maybe forty?"

"What?" Sydona stopped and dug through her bag for something reflective. But as she rifled through her stuff, she heard suppressed giggling from the other two.

Sydona rolled her eyes and held back a laugh.

Giovonna continued her questioning. "So how old are you then, Raoul?"

"I am fifty-five years young," Raoul said proudly.

"And if Sydona got you when she was eight, like most fliers do... That would make Syd--"

"Shh!" Sydona perked up. Holding her hand up flat to stop them from talking, she took a couple steps forward. She could faintly hear a barking in the distance. She stood as still as a statue and waited to hear it again, thinking it was a fluke. But not even a minute later, she confirmed a second barking along with the first. They weren't coyotes or wolves like she had heard many times before. They were hound dogs.

Raoul dashed toward the sound of the dogs and yelled back. "We need to go!"

"I think it's them again," Sydona said and took off running through the woods, dodging in and out of trees, away from the howling. Giovonna struggled to keep up with her and lagged way behind. The yells and laughs of the men filled the trees. Raoul stayed ahead of the girls to scope out places to hide. Suddenly, Sydona heard Giovonna make a loud grunting sound and fall into a pile of debris. She whipped back around to see what happened and helped her up as fast as she could. Giovonna hunched over and grabbed her knees.

"Ouch…" Giovonna moaned. "Landed on a bunch of rocks."

"Can you keep going?" Sydona asked hurricdly.

Giovonna tried to move and collapsed. "Think they're just bruised, but man does it hurt."

"There's a house up ahead! Just carry her!" Raoul yelled as he pointed in the direction of a clearing.

Rather than trying to support Giovonna by being a crutch, Sydona picked her up with a grunt and cradled her. Joking to herself, Sydona thought that if they were flying this would be a piece of cake. But the forest was so dense that there was no way to fly away without hitting branches and falling back down. Giovonna being new at flying and having bruised knees gave them especially few options. The sounds of the dogs and the truck were getting louder and so was her heart beat. Giovonna complained that she was fine and could walk, but

Sydona ignored her, fearing what would happen if they were caught. The house came into view through bushes and trees. And there was a clearing. A perfect place to fly away from. Raoul could donate as much fairy dust as he could to help Giovonna fly. If they were to do this, though, it had to be fast.

"Raoul! Wait up!" Sydona struggled to keep up with him as he zoomed well ahead of them.

Just then, she felt a sharp sting in her neck. Her vision blurred almost instantly. Sydona suddenly felt like a cement truck, and she fell to the ground as the pain got stronger. As she was lying on the ground, she faintly saw a red-headed woman holding a shotgun over her shoulder. This was it. She was done for. They were all going to be the NFA's property now. She looked around for Raoul and saw no sight of him anywhere. She hoped he got away. He was very small and quick. Surely he got away. No longer able to focus on anything, a strange feeling overcame her body, and her lids felt heavy. Words slipped out of reach, and she drifted off into a deep slumber.

Chapter Six

Sydona began to hear a familiar, gleeful voice and high pitched giggles. Reluctantly, she peeled her eyes open to look through her long eyelashes, but everything still appeared blurry. She tried sitting up and instantly felt a pounding headache, causing her to grab her head with clammy hands. Blinking, she found herself lying on a firm bed with an outdated flowery and mustard-colored bedspread. Her mind was racing, and all kinds of questions ran through it. Is this the end of the road? Where were Giovonna and Raoul? What did she get shot with? Why was she not dead? And why was this bedspread so hideous? Sydona grabbed her neck where she had been shot, and it was still painful and throbbing. She then instinctively reached her other hand to where her dagger normally resided. Gone. She silently panicked. She blinked more, and her vision finally cleared. All her senses awoke like a cat hearing a loud sound. Trying to sit up more, her head began to pound harder, and she slid back down into the suffocating yellow lilies.

"Don't ya try gittin' up, now!" said a strange Midwestern voice emerging from another room. Sydona tried scanning the room without picking up her head. She was in what appeared to be an old cabin with random things scattered all over the place. There were lots of shelves on the walls with jars of varying sizes, and nick-knacks littered the empty spaces throughout. A giant buck head was mounted on one wall with proud, branching antlers, but his eyes lacked life. There was what looked like rabbit fur spread over an end table. She noticed many other animals collected to decorate the cabin like a morbid zoo. Sydona shuttered, hoping that she was not going to end up like the buck.

She heard footsteps grow near to her bedside. "You're awake!" said a familiar female voice. Sydona turned her head slowly to see Giovonna smiling down at her. She was holding a coffee cup and sat down on a poorly painted white stool next to the bed. "You've been asleep for awhile," Giovonna said, sipping from her cup.

"'Bout two hours," said the strange voice again. She walked over casually, and Sydona instantly moved closer to Giovonna, wary of the woman's intentions.

She looked up at the heavy-set, red-haired woman. "Who are you?"

"Willow," said the woman. She held two coffee cups and handed one to Sydona with her worn, leathery hands.

But Sydona was not fooled by her hospitality. "What do you want with us?" Sydona demanded, scooting further away from Willow.

Willow handed her the cup again with a little wrinkled smile. "It's tea," she suggested rather than stated. Sydona glanced over at Giovonna who nodded her head in confirmation and took another sip. Sydona sat up and reluctantly grabbed the cup from Willow before taking a heavy sniff.

"I saved your life," Willow said as she tucked back a gray streak in her hair.

"Right. Well, whatever makes you sleep better at night," Sydona said while still examining the beverage.

Willow laughed, almost spilling her tea. "You a snarky little minx, ain't ya?"

"She called you a minx…" Giovonna snickered.

Sydona was not amused but rather annoyed by how comfortable Giovonna appeared to be in the presence of someone who would be doing god knows what to them later. She adjusted herself in the bed and kept scooting closer to Giovonna.

"So. What are you going to do with us?" Sydona asked straightforwardly.

"Do?" Willow stroked her tiny chin hairs. "Hmm. I don't know. I mean, I can cook up somethin' for ya. Do you like rabbit noodle soup?"

Both Giovonna and Sydona's faces scrunched up.

"It tastes just like chicken," Willow reassured them.

Giovonna changed her face to a smile; Sydona's stayed the same.

"Sure! I'm starving!" Giovonna stood up quickly.

"Pass," Sydona said.

Giovonna glanced back at her, confused. "What?"

"Uh, I think not, *Willow*," she said, moved her legs to the side of the bed and stood up slowly. "As much as we would love your poison ridden meat… I think we'll be leaving now."

Giovonna looked at her with disappointment. "Syd! We can't leave now! She's just about to feed us!"

Sydona grabbed her arm, walked to a corner of the tiny house, and whispered to Giovonna. "Gia… she's a hunter. She can't be trusted. All she wants from us is *us*. She's not who she appears to be."

Giovonna whispered louder, "No. you have it wrong, Syd. She's one of the good guys. She nursed us back to health. She *can* be trusted." She paused. "Don't you think if she wanted to hurt us she would've done it by now?"

Sydona took another long look at Willow who was in the kitchen cutting up an apple. Maybe Giovonna was right. They could be in a blacked out van right now with bags over their heads. But instead, they were in a warm house with food being served. Could her gut feeling be wrong about the burly woman? All signs pointed to her being an enemy, except for her kindness and warm food. Maybe she wasn't a killer.

Sydona gave a sigh and rolled her eyes at Giovonna in a loving way. Giovonna responded by squealing like a mouse and jump-hugging her. Willow returned to the main room, wiping her hands on a towel. Sydona dauntingly walked over to Willow with her head held high, chest puffed out, and her arms crossed.

"So what are you?" she asked Willow.

"Human."

"How do you know about us?"

"Army."

"Still active?"

"Retired."

"Why do you have a gun?"

"Protection and huntin'."

"Married?"

"Widowed."

"So you live alone?

"Yep."

Damn she's good... Sydona thought to herself.

"Where's my fairy?"

"Kitchen."

Sydona popped her head around Willow and saw Raoul going to town on an apple. She walked into the kitchen and stood directly above Raoul, tapping her foot.

"Raoul!" She bent over to get eye level with him.

He spun around on the cutting board, clutching an apple slice half the size of himself. "Syd! You're okay!" He grinned up at her. "You met Willow yet? She's awesome." He winked at Willow standing in the doorway.

Even though she was thankful that Raoul was okay, Sydona was still annoyed that he was vouching for Willow, too. She wondered what Willow did in order to turn her friends to the dark side. Raoul seemed way too willing to eat food from a stranger. But then, she thought it wasn't that strange actually. Food was Raoul's weakness. Giovonna's weakness was probably just being gullible and naive. She watched Raoul eat the entire slice of apple without so much as taking a breath. Was she so cold-hearted that she couldn't see the good in this perfect stranger? No. She was being perfectly rational in not trusting someone who shot her. Willow could be trying to make up for what happened, but it didn't matter to Sydona.

"Wait, can I just say something?" Giovonna entered the kitchen. "You're widowed?"

Willow released a smile. "Yes I am."

"And your name is Willow?" Giovonna put her hand on her hip.

"Accordin' to my mama."

Giovonna stared at the ceiling in deep thought. "So you're telling me that your name is Willow, and you're widowed? Willow the widowed."

Willow nodded and raised her eyebrows. "I like you."

Giovonna blushed and turned back into the main room whispering *Willow the widowed. Willow the widowed. Willow the widowed.* as fast as she could.

Sydona followed her and began turning over frilly pillows and searching under the bed for her satchel and dagger. "Where's my stuff?" Sydona glared at Willow.

Willow waddled over to a closet that stood on the other side of the main room and grabbed their belongings: the green tote and both backpacks. Peering inside the small closet, she also saw a few rifles and the shotgun from earlier. Sydona snatched her bags from Willow's hands and riffled through them, making sure everything was still there. Her special dagger was accounted for, and she placed it back on her hip. As she prepped everything to leave, she noticed Giovonna standing and watching her.

"Why aren't you packing up?" Sydona asked as she fixed her hair back into a ponytail.

"Um... because it's like midnight?" Giovonna sipped her drink again, trying to hide behind it.

Sydona peeked through the blinds to reveal pure darkness outside. As she turned around, they looked at her with concern. Even Raoul sat on Giovonna's shoulder with a worried look.

"So what? You guys want to stay the night here?" She responded to the judgmental looks aggressively. "No. Absolutely not."

"But I'm tired... And my knees still kinda hurt..." Giovonna whined.

Sydona dropped her head with a sigh. She had forgotten that Giovonna fell. It wouldn't be fair of her to force her to leave and walk for miles. She fought with herself. Sleep sounded good. And what had just happened to her, she didn't consider sleep. She still didn't know who shot her, though. Did Willow shoot her? If so, why? To invite her in and feed her and her friends? Something wasn't adding up.

She caved and removed her bags, but still kept her dagger handy. Giovonna was happy that she changed her mind. Eventually, Sydona took the cup of tea that she was offered. It was black tea, and she wasn't a fan of it. Still, the warmth felt nice going down. As she sat on the bed with Giovonna, Sydona spoke up with questions she needed to ask.

"Who shot me?"

"That would be Harold and his buddies. He's a... well, he's a bounty hunter," Willow said with hesitation.

Sydona's heart skipped a beat, and she gulped air. "A bounty hunter?"

Giovonna stepped back into the kitchen silently and looked at them with worried eyes.

"Yeah. NFA hires people to bring the fliers to them at any cost," Willow said, leaning back on the short counter and wringing a towel between her massive hands.

"Are you serious?" Giovonna quivered with tears forming in her eyes.

"Afraid I am, sweetie pie," Willow said and stared at the ground.

Sydona felt a pain in her stomach at Giovonna's reaction. She was much more emotional than Sydona understood. The gravity of what this young girl was getting into might be too much for her.

"Gia. Are you sure you want to come? You don't have to. You can still go home," Sydona said softly.

At first, Giovonna seemed to contemplate the offer, but then, she heard the word *home*. Her face hardened.

"No. I'm fine." She sniffled loudly and shook her head.

Sydona didn't feel convinced. "Are you sure?"

"I'm sure. I'm not going back home." Giovonna pursed her lips.

The tension was thick in the room, and Sydona wasn't sure what else to say. She seemed to have her mind made up. Giovonna was as stubborn as herself, and she admired it.

"Bounty hunters… But the article I read said it was encouraged to have fliers come and even bring family members. Why--"

"O'course the article said that. You thank they gonna post in national news that Eagle Lake is more like a concentration camp? Hell no!" Willow yelled angrily and almost tore the towel up.

"A concentra--" Giovonna squealed, trying to stay strong.

"No. I don't believe that…" Sydona said and crossed her arms. Meanwhile, her heart was beating even faster. She felt unsure of what she was getting herself into.

"Well, believe it, princess! I ain't never seen it, but my buddy has and I trust 'im," Willow spat.

The room stood stale after Willow spoke. Sydona stood in the doorway, biting her nails nervously, letting the news sink in. Giovonna sat at the kitchen table, playing with a hair tie on her wrist. She looked just like a ghost had passed through her, blank and staring. Raoul resided on the countertop, staring up at the ceiling and shaking his head every once in awhile. Willow made herself comfortable against a wall, picking at the towel in her hands until someone finally said something.

"Why don't you want to capture us?" Sydona asked.

"'Cause I ain't no bounty hunter. Trust me, if I was, you would know," Willow said with a tiny smile, trying to lighten the mood.

"She's part of the Sparrows!" Giovonna perked back up. "She told us earlier. Me and Raoul."

"The Sparrows? What is that?" Sydona asked.

"Where ya been, girl? It's a resistance. It's just been reunited recently from that damn article circling like a vulture 'round the media," Willow said.

A resistance group. It was unfathomable. There were non-fliers out there that were on their side. Never in her lifetime had she thought that would exist. Ever since she was a child, she thought humans were out to get her. It was so incredible to hear that she could hardly contain her excitement!

"So we'll stay here for the night, I guess..." she said nonchalantly. "But we're gone in the morning."

Raoul flew into the room and jumped on everyone's head in excitement. "Woohoo!"

Giovonna celebrated by hugging Willow tightly.

"I'll get you guys some sleepin' bags." Willow forced herself out from being squeezed so hard.

Sydona and Giovonna slept on the floor in separate sleeping bags while Willow slept on the flowery bed. Raoul made himself cozy on a sweater Willow folded up for him on the floor, next to Sydona. She lay there thinking about being in a human's home and patted the dagger she had next to her side. It was sheathed but ready in a moment's notice if anything were to happen. The animal heads mounted on the walls were haunting, and she found it hard to take her eyes off of them. She wondered if that was something she needed to be weary of. Laying in silence for what felt like hours, her lids finally grew heavy, and a familiar dream came back. This time, in more detail.

Her family lived in Southern California when the announcements surfaced about capturing fliers for experimentation. Men in white coats would stop by every house that qualified for the species type. Some of them acted like they were from the local clinics and were doing "in-house" flu shots just to get in the door. They had to use this excuse to get into Sydona's house as her parents didn't trust them at all. Her mother told Sydona to hide in the closet next to the front door. They didn't have time to think. When they invited the men in, her mother, Evelyn, offered them coffee. They refused. One man sat back down while the other began to look around.

"Can I help you find something?" her dad, Ian, asked sternly. He made a point to stand in front of the shuttered closet door where Sydona hid. The man ignored Ian and began to walk down the hallway, but Ian grabbed his arm angrily.

"Hey, I asked you a question!" Ian shouted. As that happened, the man grabbed Ian's arm in an attempt to wrap it behind his back, but he was too strong. The man's eyes widened with surprise at his strength.

Suddenly the other man jumped up to try to fight off Ian, and both the men started fighting with him. Evelyn tried to help by grabbing the men, but they were so focused on Ian that they pushed her down hard. Her next thought was to save Sydona. The brawl had been taken outside and onto the porch. Evelyn took the scared, nine year old Sydona from the closet.

"Grab Raoul. Now." Her mother kissed her forehead and pushed her out the back patio door. Sydona stumbled but kept going, wiping her tears as she ran across the backyard. Approaching the oak tree, she called for her fairy Raoul, who appeared within seconds. Evelyn joined them shortly after and shoved a green tote bag into Sydona's arms.

"Take him and run. Run as far as you can, Syd! Don't worry about us; we'll be fine. I need you to remember this. Don't trust anyone. Raoul is the only one you can trust now. Don't let them take you. You're my special girl..." Evelyn choked back back tears. She grabbed Sydona's face with both hands, and Sydona memorized her mother's eyes, fearing that she may never see them again.

"Mom!" Sydona hugged her tighter than she ever held anything.

"I love you. Go! You need to go now!" she yelled.

Sydona nodded, and Raoul flew into her tote. As she stepped backward, Evelyn faded further and further away from her reach. Sydona turned and hid in a bush.

Then, she saw cop cars with lights flashing everywhere, big white vans with no windows, and other cars. Evelyn turned back to the house, but as she ran, men in black suits grabbed her, and she struggled greatly to get away. She needed four men to get a hold of her, and she still made it hard for them.

One of the men in white coats came out the back door with a syringe and a needle, and Evelyn screamed at the top of her lungs. Sydona was frozen with fear at this sight. Raoul flew out of the bag, unable to hide any longer. Evelyn no longer had the strength to fight once she was stuck with the needle. The men in black suits carried her by her head and legs like she was a deer they just hunted, an animal. Eventually, Sydona was able to move, and she quickly ran along the hedge to the front of the house, still keeping hidden.

Then, out of the corner of her eye, she saw her father in the same state as her mom. They were put in the back of an ambulance with the men in the white coats. As Sydona watched the van drive away, she decided to run as fast as her small legs could carry her. She didn't know where she would run to, but she knew it would be away from humans. Forever.

Her eyes grew heavy as she tried to sleep through the night, but thoughts of the camp and her parents scratched in her head.

Chapter Seven

A loud pounding at the cabin door made Giovonna jump. Sydona awoke in frustration because she had finally fallen asleep. Willow threw the covers off of her quickly, grabbed a robe hanging on a nail in the wall, and opened the door angrily.

"What can I do for you, gentlemen?" Willow frowned at the four men standing on her porch as two of them held back a couple hound dogs. A scraggly man with a dirty white hat and holey shirt and jeans answered with an accent as strong as Willow's.

"Howdy, Willow," he said, attempting to look inside her house. Sydona, Giovonna, and Raoul were hiding back in the kitchen with the window closed. Sydona peeked out slightly from behind the wall but only got a glimpse of the man before she had to hide again. It was the same man from the diner. A sinking feeling crept over her as she eavesdropped on the rest of the conversation.

"What can I do for you, Harold?" Willow asked impatiently.

"You got somethin' I want."

"Is that right?" Willow held her chin up high.

"We saw them in town, so they belong to us!" Harold challenged.

"I don't think so! This is my property, and whatever enters it is my business!"

"So, they are here?"

"You betcha! And there ain't no way I'm lettin' you have 'em! And by the way, why is it you shot her yesterday, and you just now comin' to collect your prize?"

Sydona shuttered at the word Willow used to describe her.

"Never you mind what I do. And anyways, this is official NFA business, woman! I don't give a damn if it's on your property, if you marry it or kill it. They're ours!" Harold yelled. A thump and creaking sound told Sydona that Harold took control of the door. A loud slam against the wall startled her, and she peeked out of the door to see what happened. She saw him standing fully in the doorway. A menacing, crooked, yellow toothed smile crept across his face as he glared at her. A sliver of brown shown through her contacts as she stood frozen in fear. There was no use in hiding; he knew she was there.

"Told you I'd see you again, sweetheart. And I see you brought a friend. Even better."

Willow turned her head to the girls with a look of desperation on her face. But she pulled herself together quickly and used all her strength to get him out. Willow was easily twice the size of Harold and pushed him out by kneeing him the stomach. As she was able to get him back onto the porch with his friends and take control of the door again, she yelled.

"I said get the hell off my porch, asshole!" She proceeded to kick him in the groin as hard as she could. Harold hurled his upper body over his legs in pain and stomped his feet hard. Willow stood waiting for them to leave, and when they stood their ground, Sydona knew she had to do something. Harold was not going to give up easily, especially since he knew two fliers were within his reach. She glanced over at the slightly open closet door and remembered the guns inside. She focused and took the shotgun into her hands.

"It's gon take a lot more for me ta leave than--" Harold froze as he looked back up at Willow. To his surprise, Sydona stood next to her, pointing a gun fiercely at him. She glared at him with the butt end of the gun pressed against her left shoulder. Harold stood up slowly, moving his eyes back and forth between the gun and Sydona.

"If you think this is my first time using a shotgun, you'd be dead wrong. Willow said leave," Sydona threatened with a steady voice.

His arms finally left his groin and went up in the air in surrender. But then, he bravely took a step toward the women, not yet convinced anything would happen. Sydona pumped the shotgun and readjusted the end to his head. It was all Harold needed to finally leave the porch. His lackeys followed behind with a look of surrender and drove off in a hurry.

Willow slammed the door so hard the walls shook and almost knocked her knick-knacks to the floor. She rested one hand on the door while locking all the locks with the other. Sydona handed Willow the shotgun. The women only nodded at each other.

"What was that guy's problem?" Raoul said as he and Giovonna joined them in the main room.

"Yeah, you seem like you have some history with him," Sydona said.

Willow stared at the floor and grinned, while trying to calm herself down. "Oh, yeah. Me and Harold go way back. We're neighbors, if you can believe it. But of course, he's part of the National Fliers Association, and I'm part of the Sparrows." Sydona perked up at the mentioning of the Sparrows, and Willow continued. "You ain't the first fliers I had here that he's tried gettin' from me."

Wanting to know more information on this organization, Sydona asked, "What have the Sparrows done to help us?"

"Well," Willow started, "there was a family in Oregon who was captured by the NFA a few months back, and we had a team track them down. Ended up hijacking the van they were being transported in and let them escape. We tied up the agents, and the family got away."

"Oregon, huh?" Sydona asked. "You have people all the way out there?"

"Oh yeah, honey! We're all over the place. But we try to stay off the radar. The NFA don't want the people to know they can't get what they call 'shipments' to the camps. So they don't mention it anywhere in the papers," she paused, "but we are everywhere. You may have seen us around."

She approached them, removed her robe, and pulled down the sleeve around her shoulder that exposed a small tattoo: a small wing with a circle around it.

"I've seen this before." Sydona examined her tattoo carefully. "It was graffitied in my city on a wall a few days ago. I had never seen it before then. It looked pretty fresh."

"I've seen it, too, in my library. It was drawn on a bathroom stall," Giovonna said.

"How come we've never heard of you?" Raoul asked.

"Well, a while back, a newspaper did an article, and one of our Sparrows forced himself to write this piece, and it was so convincin' that everyone believed it was just a gang called 'Angel Wings'. No one looked into it since that. Made up some pretty good photos to hide it all up. Mainly, people stay away from the symbol when they see it now. But if you know what it is, it's a sign of hope. We joke sometimes and call ourselves the Angel Wings, too. It makes sense, I guess."

Sydona and Giovonna both smiled at each other briefly. Still, Sydona wasn't entirely convinced; she wanted to know more.

"How long have they been around?"

"A long time. They actually had done this before, back in the forties. Rounding up fliers and takin' them to a big lab. The species wasn't that well known back then, but some folks were real upset that they were being treated like second class citizens. I'm not sure exactly when the Sparrows officially grouped up, but it was when I had just joined the U.S. Army. When you travel as much as we did and talked to the people we did, news got around quick. Then the winged symbol started appearing randomly. It made folks curious, and then eventually, it took off."

"Why have I never seen this symbol before?" Sydona furrowed her brows, trying to understand.

"I dunno. But we are all over the country and even across seas. Could just be that you missed it. Or that the NFA was trying to suppress it. They quickly caught on, once labs and camps were bein' ambushed."

"So why is that Eagle Lake is being put in the spotlight now? If this has been going on for all these years? Why haven't the Sparrows taken it over yet?"

Willow snorted. "You sure ask a lotta questions…" She paused and waited for Sydona to do something. When Sydona didn't move a muscle, she continued on with a sigh.

"Because Eagle Lake is new, from what I gather. It's a tricky operation and is the biggest group that exists. Also, the first one that is out in the open. Most of the labs are underground or in secret facilities. Sparrows are wary of it and wondering why it's so different than most."

"What do you mean it's new?" Sydona leaned in closer to Willow, hungry for more.

"It's common for these operations to move around. Some intel will get word that we are plannin' on ambushin' it and will move in only a day. We may have a lot of people in the resistance, but they have more. They will always have more…" Willow shook her head.

"Where did it move from?" Sydona stared intently at her, wondering if it was from anywhere in California where she grew up.

"I wish I knew. But these things move around so much, sometimes never stay in one place more than twenty-four hours. I know one place it was for a while was Nevada, but that was years ago."

"How do you know it's the same one?"

"Usually by the guy runnin' it. Dr Malik is the son of the big wig of the NFA. Guess he's kinda crazy, which is why we haven't done anything yet. We don't even know what he's doin'.

"Why aren't you there now?" Sydona asked with anger in her voice.

"'Cause it's in Oregon. Do you know where we are? It's not my territory, and I haven't been called to help out there," Willow answered with sadness in her voice.

Sydona sat on the bed after grilling Willow and tried to process the load of information. She might not be alone in this after all. The vision of her parents kept popping up in her head, and she imagined them escaping a lab with Sparrows taking out the NFA. A wave of uncertainty cramped her stomach as she realized they might not even be at the camp. There had been hundreds of labs and camps over the years. Why would they be at this one? The odds were not in her favor. They could be sitting in Hawaii, sipping Mai-Tais and eating lobster. As great as that sounded for her parents, she still hoped that she could see them. Going to Eagle Lake was the best chance she had to possibly reunite with them.

"Welp! Who's hungry? I know I am!" Raoul broke the intense silence and yawned. He flew into the kitchen. Sydona shook her head, feeling as if she was the only one taking things seriously.

"Good idea!" Willow slapped her leg and happily headed to the kitchen. "How does bacon and eggs sound?"

Giovonna's eyes lit up. "Ooh! Yes please!" She ran to the table and sat down quickly.

Sydona rolled her eyes and slowly strolled over to the table as well with much less enthusiasm and a look of disgust on her face. She envied Giovonna and Raoul's sudden excitement after everything Willow just said. A dark cloud hovered above her head, and she knew it would not be going away anytime soon. Food seemed so petty in a time like this, but the thought of eating something made her mouth salivate. She realized it had been a while since she ate anything. As Willow began to cook the bacon, the strong smell filled the house and made Sydona's face scrunch up.

Giovonna glanced over at her. "What's wrong?"

"Bacon." Sydona flopped down on the chair.

Raoul sat down on the windowsill overlooking the small kitchen. "Oh, right. Sydona isn't a meat eater, Willow."

"What?!" Willow exclaimed, almost dropping the carton of eggs on the battered wooden floor. "How do you not eat meat?! It's human nature to eat innocent animals and sprinkle it with delicious seasonin's!"

Sydona twirled her blonde hair around her index finger. "I don't know. It's just easier to grow veggies and fruit. I haven't had meat since…" She stared off into space. A brief memory came back to her with the smell of bacon wafting against her nose. Sundays were usually family days when both her parents were off from work. They always made an elaborate breakfast with bacon, eggs, pancakes, fresh fruit, and the like. The memory made her smile, but the sound of Raoul shoveling eggs into his mouth made Sydona come back to earth. Willow had joined them at the table while she spaced off.

"You alright there, princess?" Willow asked as she salted her food. "Thought we lost ya."

Sydona looked down at her big plate of fried eggs and an apple Willow had cut up for her. "I'm fine. Thank you though."

Everyone quietly ate their meal. Once finished, Sydona stood up and placed her dishes in the ceramic sink.

"I think it's time for us to go now," Sydona announced to everyone and walked back into the other room to gather up her belongings. Giovonna was sad to be leaving and moved very sloth-like as she scraped her plate off and grabbed her stuff.

"Here! You may need some food for the road." Willow handed some snacks and goodies to Giovonna and Sydona.

"Thanks." Sydona nodded. She organized her tote and backpack to be able to fit everything. After getting it all settled, she strapped her backpack securely on her back and headed out the front door. The sun shone brightly between the tree branches, and Sydona took a brief second to breathe in deeply. Pine needles littered the ground, and the smell filled the air like an air freshener. Walking away from Willow's cabin, she quickly noticed Giovonna was not next to her. Neither was Raoul. She turned to see Willow standing in the doorway with her arms crossed while Giovonna and Raoul whispered to each other on the wooden stairs. Sydona sighed. She could feel a speech coming on. Trying her best to avoid this, she started walking farther away from the cabin, making it obvious how she felt.

"Syd, wait!" Giovonna called out finally.

Sydona heard this but kept walking. There was no time to argue about having Willow come along. Which is exactly what she knew they were talking about. Giovonna and Raoul caught up to her.

"Syd, stop. We need to discuss this," Raoul said shortly. His tone surprised her, and she halted.

"We should ask Willow to come with us," Giovonna said.

"Absolutely not."

"She has a car, Syd!" Raoul threw his arms up.

"I don't care! I don't know her."

"Come on. Be rational here. You didn't know me either. And now you do!" Giovonna grinned.

"Because you were going to come with me whether I wanted you to or not," Sydona retorted, making Giovonna's smile dissipate. "Plus, you're a flier. We stick up for each other and protect each other. Willow isn't a flier. I can't trust her."

Despite the fact that Willow was in a resistance group that protected people like her, her mother's last words rang in her mind. She couldn't trust humans. Although, she made an exception for some, it didn't matter anymore. And Willow could just have easily made all of that up, especially with all the knowledge she had about the NFA. It could be her tactic in order to get fliers to trust her. And once they had their backs turned, she scooped them up and turned them in. Or whatever it was they did. The information Willow gave her was enough to go off of for now.

"That's crappy. You knew Annie pretty well," said Raoul.

"I had to. She sold food that I needed. Not to mention that food was fruit that I kindly paid for you and your entire family to eat."

Raoul shook his head with disappointment and paused as he let her cold statement sink in. Once he let it roll off his back, he said, "You guys were friends. I know you were."

"Yes, we were. But you know how long it took me to really open up and talk to her? Three years. We don't have that kind of time with Willow." Sydona crossed her arms angrily.

"Well, just speed it up a little. Annie was obviously a good person, even after she found out what you were." Raoul threw his hands up again.

Sydona stayed quiet, not wanting to admit that he was right. She could argue with them until her face turned blue, but she had a feeling she was not going to win.

Giovonna spoke up. "Look. I don't know much about you, but I can tell you have serious trust issues. But does it help that Raoul trusts Willow, and you've known him for like, ever, I'm guessing? That has to say something. And I like her. I think she would be good to have around. She's also part of the Sparrows. People dedicated to helping us."

Sydona stared down at her boots, trying to come up with another reason to leave Willow behind. When she couldn't think of anything, she looked back at Willow who waved at them. Another breath of air escaped her lungs in defeat. She reluctantly nodded her head with approval.

"If she does one thing--one little thing, I will not hesitate to--" Sydona gritted her teeth.

"I know, I know. Lighten up, wouldja?" Giovonna whispered back.

Giovonna happily ran back up to Willow to tell her the good news. Sydona was left clenching her jaw, hoping that she would not regret it. She pivoted back to the cabin and joined her friends. As she approached the cabin door, Sydona leered at Willow as she gathered her things. She filled an oversized camouflage bag with some food, medical supplies, water bottles, ammo, rope, and a little pistol to put in her ankle holster. The outside of the bag also had a rolled up sleeping bag and a tent. Willow hunched under the weight of the bag; it was half her size. Sydona secretly applauded her for being so prepared, especially with a tent and everything. But she made no acknowledgement and walked down the steps to join her friends.

Willow walked around the cabin, making sure she had everything she needed while everyone else waited next to a white SUV. The SUV was so obnoxiously large that it could easily fit a small classroom inside. In the daytime, it was much easier to see how cluttered her place was. She had a shed to the left of her cabin filled with enough items to have a neighborhood garage sale. The cabin seemed empty compared to the amount of stuff shoved into the shed, even with all the animal heads hanging up.

Willow opened the back hatch of her car and loaded it up as the girls followed suit. Sydona kept her green tote strapped across her body.

"Come'ere. Got something to show ya." Willow motioned at Giovonna who was handing Sydona her yellow backpack.

Giovonna perked up and dropped her backpack on the ground, leaving Sydona to deal with it. She excitedly followed Willow behind the cabin to the shed. A knot suddenly formed in Sydona's throat as Giovonna disappeared into the darkness. What could Willow be showing her that she needed to be alone for? Her feet slowly made their way back to the shed, and her gaze narrowed in on the slightly opened door. Subconsciously, her right hand made its way down to her dagger, and she gripped it tightly. As she got closer, she heard their voices and then a squeal from Giovonna. Her heart gasped and pulse raced through her body. Sydona kicked the door open, almost shattering the window. She had her dagger out and ready.

"Gia--"

"Look, Syd! It's a crossbow!" Giovonna exclaimed with a huge smile.

Sydona dropped her arm holding the knife and then dropped her head. Resheathing her dagger, on her hip, she sighed deeply and stormed out of the shed. Her face felt hot from embarrassment and thinking something much worse was going on. Conflict over why she felt she needed to save the teenage girl ate at her.

Giovonna ran up beside her, still holding the bow like a prize she had just won at the fair.

"What's going on?" Giovonna asked with a small voice.

Sydona clenched her jaw. "Why did she give you that?"

Giovonna shrugged. "I dunno. She just did."

Sydona heard footsteps from behind her and knew they were Willow's, so she ceased the conversation.

"Y'all ready?" Willow called up to the car.

"Shotgun!" Giovonna cried out so loud birds flew out of the trees.

Sydona flinched as she yelled because she was standing right beside her. Giovonna glanced at her with an apologetic look. Sydona tried to smile, knowing that she wasn't being obnoxious on purpose, but being stuck with a teenager was still new to her. At least at home, Sydona didn't have to be around the adolescent fairies all the time. Their parents were usually around to keep them in line, though.

Sydona was glad to sit in the backseat because she wanted to be further away from Willow. Still, she sat on the opposite side to keep an eye on her. As Giovonna put her new crossbow in the back, she raved about it with Raoul. Raoul was just as excited as her, and it was like listening to two giddy schoolgirls. Sydona always admired Raoul and his ability to open himself up to strangers. Ever since they grew up together, they went through a lot of the same things, but Raoul always had more of an optimistic outlook. Not many people knew he existed, and he relished the moments he could talk to someone other than Sydona or his family.

As she waited for Willow and Giovonna to get in the car, she gandered at all the supplies. There was another tent, firewood, cooking supplies, lanterns, umbrellas, canned food, and blankets. It was enough supplies to live in the wilderness for about a week. It seemed that she had this stuff all ready to go in a moment's notice, and somehow, that made Sydona more comfortable. Maybe Willow was with the Sparrows and had to be ready to leave quickly with short notice. She was sure Willow didn't normally get much notice when those calls came in.

Raoul made himself a spot in the middle console, complete with a soft rag for him to sit on. Once everyone was buckled in and set, Willow started the car up with a loud rumble and backed out of the long driveway.

"How long until we get there?" Giovonna asked.

"Hopefully a day. If we don't run into any car troubles or anythin'," Willow answered.

Giovonna asked Sydona to grab a fiction book from her backpack in anticipation of the long trip. Willow had the radio turned down low to where Sydona couldn't understand the songs, but the melody soothed her. Sydona kept an eye on Willow for a few hours in the car, but soon she grew bored and tired. The smell of rain wafted through Giovonna's open window, and Sydona sighed happily. She loved the aroma and sound of rain. The sky darkened and thunder crackled in the distance as rain began to pour down. As she stared out of her window, listening to the pitter patter on the outside of the car, her eyes grew heavy, and she drifted off to sleep.

Sydona hid in a kid's treehouse a few houses down from her own. When her parents were taken away, she wanted to run far away but also wanted to go back to the house eventually. She cried for days and rage pulsed through her, but Raoul was able to calm her down to keep her from doing anything rash. She could see her house from the tree, but it was surrounded by agents for days. Finally, when they gave up and couldn't find anyone else, they left. Sydona and Raoul cautiously walked back down to the house and through the open back door. The house was destroyed. Broken glass was everywhere, things were thrown from the cabinets, furniture was severely damaged, and many items were missing. Sydona walked slowly through the house, and tears quickly started streaming down her face. She headed up the stairs to find that her bedroom was the most devastating room of all. Her mattress was torn to shreds, feathers covered the scraped up wooden floor, the mirror above her small vanity desk was shattered, and many of her things were broken, including pictures she had of her family.

"Animals," she whispered as she noticed a picture of herself taken by her mom was ripped in half. It showed only the top part of her face, and her small purple eyes were smiling.

She straightened up and wiped off her tears. Her eyes flared green as she stormed through the house and grabbed a giant bag from her parent's room. She filled it with food from the kitchen that wasn't touched, clothes in her room, and a random assortment of other items she thought she may need for a few weeks. Raoul sat on her shoulder, trying to hold on and not saying a word. There was nothing to be said. She went into her parents' room again and looked for any sort of memento that she could hold onto. Everything seemed to be gone. Not only had they destroyed their peace of mind, but they also stole everything of value in the house. She grabbed a pillow off their bed and started hitting things in the room with it. Raoul flew out of the room quickly, afraid that he would get hit. With one last outburst of rage, she kicked her parents king size bed, and it moved slightly.

She looked under it curiously to see if there was anything underneath and noticed a piece of the wooden floor sticking up slightly. Pushing the bed over to the other side of the room, she then wedged her fingers into the edge of the board and lifted. The hole was very narrow, and she felt around for other boards that could be moved. As she moved back four more, she reached down and felt a large metal box. It was heavy and took all of her strength and Raoul's fairy dust to lift it out. On one side there was a circular lock that had numbers on the edge.

Sydona stared at it, trying to figure out the combination.

"Try your birthday," Raoul whispered.

She dialed the numbers '11, 15, 34'.

The metal door squeaked open, and Sydona's jaw dropped. Sparkles from emeralds, rubies, diamonds, and other jewels shone in her eyes. There were also gold coins, stacks of cash, and currencies from other countries she had never heard of.

"Buzz around the tree was that your parents and a family friend had flown to Saudi Arabia a long time ago. And while they were there, they discovered a cave that was filled with treasures. Your parents said they were going to keep it if they ever had a baby," Raoul said softly.

As she searched through the safe, she found a piece of paper with her name written on it. Curiously, she unfolded it, and tears ran down her face once more as she read it to herself.

Dear Sydona,

You may not be born yet, but we decided to save our findings from our adventures to use towards your college education when you grow up. The doctors say you're very healthy and will come to visit us in just a few short weeks! We hope that this serves you well and that you will be the first Wilder to attend college. Make us proud, baby girl.

Love always, Mom and Dad

She hugged the letter, curled up on the wooden floor, and lay there for hours. Raoul snuggled up next to her, singing a lullaby her mother used to sing to her until she fell asleep.

Chapter Eight

A sharp turn from the car startled Sydona awake. Opening her eyes to bright scenery, she saw the rain had stopped. The road and trees were soaking still, and birds played in puddles. Peeking up at the radio with a digital clock, she noticed she had slept for several hours. Raoul was no longer in the middle console but zonked out on the other passenger seat. A tiny nudge from Sydona made Raoul stretch, open his eyes, and let out a yawn.

"Hey. How are you doing?" Sydona whispered low enough to avoid having Willow and Giovonna overhear.

"I'm tired." Raoul rubbed his sleepy brown eyes.

"No, I mean how are you doing? You miss home?" Sydona asked.

Raoul nodded as he stared off and thought about his family.

"Me, too. I wonder how everyone is doing."

"I'm sure they're fine. They might miss all the fruit you normally get, but they can eat the veggies in the garden. Even though a lot of them don't like them because they're not sweet. It would be helpful if you had tomatoes, though."

"Yeah, but you can't grow tomatoes in May. Just like you can't grow corn in the spring." She winked with a grin.

"How long are you gonna hold that against me?" Raoul crossed his arms.

"As long as it's still funny."

She accidently let out a burst of laughter at Raoul's sour face and caught Willow's gaze in the rearview mirror. Sydona's face returned to normal, and she looked back out of her window.

Willow then cleared her raspy throat.

"So how'd y'all meet?" Willow glanced over at Giovonna who had a book propped up on her knees. Giovonna shut her book and grinned at the both of them.

"Well. I just had a stupid argument with my dad about school crap for the thousandth time. Did you know I get A's on most of my papers, and if I screw up just a little and get a B, he bites my freaking head off?" Giovonna grumbled while waving her hands around with anger. She then composed herself and continued on. "Anyways, I was so mad at him for that whole thing, so I left my house. Then I saw this cute little diner down the road and wanted to go in. And wouldn't you know it, only twenty minutes later a tall blonde walks in wearing sunglasses. Next thing I know, that Harold guy is causing a scene and bumps her glasses off! Then I see her eyes! I knew I had to talk to her..."

Sydona sweat just thinking about that whole thing, and it irritated her that Gia brought it up in front of Willow.

"When she left, I followed her but at a distance. I didn't want to seem creepy. But I've never seen anyone with eyes like mine before. Of course, then she thought I was a human 'cause of my contacts. But I showed her and convinced her I was a flier like her. And of course, she begged me to come along with her."

"Excuse me, I did not beg you..." Sydona interjected, even more annoyed than before.

"That's not what I heard," Giovonna chuckled and gave Sydona a look.

"I did not--okay. Haha." Sydona turned her head to face the window again.

Giovonna laughed harder. "No, okay, she didn't beg me. But I did kinda beg her."

"Kinda? You were going to follow me like a lost little puppy dog!" Sydona yelled. But then quickly realized that Giovonna was only messing with her. After she yelled, the car got quiet, and Giovonna stopped laughing.

"Sorry," Sydona said softly.

"No, it's okay. You're right. I was gonna follow you. Meeting you was too big of a sign for me to ignore, and I wasn't letting go of it that easily." She flashed Sydona a smile. The tension in the car disappeared, but it was followed by more silence. As a change of subject, since apparently she didn't have an off button, Giovonna turned around more to face Sydona.

"Hey, so, tell me about us. How were we created? I've always wanted to know."

"Well," Raoul cleared his throat and landed on the middle console, "our tree is full of traditions, one of them being a story that is told every year of how the first flier came to be." He cleared his throat again, puffed out his chest, and lowered his voice to imitate Shaman Faro.

"A long, long time ago, back before my great great grandparents were born, there was an island named Nebulous Isle that was inhabited by fairies. They were happy here, peaceful and protected. The island held many fruit trees that did more than satisfy the fairies that lived there. They homed many trees and lived there for centuries, unwavered. Until one day, a lone wanderer named Grace crashed her boat along the sand during a bad storm. The fairies did not know what to do as they had never come across a human before, and considering her size, they were terrified. But the woman showed no signs of harm; she was just hungry and lost. Grace took shelter in a cave on the opposite side of the island to prove that she did not want to hurt them. After several weeks, one fairy in particular took an interest in her, wanting to know more about this foreign species. His name was Valerio, and he had violet colored eyes. They spent every day together, and it didn't take long before the two fell in love. Grace was then invited to live amongst the fairy community, and she did for many years.

Soon, Grace and Valerio decided they wanted a family and did not let their differences hold them back. One of the village shamans tried everything in his power to help them but failed after many attempts. The couple thought a baby would never be a possibility, and the island became dark and cloudy. Eventually, many of the fairies rallied for them and were able to convince two of the most powerful shamans on Nebulous Isle to contribute their powers. One of the shamans was named Dario, and he had bright green eyes and a serious temper. Although he was hotheaded and unpredictable, he was one of the greats. Bazel was his counterpart and showed off his more sensitive side. As great as Bazel was, he was afraid of many things and often scared of the unknown. His eyes were a timid auburn color.

Dario, Bazel, and Valerio all came together as one to complete one of the most complicated spells they've ever attempted. After several days and tedious chantings, it was finally a success. Nine months later, Grace had a baby girl named Nova. They were surprised to learn that she had developed Valerio's violet eyes. And at only eight years of age, her eyes changed colors depending on Nova's mood. Not to mention, she could now fly.

We now celebrate the blessed day that brought the two loving creatures together. Despite their clear differences, love was the only thing that mattered, and from love, came life. We are proud of this species and have been honored to have them by our side since the beginning.

And then we all do shots."

Raoul bowed, waiting for a reaction.

Giovonna giggled and waited for the punchline.

"Okay, we don't do shots, but I had to put something in there at the end. That story is so boring." Raoul took a deep breath and sat down.

"I thought it was fascinating!" Giovonna exclaimed. "Thanks Raoul. I love a good origin story."

He nodded his head.

Sydona loved the story. She had only heard it a handful of times, but she knew that Raoul heard it way too many times in his life. She imagined herself a lot like Grace: living alone with nothing but fairies in a place where they would never be disturbed. She never fell in love with a fairy the way Grace did. Not to be prejudice but she preferred men that were at least the same height as herself.

As she stared out of the window, dreaming about the perfect island, Giovonna was busy messing with the radio stations.

"This is my favorite song!" Giovonna exclaimed. She adjusted the volume knob on the radio so loud that it made Sydona and Willow jump. Raoul hid himself in the very back of the car under all the bags and luggage. Giovonna bounced around in her seat and sang loudly while playing an air guitar. Sydona covered her ears to help block out some of the noise. She had never heard the song before, but Giovonna seemed to be making it worse.

Willow asked her several times to have her turn it down, but Giovonna argued that it was almost over. Every time Willow would reach over to turn it down, Giovonna would turn it back up. Sydona rolled her eyes at the scene, and her ears pounded each time Giovonna turned it up, making it louder every time.

"Gia! Would you stop!" Willow yelled.

"Just a second. It's just getting to the good part." Giovonna fought with Willow's hand.

As Willow was focusing half on the road, half on controlling the radio, she barely kept her eyes on the road. Sydona happened to look out the windshield as the arguing continued, and she tensed up as she saw a deer standing in the road.

"Willow!" Sydona screamed and pointed up front.

It felt like slow motion. Willow's head snapped around as Sydona yelled. She didn't have time to use the brakes. She tried to swerve, but the deer jumped in the same direction. Panicking, she maneuvered to the other side. The road was still slick from the rainstorm, and her tires skid uncontrollably, forcing the SUV into the edge of a metal railing. Screams from Giovonna rang throughout the vehicle, the tires squealed, and Willow cursed every other word. Sydona squeezed her seat belt tightly and braced for impact.

As they hit the railing with an ear-crunching sound, the airbags went off instantly in front of Willow and Giovonna with a loud pop. Sydona wasn't sure what caused the next thing to happen, but soon they were upside down, rolling over and over down a hill. There must've been a downed tree or boulder to cause the giant vehicle to overturn with ease. Her heart raced as she thought about Raoul who wasn't buckled in or anything. Supplies from the trunk were roaming about the cabin freely, hitting Sydona in the head and body. Luckily, nothing hard enough to do any real damage. The screaming and cursing stopped as the SUV landed at the bottom of the hill on it's side.

Sydona sat still for a moment, in shock from the impact and still gripping her seat belt. The sounds of pipes whistling, airbags deflating, and Giovonna moaning were loud in her ears. Finally feeling safe enough to open her eyes, she took everything in. The window underneath her was shattered. The glass made several cuts in her right arm, and she could feel the throbbing intensifying. Her neck ached from being tossed around like a bobble head, causing her head to hurt, too. Their supplies were scattered all around the car. A few logs laid on her chest and made it hard to breathe. The lantern was broken, and a medical kit had burst and thrown its contents everywhere.

She searched for the buckle on her seat belt. Once she freed herself, she pushed everything off and threw it in the back.

She examined her arms and legs and found only a few scratches. She could feel bruises that weren't visible yet. The silence worried her. She knew that they had probably gotten much more damage than she did and began to climb out the other side. Cranking the other passenger window down, she hoisted herself out, sat on the top, and gasped for fresh air. Fresh, muddy tire marks weaved down to the scene of the accident. The guard rail was severely bent, and the deer was nowhere in sight. A part of her was glad that Willow dodged out of the way instead of hitting it. She knew her SUV would take little damage compared to the animal. Maybe Willow had a soft spot for it. Knowing this helped her like Willow just an inkling more.

Just then, she heard coughing from back inside the sideways car. It was a small cough, and she knew instantly that it was Raoul. She slid off the car and hobbled back to the trunk where she assumed he was trapped. She popped open the trunk and rummaged through everything, listening intently for the cough. Lifting up a blanket, she uncovered Raoul stuck underneath a log of wood.

"Are you okay?" Sydona asked with a sigh of relief. She threw the log off him effortlessly.

"I am now." Raoul slowly stood up and fluttered his wings. He examined the one red wing that was torn and sighed. Testing his wings out, he discovered it wasn't bad enough to prevent him from flying.

"Okay, good," Sydona said. "I'm gonna go help them. You gonna be okay?"

Raoul gave her a thumbs up while he massaged his shoulder.

Her muscles ached, and her neck still cramped, making it hard to move quickly. She knew she had to crawl back on top of the car in order to help them, though. Managing to make it back on top, she looked down Willow's rolled up window to see her hanging sideways by her seatbelt with blood on her head.

She was so large that she couldn't see Giovonna at all. Willow wasn't moving or anything. Sydona grabbed the door handle, but it was locked. With frustration from it not opening and her injuries, she grudgingly went back inside the opened window she came out of. She was now able to see Giovonna and her condition, and it didn't look good.

"Gia," Sydona called and shook her shoulder. Giovonna suddenly moved and opened her eyes. The noise woke up Willow as well.

"Is everyone alright?" Sydona asked while helping Giovonna out of her seat.

They nodded, but each movement they made caused them to moan and grumble in pain. Giovonna struggled with unbuckling herself, but Sydona helped her with it. They told Willow to stay put, fearing she would fall and crush Giovonna. Giovonna cried out in pain as she put her scraped up arms around Sydona who pulled her out. Tears streamed down her smooth caramel skin, and her eyes were bloodshot with pain. Sydona led Giovonna to a patch of soft wet grass where she tended to the bloody wound on her leg. Her jeans showed damp, red patches near her calf. Sydona barked at Raoul to help Giovonna while she went to help Willow.

This was going to be a challenge. She guessed Willow weighed close to two-hundred and fifty pounds and was dreading lifting her out. The seatbelt that held her in place made getting her out extremely difficult. With the door opened, Willow gripped the side of the car and tried to pull herself out as Sydona tugged on her clothes. She could tell Willow was in serious pain because her arms shook as she tried to lift herself up.

"Raoul!" Sydona yelled back at him. He was tending to Giovonna still. She motioned her head towards them, hinting that they needed his help.

"Can you dust her?"

Raoul looked wide-eyed at Sydona as he glanced back and forth between her and Willow.

"...I'll try."

Raoul then sprinkled his red and orange fairy dust on Willow. Afraid of getting the dust in her eyes, she squeezed them shut, but the magic dust disappeared as soon as it touched her skin. After Raoul was satisfied that he gave her enough, he gave his approval to Sydona to try lifting again. Raoul flew over and unbuckled her as Sydona held onto Willow. With another tug and grunt, Willow's weight felt more like a small child's, and Sydona pulled her out with ease.

Finally, Willow was out.

"I feel like air!" Willow exclaimed.

Sydona smiled at her reaction to the dust and helped her down off the SUV. She still landed with a thud, but Willow couldn't tell the difference.

"How long this stuff last for?" Willow asked Raoul with amazement.

"Never as long as you want it to," Raoul laughed.

"That's a shame. Could I fly right now?" Willow looked up at the sky.

"No, and please don't try," Raoul warned. Sydona knew it wasn't the first time he dusted someone who wanted to fly. Last time, it ended very badly.

Sydona grinned and headed over to Giovonna who was fixing herself up.

"How are you feeling?" She sat next to her in the muddy grass.

"Not as good as Willow," Giovonna said.

"Yeah, it'll wear off soon, and she'll be feeling her injuries more," Sydona said and laughed as she watched Willow try to jump. She knew she would regret it soon. When she looked back, she found Giovonna staring at the ground and crying.

"It's all my fault..." she whimpered.

Sydona's stomach twisted; she felt uncomfortable around weepy people. Between the deer and the slick road, the accident probably would have happened even if Giovonna hadn't distracted Willow.

"It's no one's fault. These things just happen," Sydona said.

"But if I would have just turned it down, Willow wouldn't have been fighting with me, and she would have seen it."

"Everything happens for a reason," Sydona said. Even though it sounded cliché, that's how she felt about many things in her life. Sometimes there was no way to control anything that happened. As an adult, she knew this, but understood at Giovonna's young age, it was hard to accept.

Giovonna scoffed and wiped her cheeks. "Yeah. Whatever," she mumbled as she slowly stood back up and limped over to the vehicle. She followed her back to the car at a safe distance. Her words didn't comfort Giovonna like she hoped they would, and it somehow made her feel sad.

Willow was patching herself up and had a big white cotton square on her forehead covered by tape. Raoul was busy organizing everything and getting the medical supplies back in the first aid kit. Willow searched around in her oversized pack for a pill bottle, and once she found it, she took one pill for herself and handed one to Giovonna.

For the next hour or so, the group gathered up their items and decided what they could bring and what needed to leave behind. The SUV was too badly damaged to try to fix. Willow was very upset that her car was totaled, but she was less angry than Sydona anticipated.

"So where do we go from here?" Raoul made himself comfy on Sydona's shoulder as she sat on a log.

"Well, we can't drive there anymore!" Willow yelled and kicked a tire.

"I think I remember seeing a sign for a train station just a few miles from here," Giovonna said as she adjusted her yellow headband.

Sydona laughed softly and then louder the more she thought about her suggestion. "I needed that, thank you." She sighed and began hiking up the hill to the road. Raoul flew off her shoulder and stayed back with the others.

"Why is that funny?" Giovonna asked after her.

"Because it's a joke. Jokes are supposed to be funny, right?" Sydona said as she kept walking.

"Honey, do you know where we are?" Willow yelled angrily enough to slow Sydona's walk and make her turn her head. "We ain't even to Wyoming yet. And you wanna walk the rest of the way? Huh-uh. No way in hell."

Sleeping the whole ride pulled the wool over her eyes. They were much farther away than she thought, and she clenched her fists. Standing on the edge of the road next to the bent railing, she looked down at Willow and Giovonna who had their arms crossed. Even Raoul was on their side, and she felt like the outsider. She didn't think she was being that unreasonable by not wanting to board a train with dozens of passengers and no way to escape. It was suicide.

The vote was three against one, and she wondered why she was always on the losing side. So much of her wanted to leave on her own because she felt like she was the only one being smart and rational. It was as if they couldn't grasp the seriousness of the situation, and she was trying her best to avoid people on the way there. But in a world where humans populated ninety-nine percent of the planet, she was bound to run into them at some point.

After fighting with herself, she couldn't bring herself to leave Raoul and Giovonna. Willow she couldn't care less about, and she knew she could handle herself.

"Let's get going then," she finally said and walked back down the hill. The group stayed back in the forest but still close enough to the road to look out for signs.

The woods were still soggy, and they had to maneuver around puddles rippling from the raindrops in the trees. Willow hung back while Giovonna and Sydona walked side by side. Raoul hitched a ride on Giovonna's fluffy, curly black hair. Even as the sun was going down, the humidity hung in the air, making it miserable and hot. Mosquitoes took advantage of the humidity as well and latched onto Sydona's arms and caused her skin to become itchy.

The sun was getting ready for bed, and Sydona was getting tired as well. She was now much farther in front of them. Giovonna and Willow held onto each other and limped along. As much as she wanted to walk faster, she felt that telling them to hurry before the sun went down would be too harsh. She already felt like the bad guy and the only one who didn't trust people. Maybe she should try to lighten up. Just as she was internally mustering up some kind of small talk, Raoul called back to them about seeing the edge of a town.

"Thank god!" Giovonna gasped.

"What's the name of this place, Raoul?" Willow spoke up, clearly out of breath and ready to pass out.

"Norrisville!" Raoul exclaimed, happy to be done, too. Although, he spent most of the time sitting or lying on Giovonna's head.

"Come on, you know the drill," Sydona said to Raoul as they were in sight of buildings and houses. Raoul reluctantly dove into her bag.

"Let's get some damn tickets, shall we?" Willow said as she limped up to the front of the girls and took the lead. Sydona took over as Giovonna's crutch as they crossed the rusty railroad tracks to the lonely train station. The town appeared smaller than Mayfield with very few buildings around, and the ones that were still standing seemed run down and abandoned. A porch with a few stairs introduced the train station. Skinny metal columns held up the roof, and the railing was rusting in several places. Trash was tucked away in the corners. It obvious that the station wasn't used very much or well taken care of. A tattered wooden bench stood next to the entrance with a dated newspaper box next to it.

Following Willow to the entrance of the station, she led Giovonna over to the bench to rest. Willow went inside to purchase tickets as the rest of them waited outside. Sydona peeked inside the newspaper box, and even though the box looked old, the paper was to date. The headline read: <u>10 'Fliers' Found in Cellar of Private Home in Seattle, WA</u>.

She closed her eyes with disbelief and hung her head low. Rubbing her eyebrows softly, she leaned against the railing of the porch and gave a slight laugh.

Giovonna, who sat across from her on the bench with her leg propped up, mimicked Sydona's laugh. "What?"

"Am I crazy?" she asked softly.

Raoul took this opportunity to exit the tote bag and join the conversation. He quickly caught on that she was referring the headline on the newspaper hiding behind the dirty glass.

"I dunno. But if you're crazy, I guess I am, too," Giovonna said.

Trying to keep her mind light, Sydona grinned and decided to change the subject. She noticed Giovonna wincing as she tended to her leg.

"How's it doing?"

"Hurts. Still." Giovonna visibly clenched her jaw in pain.

Sydona nodded and tried to think of a story to get Giovonna's mind off the pain while they waited for Willow.

"When I was seven, we had this awesome tire swing set up in the backyard. My dad had just rigged it up for me, and it was so much fun. Well, I, being an impatient seven year old, wanted to try flying before I was supposed to. The swing went really high, and I thought it was the perfect platform to try it out. I waited until mom and dad weren't around because I knew as soon as they saw me on the top of the swing, they would try to stop me. So I went for it. And of course, I didn't fly. But I did break my arm in three places when I came crashing down. My dad was maaad. Needless to say, they took the swing down after that." Sydona laughed.

"You were such a little rebel!" Giovonna giggled. "I can't believe you actually thought that would work."

"I know!" Sydona said. "It hurt sooo bad. Never been in that much pain before."

"Where was Raoul when this all happened?" Giovonna turned to him.

"I wasn't born yet. Otherwise, I would have kicked her butt!" Raoul belted.

"I think my broken arm was punishment enough," Sydona said while rubbing her arm and reliving the incident.

The mood felt lighter and made Sydona relax a little more. The train was becoming more desirable and practical the more time went on. She was starting to open up more to Giovonna, and it felt like a big step for her. Never in her adult life would she think about being friends with a teenager. But times were changing, and she needed to try to change with it.

"Alright y'all, the train should be here in 'bout five minutes," Willow announced as she stepped back outside on the porch. Raoul hid himself back in the bag without being told, and the girls went inside. The train station was small and fairly quiet. Small rows of benches for waiting passengers lined the center of the lobby. One of the two ticket windows had a closed sign, and the other held a bored-looking older woman leaning back in her chair and lazily admiring her manicured nails.

Sydona wrinkled her nose at the old, mildew smell of the station. The old building clearly had history, but it didn't seem to be kept very well. Dust lined the open-brick walls, and cobwebs hung from the ceiling like Halloween decorations. The train schedule was not electronic but written in yellow on an overused green chalkboard. An old TV hung from the ceiling facing towards the benches. They were broadcasting an episode of *Leave it to Beaver,* but the volume was muted. A single vending machine rested against the opposite wall.

"Ooh Oreos!" Giovonna limped over to the flickering snack machine while pulling out a dollar from her blue velcro wallet.

"Where is this going?" Sydona asked as she looked around the station with her arms crossed.

Willow looked at the tickets again and handed one to her and Giovonna. "Temple. Closest place I could find to, *ya know,*" she whispered the last part because of the ticket master staring curiously over at them.

"Okay, so how close is it?" Sydona asked.

"Uh, not very. But it will get us farther west. Just more north than I would like," Willow rubbed the back of her neck and groaned. "I don't care as long as we can take a break from carrying all this crap for a while."

Sydona sighed. "Well, I guess it's better than nothing."

At 7:35 sharp, the train screeched to a halt in front of the station and the doors slid open as the breaks sighed and expelled steam from underneath. For a century old train station, the train itself looked fairly new, which helped Sydona feel more at ease. Willow was in the lead again while Sydona helped Giovonna into the train. Even though she knew Giovonna could walk, she felt guilty for pressing ahead in the woods and wanted to make it up to her. The entrance to the train was narrow, and Giovonna insisted that Sydona go in front of her. Dreading the fact that she would be in the middle, trapped almost, made her nervous again.

She then felt a knot in her throat and rested her hand on her knife for security. Giovonna nudged her forward as gently as she could, but it made her trip over herself, and she suddenly noticed the train was almost completely packed full of people. Sydona scanned every single passenger and felt all of their eyes glued to her. They all moved their heads in unison to follow her as she walked past them down the hall. This was it. She was done. They knew. They all knew. It was a trap! Why did she fall for this?! She squeezed her eyes shut as negative thoughts ran through her mind.

Sydona then hesitantly opened her eyes to see the passengers looking forward or down at their laps. None of them seemed to care about her in the least. She then caught a glimpse of a man wearing a jacket with the Sparrow wing embroidered on his arm. The sight of this alone helped her relax, and her heart began to beat normally.

Finally arriving at their seats, she sat next to the window while Giovonna sat opposite her across a mahogany colored table. Willow flopped down next to Sydona, barely fitting in her own seat. The girls piled all of their belongings on the table, including the tote Raoul was in. She built a barrier to block any kind of passersby from seeing a fairy sleeping on a sweatshirt. Raoul fluffed up a part of the blue sweater, lay down facing the window, and fell asleep before the train even started moving. Sydona nervously tapped her fingers on the armrest and tried to only look out of her window. The train whistle blew again, and they all shook in place as they took off to their next destination.

Chapter Nine

It was pitch black outside, and Sydona was only able to see her reflection in the mirror from the lights on the train. She had never been to this part of the country before and hoped she could catch a glimpse of the new landscape. Glancing through darker areas and trying to see out, she kept looking back at herself and eventually at her eyes. With everything going on, she had almost forgotten they were a different color. She looked away, still unsure about seeing herself that way. Although, it did seem to be working. No one on the train seemed to look twice at her, and no one seemed hostile. She felt a little embarrassed that she had not thought of this before or even knew colored contacts existed.

Across from her, Giovonna peacefully read a book with a robotic looking face on the cover. It looked intriguing, and she was unsure if it was a fiction book. Willow was passed out next to her and sitting in a position that pressed Sydona against the window. With every big bump they came across, Willow's snoring echoed through the cabin. Sydona did her best to push Willow off of her, but she kept sliding back towards her. And of course Raoul was sound asleep, wrapped inside a sweater and out of sight.

It was so quiet. Despite Willow's snoring, the clacking from the rails below was soothing in her eardrums. There was little conversation amongst passengers as most were either sleeping or reading. After a while she heard a man talking on a television in the distance. It seemed to be a news story of some kind.

"Yeah, did you hear about that?" Giovonna was suddenly looking back and forth between her and the television.

"What?" Sydona asked as she tried paying closer attention to the story.

"That news story about a father drowning his ten year old son in a kiddie pool. I mean, what kind of psycho would do that? And only ten years old! Just insane… this world. Make it sound so easy to take a life…" Giovonna shuttered.

"Oh my god. When did that happen?" Sydona asked, wide eyed as she looked at the program again and saw shots of pictures from the crime scene. One was of a blue little pool in the backyard of a run down house and then another of yellow tape crossing the area off.

"Sometime last week. It was down in Florida." Giovonna shook her head.

"Yeah… I can't imagine anyone doing that to a child," Sydona mumbled as she suddenly remembered a dark memory as a child. Her stomach twisted at the thought of this being brought up again and how much she wished it didn't happen. She couldn't help but to relive the painful day that happened only weeks after her parents had been taken away.

"There he is!" Raoul whispered loudly to Sydona from behind her head.

Her eyes narrowed as she pointed the bow in his direction, up in the tree. "Gotcha." The arrow lined up perfectly with him.

Pfft! The squirrel was pinned to the tree. Sydona smiled with satisfaction. "Dinner is served."

She climbed up a few branches of the oak tree to grab what she hunted. She retrieved her arrow and put the little gray squirrel in her tote and jumped back down to the leafy ground. Stopping after only a few steps, she heard a rustling in the bushes nearby. Her eyes turned auburn with fear that a predator might have tracked her down as well. Walking as quietly as she could and readying her bow, she approached the shrubs. She concentrated intently into a hole in the bush and noticed a pair of eyes looking back at her. It was a person, and a small one at that.

"Show yourself!" Sydona commanded with her tiny voice. Raoul hid in her pocket as he was not fond of sharing a space with a dead rodent.

The little boy stood up as quickly as he could, looking as frightened as the squirrel as he stared at her weapon.

"Oh, sorry!" She lowered her bow. "I was just doing some hunting."

Her eyes soon turned back to normal as she observed the person. He was young and unarmed, letting Sydona feel more relaxed. But his face seemed frozen in fear, and he was unable to take his wide eyes off of hers.

"My name is Sydona, but you can call me Syd." She smiled, happy to see a person her age. "What's your name?"

"Sam," the little boy squeaked.

"What are you doing way out here, Sam?" Sydona asked.

"Nothing," he retorted quickly.

"Oh," Sydona shuffled her feet and adjusted her bag. She continued, "Well I'm..."

"Are you a flier?" Sam blurted out.

Sydona stopped breathing for a second and tried to choose her words carefully. Why would he ask her that? Did she look like a flier? She always thought she looked very similar to other humans. Was it her blonde hair, her fair skin, her purple eyes--

"My eyes," she whispered to herself. She never thought of her eyes always being a different color than other people's.

The little boy took her silence as a yes and bolted toward the town. Sydona's heart was beating rapidly, and her adrenaline soared. She needed to stop him; he could tell the wrong person and then what would happen to her?

She ran as fast as her small legs could carry her after Sam. He looked back and saw her running closely behind him, which made him panic and trip.

Now was her chance. She lifted him by his shirt and begged, "Please! Please don't tell anyone, Sam!"

"Let go of me!" Sam struggled to get her off, but she was surprisingly strong for her age.

"Please!" Sydona insisted as her eyes turned a teal, then an olive green color.

Sam saw her eyes change color and was even more frightened. "Get off me!"

"No! You have to promise me you won't tell anyone!" Sydona was shaking him hard to try to control him. Her anger clouded her judgment, and she pushed him hard, causing him to fall down. He looked behind him. He was very close to the edge of a big pond in the middle of the field. He scrambled to get up with a look of terror and surrender. He was finally able to stand up, but Sydona pushed him again, right into the water.

He bobbed up and down in the water, gasping for air. "Help!" Sam squeaked loudly. "I can't swim!" he choked.

Sydona panicked at the sight. She rushed to the edge of the water and tried to grab him, but he had moved too far out. Sydona flattened herself out in order to reach out further, but the more Sam flailed, the worse it got.

"Take my hand!" Sydona urged, but the boy was too scared and had fear in his eyes.

Sydona stared at the flailing boy in the water and couldn't seem to make herself move. Raoul popped out of her pocket and buzzed in the direction of the town and heard people yelling his name.

Sydona could hear them slightly, too, and her heart beat even faster. She looked out towards the voices, trying to figure out what to do. But the next thing she knew, Sam was gone.

"Sam?" Sydona asked herself as she looked at the water again, and all she saw were tiny bubbles, a few lasting ripples, and tiny waves crashing over the cattails. Raoul grabbed her shirt, hinting that she needed to leave. Without thinking, her feet began to move away from the screaming woman, and then, she ran faster and faster into the depths of the nearby forest with Raoul flying right beside her. Her thoughts traveled faster than her legs, and she couldn't wrap her head around what just happened. But she couldn't deny it. She had killed someone at only ten years old.

The train blew its whistle again as the announcer spoke over the intercom. "Good evening ladies and gentleman. We have arrived at Temple, Wyoming, and it's approximately 10:40 p.m. Please make sure to grab all of your belongings and stay seated until the train comes to a complete stop. Thank you and enjoy the rest of your night."

Sydona nudged Willow hard to wake her up, and the group gathered all of their bags and supplies. The train came to a slow, squeaky halt at the station in Temple. Willow grabbed her giant camouflaged backpack and adjusted the straps with a big yawn. Sydona, Giovonna, and Willow wobbled out of the train with shoulders, arms, and hands full of stuff.

"See! That wasn't so bad, right? No one tried to kill you or anything!" Giovonna smiled at Sydona, trying to make her feel better.

Sydona chuckled as she entered the lobby of another small station. It put her mind at ease that this town was also smaller and not a big city. It was hard enough being on a train full of strangers with no way out; this was like a breath of fresh air. Helping Giovonna to the exit of the station, she looked around and noticed a lone pay phone sitting in the corner. Enough time had passed to where Sydona felt Giovonna's parents should have an update. It wasn't clear how long Giovonna told them she would be gone, and Sydona knew her parents would begin to worry. If it was herself, she knew her parents would want several updates. But then again, she was never old enough to go out on her own when her parents were still around. She whispered to Giovonna.

"Hey. I think you should give your parents a call."

Giovonna sighed and rolled her eyes.

"We're not going anywhere until you call them."

"And say what?" Giovonna spat. "That I'm not at a friend's house but on my way across the country with two older ladies and a fairy? Yeah, that'll go over real nice."

Sydona shushed her, afraid the folks still getting off the train would overhear. A couple of people walked by with puzzled expressions, and she suddenly felt uneasy again.

"I'm not going to ask you again," Sydona said as she took Giovonna's arm off of her shoulders and nudged her over to the phone.

As Willow turned back towards the girls, Giovonna reluctantly made her way over to the pay phone. Sydona and Willow waited on the bench while she made her call. The building was empty, leaving just the three of them.

"Hi. It's me."

"Is mom there?"

Giovonna pulled the phone away from her head and sighed loudly.

"I was calling to see if I can stay at Suzanna's house a couple more days."

"Because she's my friend and--it's nice being in a different house."

"I'm in highschool now, dad. You don't need to keep treating me like a child."

"Dad!"

"Please. I never ask to do anything!"

She was silent for a few minutes, and Sydona guessed her father was busy yelling at her.

"But--"

"Uuhg, dad!"

"You make me go home right now, and I will tell mom you're having an affair."

"Oh, yes I would."

"Fine. I will!"

"I wouldn't have to look at your face anymore!"

"Fine!"

She slammed the phone over and over and then hunched over to a nearby chair with her face in her hands. The train station echoed with sobbing while Sydona and Willow slowly made their way over to her.

"What'd he say?" Sydona asked softly.

Giovonna didn't answer as she was too busy choking back tears. Willow and Sydona exchanged worried looks and mutually decided to leave her be. As they walked back towards their bags they left on the bench, Giovonna answered.

"He told me to not worry about coming back..." she said between breaths.

"Yer pop actually said that to you? What a piece of--horse manure," Willow answered quickly as she turned back to face the girl.

"I'm sure he didn't mean it," Sydona said and made her way over to her.

Giovonna scoffed and wiped her face.

"He just cares about you and wants you to be safe. I'm sure he was just angry when he said that," Sydona said.

Giovonna shook her head and spoke up.

"I'm adopted--" Giovonna started, "when I was only a year old. And when my eye color changed, they freaked. It's like they didn't know what to do with me. They sheltered me because of bullying at schools. I never learned to fly, never knew anything about who I really was. My dad--he and I have never been close. He only tolerates me because of my mom. And even then, mom's not the best either... She doesn't defend me. I'm better off without them."

Sydona shook her head in disappointment. She was starting to see where her anger stemmed from now. Flying was the best feeling imaginable, and to not let your child experience it seemed cruel. To suppress her for being unique and different from them was beyond her comprehension. Sydona was raised to be proud of who she was and proud of being different than the neighborhood kids. Her mother said the world would be very dull if everyone looked and behaved the same way. She wished she could understand what Giovonna was going through. If her own father ever said that to her, she would probably have an equal reaction. Sydona liked to stay out of sticky situations unless it was her own, but there was something about this girl. Her adopted parents had never accepted her for who she was, but Sydona felt she had a chance to fill that gap.

Sydona sat down next to her, and Giovonna immediately wrapped her arms around her. Sydona used one of her free hands to awkwardly tap her arm. Giovonna cried into Sydona's shirt, muffling the sniffles. Normally, she would be very uncomfortable with being the shoulder to cry on, but this time she felt an odd feeling. She felt needed. And she smiled.

The girls sat for a few moments without words. Sydona didn't know what else to say to her, but not saying anything was sometimes a good thing. She caught a glimpse of Willow who stood by the exit and yawned heavily. It was almost midnight, and she could feel Raoul getting antsy in her bag. They needed to find a place to crash for the night and let Giovonna rest her leg for a while, too. Moving slowly, Sydona coaxed Giovonna into getting up so they could leave.

As the girls gathered up their belongings, Sydona mentioned they needed to find a place to sleep for the night.

"Can your tent fit three people?" Sydona asked.

"I brought two. One sleeps just one. The other is a bit bigger," Willow answered as she walked outside.

"A tent?" Giovonna sighed.

"Unless you wanna lay on the wet muddy ground." Willow jabbed her.

"What, we can't stay at a hotel or something? I saw that there's a bed and breakfast near here," Giovonna said and limped behind them. Sydona lagged back to be her crutch once again.

Sydona smirked and laughed. "No. No hotels. Willow's tents will do just fine."

"But I need a shower…" Giovonna whined.

Sydona rolled her eyes. "Don't we all."

Low lit street lights guided them along with their soft buzzing, and crickets began their night songs, deafening the distant train horn. Sydona let Raoul out while they made their way, and he hid under her hair when they caught sight of anyone. Only one car had passed by them, but Raoul was in desperate need of fresh air. Giovonna's leg was throbbing so much that she had to stop for a minute. Sydona suggested she hop on her back for a while.

"You wanna give me a piggyback ride?" Giovonna grinned.

Sydona smirked and removed her backpack. She handed it over to Willow, even though she was already carrying an oversized bag. She squatted down to let Giovonna climb up and grunted as she stood. Starting at a slow pace, with her arms wrapped securely around Giovonna's legs, she thought she would have some fun and run. Hearing Giovonna laughing made her smile, and Sydona hoped it cheered her up after the phone call with her dad.

Back into the depths of the forest, as far away from the road as they could get, they found a flat area to set up camp. Judging by the direction of the moon, Sydona guessed it was about one in the morning. Everyone felt exhausted and dreaded setting up the tents. Raoul was the most awake since he slept more than everyone on the train, so he helped by giving everyone equipment. Willow decided to sleep in the one-person tent by herself and passed out with her feet sticking out.

"You know, for being in the military and part of the resistance, she sure wears out quickly, huh?" Raoul said to the girls.

"Thanks for your help, buddy." Sydona yawned. "See you in the morning."

"You're going to bed already?" Raoul asked as he zipped around her.

"Yes, you coming?" Sydona took off her red shirt and left the white tank top on.

"But I'm not tired."

"Okay, well. You can be on lookout for bears then." Sydona lay down next to Giovonna who was already asleep.

"Bears?!" Raoul whispered.

Sydona shut her eyes and answered, "Yeah…"

"Syd! Wake up! No one said anything about bears being out here!" Raoul flew around the tent in a frenzy.

Sydona furrowed her brows with her eyes still shut. "Sh--it's fine Raoul. I'm sure they won't be coming here. Just--go to--sleep…" She barely said this before she passed out.

It felt like only a few hours later when a beam of sunlight came bursting through the tent and into her vision. Her eyes still felt heavy from the short sleep and her body sweaty from the sleeping bag. Squinting her eyes, she saw Giovonna was still asleep with a shirt over her face. And Raoul was on the other side, curled up into a ball. Sydona lay in her sleeping bag, taking a few minutes to relax and enjoy the peace and quiet. The crunching of leaves and twigs outside the tent put Sydona on high alert.

"Excuse me. Hello?" a man's voice called out softly.

Sydona's heart began to pound out of her chest as she grabbed her dagger. She stayed still, hoping that the stranger would move on.

"Anyone?" he asked again as he walked around the site.

Sydona could see his shadow coming through the tent walls as she followed him around. She positioned herself into a crouch with her knife stiffly ahead, staying as quiet as a mouse.

"Please. I'm lost and haven't eaten in days," he pleaded.

Sydona gulped loudly and bounced on her feet, conflicted on if she should help the stranger. Her first thought was that he was a bounty hunter. But they didn't see anything or anyone on their way to the site. He must have come from miles away. What were the odds that he ended up at their campsite? Raoul and Giovonna were still both sound asleep. She wanted to wake them up but couldn't be sure they wouldn't make a lot of noise.

She peeked into her bag, found a couple apples, and grabbed one. Staring at it and wiping off the skin, she sighed. She unzipped the bottom of the opening just big enough to roll the apple out and zipped it back up.

"Oh my, thank you!" the man said loudly and took a bite.

Sydona faced the area where she thought he stood and grabbed her dagger again. "You got food. Now please leave."

He took a few more bites. "I can't express how glad I am I came across your site. And you gave me food! There aren't many people like you left in the world."

Sydona rolled her eyes and didn't respond. It was just what he wanted. Giovonna rolled over and opened her eyes.

"What's going on?" she mumbled.

Sydona put her hand up to the girl's mouth. Giovonna furrowed her brows and then heard the crunching of an apple outside of their tent. Raoul yawned loudly.

"Who are you talking to, Syd?" Raoul asked sleepily.

"Shh!" she said quickly, frustrated at exactly what she feared they would do.

"Oh, your name's Syd? I'm Peter," the man said more loudly. "I would like to thank you properly, if that's alright?"

Sydona, Raoul, and Giovonna exchanged looks and silently argued over what to do about the stranger. By Giovonna's expressions, Sydona assumed she thought he was just a normal guy who wanted to thank her. Then, she opened her mouth.

"Just a minute, Peter," Giovonna called out to him.

Sydona widened her eyes at Giovonna with anger.

Raoul whispered in Sydona's ear, "I'll try to throw him off."

Sydona shook her head quickly, but Raoul didn't listen.

He flew up to the entrance of the tent, only a few inches from his face, put his hands on his mouth and puffed his chest.

"Listen pal. My friend said leave. So you better go before we make you." A deep, booming voice came from Raoul, making the girls heads twirl. He sounded like a six-foot tall man.

Sydona had never heard him do this voice before, and she would have been impressed if it wasn't a such stupid idea.

"Hey, I don't want any trouble. Just wanna thank your friend. I don't think I'm asking a whole lot here," said Peter, sounding less friendly.

Raoul looked back at Sydona with a shrug. Sydona responded with an eye roll and thin lips.

The three stayed quiet in the tent, unsure of what to do next and hoping that he would get bored and move on. Sydona wondered what Willow was doing in her tent. Not so much as a peep came from her side. Willow didn't seem like the rash type that would burst out and attack. Her strategy seemed to be the same as theirs: wait for him to leave.

"I'm not going to leave without thanking you," Peter said shortly. Then a sound like a gun being cocked echoed in Sydona's ears.

Sydona caught a glimpse of Giovonna whose eyes turned wet from tears. Raoul looked up at Sydona longingly, stuck on how to get out of the sudden hostage situation. Sydona slowly and quietly equipped her knife on her hip and tied up her boots. She grabbed a black jacket with a hood and had Raoul hide inside of it.

"Still there, Syd?" Peter stepped closer to the tent.

"Yes. I'm coming out," she said and took a deep breath.

The sun blinded her as she unzipped the tent, but she could make out a large, bald man in a white t-shirt aiming a pistol at her.

"Slowly now. This isn't a race," Peter said.

Sydona's eyes turned green underneath the contacts as she clenched her jaw. She put her hands up to show him she meant no harm.

"The other two in there, too," he said.

"She's injured. Can't walk," Sydona blurted.

Peter looked her in the eyes and grinned. His skin was weathered and face covered in frown lines. The pistol was small compared to his massive hands, and his shirt stretched so much she could see his chest hair through it. He would be a good match for Willow.

"What about the guy? Or is he injured too?"

"That was me," Sydona avoided eye contact.

Peter didn't seem to be easily fooled. "Who's in here?" he pointed at Willow's tent.

"No one. It's for our supplies," Sydona lied.

"Oh. So you won't care if I open it then?" Peter walked towards it with his pistol still glued on Sydona.

She stood silently and tried to come up with something quickly.

"Wait," Sydona shouted. "I lied. It's not supplies. It's my grandmother. She was recently widowed and is severely depressed. Plus, she hates when people wake her up. Gets a bit cranky."

Peter smiled wider. "Your grandmother. You expect me to believe that?"

He laughed and bent down to unzip the tent regardless of her warning. As he pushed the flap back, he found Willow sitting on the ground with a loaded crossbow aimed directly at him.

"Get off my lawn!" Willow cried out and shot the arrow into his shoulder.

Raoul took the small opportunity to grab the gun from Peter and fly it back to Sydona. Peter clutched his shoulder and cried out in pain as he examined the arrow sticking through his body. Switching roles, Sydona held the pistol at Peter in case he tried anything foolish. This action only aggravated him further like a grizzly bear. He turned to face Sydona with bared teeth and growls coming from him. As he took a step towards her, Sydona fired the gun at his thigh and caused him to drop to the ground in defeat. Sydona lifted her chin, proud that she was able to disarm the threat.

"Drop it!" a female voice called out through the trees.

Sydona perked up and stuck the gun out straight as she circled in one spot around her, searching for the voice. Suddenly a younger man and female appeared from behind the trees in the distance. Both had guns in hand. As they approached the site, Sydona's stomach twisted, and her hands shook, making it difficult to hold the gun steady. Willow exited her tent with the empty crossbow while Raoul hid back in Sydona's hood.

"You're outnumbered. Just drop it!" the woman called out again, coming into full view. She was of Asian descent with dark eyes that matched her jet black, short hair. The man who accompanied her stood on the other side of the campsite, making it hard to watch both of them at once. The man had dark brown skin, short dreadlocks, and a murderous look in his eyes.

"Did you really think I came without backup?" Peter groaned. Willow kicked him.

"Who are you people?" Sydona asked, needing a confirmation.

"Drop your damn gun!" the woman shouted and stepped closer.

Sydona grinded her teeth, set the gun on the ground, and returned her hands to the air.

The woman nodded her head but remained steady.

"We're with the NFA. We're not here to hurt you. The guns are just a precaution," she said calmly.

The man grabbed the extra gun and put it in the waistband of his jeans.

"How'd you know we were here?" Sydona asked.

"Not important. Can she walk?" the man asked, looking inside the tent at Giovonna who sobbed uncontrollably.

"Not well," Willow answered.

"Can you carry her?" the woman asked.

Sydona squeezed her fists until her knuckles turned white.

"We're not who you think we are," Sydona blurted. "Look at our eyes. If you're looking for fliers, you've got the wrong people."

The man and woman looked at each other with uncertainty.

"Yeah! We're just out here campin', mindin' our own business. How can ya be so sure?" Willow said, going along with Sydona.

"Shut up!" the woman yelled. "Get that girl out of the tent. You. Carry her. Let's go!"

She directed Willow to carry Giovonna.

Sydona was out of options. If these people were from the NFA, they wouldn't want to bring in dead fliers, but what was stopping them from hurting her and her friends? And how did they find her? They were in the middle of nowhere. She made sure of that.

"Did Harold send you?" Sydona asked as she began to walk away from the campsite with a gun at her back.

"Stop asking questions." The man jabbed her harder in the back.

Willow helped Giovonna out of the tent, and Giovonna held onto Willow's side and limped beside her. Her face was covered in tears and her forehead with sweat. Giovonna's cries made Sydona's stomach twist. The man directed Sydona as the woman herded Willow and Giovonna in front of her.

"Where are we going?" Giovonna sniffled.

"Our van, about a mile away," the man answered. Giovonna cried out once more.

"I don't think so," another man said from behind the group.

Sydona turned around to find a younger man with shaggy black hair had a gun to her captor's head. What stood out more than anything, though, were his violet eyes.

Chapter Ten

"Nobody move." The new guy gritted his teeth.

The woman turned around and gasped at the site of her partner being held up by a gun. "Jordan…" she cried, pointing the gun at the stranger.

Sydona froze, unsure of what exactly was going on. Where did this mysterious stranger come from? Judging by his gangly appearance, he could possibly be homeless. His hair was so long and unkempt that it covered most of one eye. The hand he gripped his gun with looked rough and filthy, matching his moth eaten and baggy clothes.

"Let him go!" the woman yelled, bearing her white teeth.

"Not until you drop your guns and let them go," the stranger said calmly.

The woman shook with anger and fear, trying to hold back tears. As she tried to decide what to do, Sydona remembered the dagger on her hip and slowly worked her fingers to the handle.

"Meg, just do what he says," Jordan said.

"No! This wasn't how it was supposed to go!" Meg yelled.

"Meg, please. They're going to kill us like they tried killing Peter… Nathan will never get the help he needs if you're dead," Jordan said.

The woman began to cry harder but still kept her gun aimed. Giovonna and Willow stood quietly behind Sydona as they waited for a chance to change the outcome. Sydona took the opportunity to walk backwards, away from Meg, and get behind her without her noticing.

"I need this money, Jordan! *For* Nathan… Which is why I can't let them go," she yelled.

"Drop your gun, now!" the stranger bellowed.

Meg screamed at him as tears poured down her face, and Sydona moved closer behind her and kicked Meg's feet from under her. Meg went flying back as the gun shot into the air, making everyone jump. She landed on her back with a thud. Sydona kicked the gun from her hand as Meg arched her back in pain. She pressed her dagger against the hysterical woman's neck, and as she straddled her to the ground, Sydona stared into her eyes.

"How did you know we were here?" Sydona tightened her jaw. She could faintly hear Giovonna sniffling and Willow comforting her.

Meg wrinkled up her nose and lips, then hacked up a wad of saliva and spit it right in Sydona's face. Sydona wiped it off with her sleeve, grinned, and punched Meg square in her temple, hard enough to knock her unconscious. Taking a deep breath and cleaning her face more, Sydona looked back at Jordan who was still in the stranger's control.

"Meg?" Jordan asked, trying to peek over Sydona.

"What do ya think we should do with them?" Willow spoke up.

"Please. Let us go. We won't come back. I promise," Jordan begged.

"Now, why don't I believe you?" the stranger asked, still holding a gun to Jordan's head.

"I swear on my mother's grave that we won't. You have to believe me. Please!" he pleaded more.

Sydona unstrattled herself from Meg and grabbed the gun off the ground. Placing the dagger back in her holster, she glanced at Giovonna who looked traumatized. Approaching her like a timid deer, Sydona had to know if she was alright.

"You okay?" Sydona whispered. Giovonna nodded with tears glistening in her eyes.

"Are you good to go back to the site alone?" Sydona asked.

"No, what if more come?" Giovonna sniffled.

She was understandably scared, but she needed to do something with the other two first. Killing them might be the only solution, and she didn't want to expose Giovonna to that. This new stranger guy seemed to be able to hold his own, but he was still the only one pointing a gun at anyone.

"Go with her," Sydona told Willow and motioned her head to the campsite.

"Ya sure?" Willow placed her hand on Sydona's shoulder.

"Yeah. I'm fine," Sydona said.

As they limped back to the site, Sydona turned her attention back to the guys.

"What do you wanna do with them, then?" the stranger asked.

Sydona looked Jordan in his brown eyes. "We can't let you go. You're bounty hunters. It's your job to hunt us down. What would they say when you come back with one less person and no fliers?"

Jordan dropped his head in defeat.

"What if they don't go back?" Raoul asked from inside Sydona's hoodie.

Both Jordan and the other man stared at Raoul's orange glow with awe. Raoul landed on Sydona's shoulder and stretched his body like a feline.

"What do you mean?" Sydona asked.

"I mean, what if they don't go back? We keep them here. I'm sure Willow has rope or something."

Sydona flashed a smile as if a lightbulb had gone off in her head.

"Willow! You have rope in your bag?" Sydona called as Willow helped Giovonna back into the tent.

"Of course I do," Willow answered with a matter of fact tone.

"Great. We're gonna need it. And grab that douchebag by your tent, would ya?"

Willow grabbed Peter and forced him to stand up. He whimpered in pain. Willow searched through her bag for a thick rope and wrapped it around her other arm.

"Can you at least take this arrow out of my shoulder?!" Peter exclaimed.

"Sure, if you wanna be in even more pain and bleed out. It would be my pleasure!" Willow smiled as her large hands gripped him so tightly that Sydona could see the indents from twenty feet away. Peter responded to her with a grumble and continued to limp towards Sydona.

Sydona nodded as Willow approached with the bleeding bounty hunter. She then turned her attention to the new stranger. "Hey. Would you mind, uh--"

"Silas," the man spoke up as he waited for Sydona's instructions.

"Would you mind taking him this way, Silas?" Sydona asked and nodded her head away from the camp.

"Lead the way," Silas answered with a small grin, making Sydona unintentionally smile in return. She refocused.

Looking at Meg on the ground, she noticed movement and quickly returned to her. Sydona pointed the pistol at Meg as her eyes finally opened. Meg quickly stood up with furrowed brows as she glanced at the defeated men in her party.

"Walk." Sydona glared at Meg who returned the glare but did as she said.

Sydona led the group deeper into the woods until they could no longer spot the artificial green and blue of the tents. With the help of Willow and Silas, Sydona tied each bounty hunter to separate trees, so it would be more difficult to untie each other. Sydona used her blade to cut each section of the rope, and Willow made sure to tighten the ropes until each hunter could barely squirm against the trees.

Once they were secured, Sydona bent down in front of Jordan, hoping he would be the reasonable one in the group and give her answers.

"How did you find us?" Sydona asked.

Jordan avoided eye contact and looked less angry than the other two. He took a moment to answer, almost as if he was willing to say but didn't want his companions to overhear.

"We tracked you," Jordan answered softly.

Sydona rolled her eyes. "I assumed that--"

"No. I mean, we tracked you. With a device."

"A device?" Raoul asked.

"Yeah."

Sydona narrowed her eyes and glanced at Raoul and Willow who both had no idea what device he was talking about.

"Who sent you?" Willow spoke up in her raspy voice.

Jordan looked over at Meg who was thrashing around like an angry hornet glued to a tree.

"Don't you tell them, Jordan! Don't!"

Jordan looked down at the ground and shook his head.

"Was it Harold?" Raoul asked shortly.

Jordan kept still except for one single nod, and it was all Sydona needed.

"Son of a bitch." She stood up so quickly that Raoul almost fell off her shoulder.

"I knew it. That man is the biggest thorn in my side..." Willow huffed.

Sydona went over in her head how on earth Harold would have put a tracking device on her. When he arrived at the cabin, the closest she ever got to him was in the doorway, and the shotgun was closer to him than her. He never touched that gun to put anything on it, and if he did, Willow surely would've seen it. The only other encounter she had with him was in the diner in Mayfield, and even then, he didn't touch her at all. Except for...

"My sunglasses. That has to be it!" Sydona exclaimed and ran back to the campsite. Raoul flew directly behind her.

She headed to the tent that Giovonna was in and rifled through her bag.

"What's going on?" Giovonna sat up in her sleeping bag with wide eyes.

"Harold's been tracking us. Ever since Mayfield!" Raoul informed her.

"Seriously?! How?" Giovonna asked.

"With these." Sydona held her glasses up.

Feeling like an idiot, she immediately noticed the device on the face of the glasses. In the upper right hand corner laid a small, black sticker that blended in well with the plastic of the glasses. It shone in a different way than her glasses, and it seemed so obvious looking at it now. Using her nail, she peeled off the sticker and revealed underneath a red, barely visible blinking light. The new technology fascinated her but she felt infuriated for being so oblivious. Harold placed it so perfectly and quickly, she wondered how he accomplished this with such precision. He must have been doing this bounty hunting thing for a long time.

Just then, she had an idea. She stuck the tracker back on the glasses and exited the tent. Walking briskly back to the hostages where Willow and Silas stood guard, she put the glasses on Meg.

"Tell Harold we said 'nice try'." Sydona grinned and turned away from her as Meg haucked another wad of spit that just missed her shoe. Raoul responded with pulling Meg's hair and jerking her head backwards. He then stuck his tongue out at her.

"And you," Sydona looked at Peter, sweating bullets and breathing heavy. "I try to be nice and look where it got me. I hope you bleed out."

Sydona wiped her brow as she took another moment to tighten their restraints again.

"Well. If all is good, I'll be taking off," Silas announced as he walked away from the group.

Sydona's heart jumped; she completely forgot he was still there.

"Wait up," she called out.

Sydona followed him with Raoul on her shoulder and Willow slightly behind them.

"Can I ask what you're doing way out here, too?" Sydona pried, still suspicious of how he was there at the same time as the hunters.

"Well, I'm not with them if that's what you're worried about," Silas said as he adjusted the hatchet that hung from a loop in his jeans.

"So where'd you come from, huh?" Willow asked with a sharp tone. She was just as untrusting as Sydona, even if he was a flier.

"Seems awfully convenient," Raoul said.

The man laughed as they continued walking. "Yeah, it was convenient that I saved you all from being slaves. I don't think I heard a 'thank you' yet."

Sydona scoffed. "I had it handled."

"Right," Silas chuckled.

Sydona didn't respond because she knew she owed him a token of gratitude. If he hadn't been there for whatever reason, they would be in serious trouble. The walk back to the tent was quiet and tense. The crunching of leaves and twigs were the only sounds between them. Sydona battled with herself over thanking the stranger. Anymore communication with him would make him stay longer, and she wanted to head out right away to continue on their mission. When they reached the camp, they found Giovonna sitting on a log messing with a fire she made.

"Oh good. There you are!" Giovonna exclaimed, her face bright with joy. "What happened to the other guys?" Willow silently agreed with Sydona that she would talk to her about it. Sydona didn't know how to tell her that they basically left them for dead.

Silas cleared his throat. "Welp, take care," he said as he continued to walk away from the site.

Raoul flew in front of Sydona's face with a stern look.

"Are we going to just let him walk away? He did save our lives, Syd."

Sydona looked back at him with confusion. "I thought you were on my side. He's a stranger who came from nowhere. How do you suddenly trust a person like that?"

"Because he had every opportunity in the book to harm us, and he didn't. Stop being so proud Syd and thank the man." Raoul crossed his arms.

Sydona bit her lip in frustration. She hated when Raoul behaved like her conscience, and half the time he was correct. Rolling her eyes, she spoke up before Silas got too far.

"Thank you!" Sydona yelled out, making him stop.

He turned around with a small grin. "You're welcome."

Sydona blushed at his smile, making her feel warm and tingly.

"You hungry?" she asked softly as he made his way back to their site.

"Yeah. But I have my own food." He motioned his head away from the camp.

"What kind of food?" Giovonna and Raoul asked simultaneously.

Silas laughed. "Um, I don't know. Mostly junk food but it's tasty."

"Any fruit?" Raoul flew closer to him and Sydona.

"I think some bananas and pears? Maybe oranges?"

"Let's go, Syd!" Raoul swiveled around.

"Yeah. All Willow has left are space food packs. Dried up grossness." Giovonna stuck out her tongue as Willow glared at her.

The group agreed to go to Silas's camp and began to gather up their supplies. As the girls walked around, grabbed their things, and took down tents, Silas spoke up.

"How'd you find a fairy?" he asked as he admired Raoul. "Lost mine ages ago."

Sydona straightened up and grabbed her pack. "I didn't. Had him since I was little."

"Really?" Silas asked in wonderment.

"What happened to yours?" Raoul asked curiously.

Silas frowned. "Oh, I probably shouldn't say…"

"Why?" Sydona asked as she gathered supplies for Giovonna.

"It might freak you out." Silas laughed.

"Tell me!" Raoul shouted.

"Okay, you asked," Silas said. "Few years ago, I was fishing with my fairy, Jessabelle, off the edge of a dock in Washington. As I was fishing, she was being goofy and flying over the water, trying to see fish swimming underneath. Well, apparently her colors were very similar to that of a dragonfly's and--gulp. This huge monster of a fish jumped out of the water and swallowed her whole!"

Sydona stood gaping at his story and then glanced at Raoul who was white as a ghost. He looked as if he was about to faint.

Silas threw his head back in laughter. "I'm just kidding. She died of old age."

"Not funny!" Raoul yelled and flew off away from Silas.

Silas laughed at his abrupt reaction. "He's a bit dramatic, isn't he?

"You have no idea…" Sydona smiled with pink cheeks.

Over the next hour, they finished packing up their things to head towards Silas's campsite. Sydona knew that if Raoul didn't eat anything soon, he would be the most annoying thing ever. He would buzz around just out of reach like a mosquito, groaning and complaining until he ate. Sydona noticed Giovonna could walk without the assistance of herself or Willow. Either the pain pills were working, or her wound healed enough. It was good timing. She needed to be in good health if they went through with their plan. Sydona anticipated a lot of running and flying.

The sun rose higher in the sky and the air became warmer. Birds of all kinds happily sang their songs or complained about the heat. It was hard to tell if birds were ever upset. Sydona always took it as a good thing when they sang, and it made her feel at home again. The forest was much different than hers, though. Oaks, gum trees, and coffeetrees were abundant in her area. But this forest had more pines and maple trees, and she took in the new fresh scent. It was the first time she was able to enjoy her surroundings without being on the verge of passing out from exhaustion or hunted down.

The walk was long and boring. Silas led the way while the girls walked slowly behind him and recovered from earlier. He said it was only a half mile, but it felt more like a thousand. As she walked alone, she began to go over the plan of action in her head. Willow said they were only in Wyoming and still needed to go through Idaho. Unsure of how big the state was, she set aside another full day to arrive in Oregon. And that was only if they had reliable transportation. Walking would take way too long, especially with Giovonna's injury. She hoped that Silas had a way of getting around and prayed that he wasn't a wild man living in the forest. Although, with his scent, she feared the worst.

They finally approached his campsite, and she was in luck. A little red truck sat beside a small gray tent surrounded by junk. It was identical to Willow's driveway: cluttered with random things collected over the years. Maybe he did live there, and maybe it had been years. Maybe the truck was part of the collection and didn't even run anymore. Her heart sank just thinking about it.

"Well, here we are! Home sweet home," Silas said to the group with pride. He dropped the bags off near his tent and then made a B-line for a giant, metal box. It looked as if it was permanent, and he had to open it with a special latch.

"Got… beans, green beans, licorice, soup in a can, lots of jerky, protein bars--lots of protein bars, cereal, oatmeal, raisins, apples, dried apricots and--bananas." Silas grabbed a banana and pointed it at Raoul. He flew over to it as if it had a magnet inside.

"What would you like, uh--I don't think I know your name." Silas held out his hand to Sydona with a smile.

"Dried apricots and Sydona," she answered, holding back a smile.

"I don't think I have any Sydona's... Is that like samosas? Oh, wait, that's your--I see now." He winked and handed her the bag of fruit.

Sydona blushed and grabbed it from his hands.

"Speaking of, I don't think I really got any of your names," Silas said as he stepped aside and let Willow and Giovonna pick something.

"I'm Gia." She shook his hand firmly.

"And I'm Willow." Willow nodded quickly and went back to searching for food.

"The fruit lover is Raoul," Sydona added as she sucked on a piece of apricot.

"Nice to meet you all," Silas announced as he sat in a severely rusted folding chair.

Sydona noticed another empty folding chair next to his and sat down as everyone chowed down.

"Sorry about your fairy," Sydona said and cleared her throat. "I can't imagine what I'd do without Raoul. He's like my other half."

"Thank you. And uh, don't tell Raoul but--that fish story was true." Silas cringed.

Sydona gasped quietly and hit his arm. "You're kidding!"

Silas laughed again. "I wish I was. I was devastated..."

Sydona's cheeks were sore from smiling, and her face was suddenly warm--it wasn't from the sun. She glanced over at Raoul who was almost done with his banana and happily bobbing along with his chewing.

"Sorry we didn't have anything to offer you for saving us. Instead, you're helping us, again," Sydona said.

"No worries. It's nice having people to talk to." Silas took a bite of jerky.

Willow and Giovonna pulled up their makeshift seats at this point, and Giovonna spoke up.

"How long have you been out here?"

Silas took a deep breath. "Oh I don't know. Few weeks, I think?"

"Why?" Willow asked while scraping out a can of beans.

"Well, if you must know, my girlfriend kicked me out. I was living with her for a couple years, so all my stuff was there.

I guess she was expecting me to propose and even gave me an ultimatum. Long story short, I didn't propose, and she kicked me out. Then, I was fired from my job because of the breakup, and I was distracted. Construction and relationship drama is not a good mix. Anyways, I decided to get out of all of that, go camping for a while, and renew myself. Then I found out about Eagle Lake and well… you can probably fill in the rest." Silas exhaled.

"Damn." Willow shook her head.

"No, it's fine. I feel better than I've felt in a long time," Silas said.

Sydona grinned to herself, enjoying getting to know someone she felt she could connect with easily. The group ate their food quietly until they felt satisfied enough. His stockpile wasn't so large that they could eat a whole meal, so they ate what they needed for their stomachs to stop growling. Willow of course needed a bit more than the rest of them to feel it, but Silas was generous enough to accommodate. Giovonna was able to rest her leg for a few hours, and she began to feel much better. The wound was already starting to scab up, and she could put more pressure on it. Sydona still worried how Giovonna would be of help when going to the camp.

As Silas left to go check on his traps that he set for rabbits and other small creatures, the group had a discussion.

"Do you think that truck works?" Sydona pointed to the rusted red vehicle.

Willow shrugged. "Only one way to find out." She stood up and walked over to the truck and examined it closely. She kicked the tires, which seemed inflated, and checked for anything dripping underneath the truck. Then, she peeked in the window and saw keys in the ignition.

"Why are we looking at his truck?" Giovonna asked.

"We're an entire state away from our destination. We need another way to get there besides walking and piggyback rides," Sydona answered as she looked it over, too.

"And we can't fly because Willow can't, and you're still injured," Raoul added.

"So we're gonna steal his truck?" Giovonna asked loudly.

"No one said anything about stealing." Sydona glared at Giovonna with a sour face.

"So why don't you guys just ask him?"

"You didn't see the look on his face when Willow mentioned Eagle Lake," Sydona said. "That is the probably the last place he would want to go."

"Sure sounds like you wanna steal his car, princess." Willow put her hands on her hips and looked down at her.

Sydona gawked at the accusations, and her face felt hot. "I can't believe you all think I'm trying to steal his car!"

Raoul flew closer to her and took a deep breath. "Well, Syd, what *are* you trying to do?"

Sydona stared at all three of them. Willow stood next to the truck with a look of serious judgment, and Giovonna sat with her leg propped up on a chair and arms crossed. Sydona's eyes turned green, and she felt as if she could explode. The feeling of being left out and ganged up on was at its limit, and she belted out.

"I'm sorry that I am the only one here who wants to get to this place as soon as possible! And I'm sick of being the one who is left out and wants to get this journey over with. This isn't a vacation for me; we're not out to stay at cute little B&B's and have our nails done! I am trying to rescue my people and find my parents that I haven't seen in like fifty years! So excuse me if I'm not letting anything stop me from moving on. Because walking there could take another week, and there's no way in hell I'm waiting that long."

The looks on their faces burned into her mind. As they stared at her in fear, she noticed their eyes focused on something else behind her. She turned her head and saw Silas standing frozen and holding a dead rabbit.

Her throat swelled up and stomach wrenched with pain knowing that he just heard everything she said. As she was thinking of ways to run away from the tense situation, he said something she never would have guessed he would say.

"You can have my truck."

Chapter Eleven

Silas reminded her of a lost puppy as he stood there alone with a soft, gentle expression. He wasn't angry, he wasn't upset, and he wasn't judging. Sydona bit her lip nervously, unsure of his calm nature toward someone wanting to steal his property. Sydona stood without moving a muscle as she stared at Silas. Giovonna, Willow, and Raoul soon came to her side.

"What?" Sydona said at last.

"Take it." Silas walked past them and began to build a fire for his food.

"You're letting us take your car?" Giovonna asked curiously.

"Yep," he answered while gathering up branches and throwing them into the pit.

The group exchanged worried glances. Sydona tried to talk to him.

"Is there some kind of--catch?" Sydona asked with uncertainty.

"Catch?" Silas stopped what he was doing. "You think there's a catch to me giving you my car? After I already saved you from bounty hunters, gave you food, and let you rest here? Why would me giving you my truck be any different?"

Sydona felt a sharp pain run up and down her chest at his response. He was right. He had been very helpful so far, and they repaid him by planning to steal his truck. Sydona fought with herself as she tried to think of a better plan to get to Eagle Lake, but this car was the best option they had. Walking was out of the question with Giovonna's injury, and flying was too risky. There was only one solution left, but Sydona didn't want to be a thief.

"What if you came with us?" Sydona whispered.

Silas smirked. "What if I came with you?"

Giovonna perked up with bright eyes. "Yeah! You should come with us!"

"Come with you? To a place that wants to use us like lab rats? You're more delusional than I thought…" Silas broke a thick branch over his knee a couple times.

"You scared?" Willow asked in her booming voice.

"Well--Yeah! You should all be scared," Silas said angrily.

Of all of the emotions that Sydona had throughout the entire trip, being scared wasn't even in the top five. She felt anger, disbelief, vengefulness, remorse, and hate--but never scared. It was understandable why it would be an appropriate emotion since he didn't come from the same background as herself, but it took her a minute to respond.

"You should be angry. Like I am. They--" she choked. A flood of emotions came pouring through her that came from nowhere. "--they made me an orphan when I was nine. Ripped my parents away from me. Tied them up and drugged them and put them in a van. I have been living alone for my entire life, pissed off for what they put me through." Sydona held back tears as she clenched her fists so tight that her hands shook. Pausing to compose herself, she continued on as the group stood quietly and listened. "Willow--Willow said this is the biggest camp that has ever been assembled with hundreds of fliers there. She's part of a group of resistance fighters called Sparrows, and they deal with these kinds of things. But with a place of this size, we could use all the help we can get. I know that it might be scary to you, but you need to be angry and fight. We need to put a stop to this… once and for all.”

As she finished, she took a deep breath and held her chin up high. Giovonna smiled at her with tears streaming down her face, and Willow gave her a smirk as well along with a respective nod. Raoul clapped, but she barely heard it. She saw Silas grin, turn away shyly, and pick up branches again. She felt confident that she got through to him, but she needed to be patient.

The whole group seemed to be in a better mood. Silas didn't bring it up for several hours as he prepared the rabbit for eating. Willow realized that one little rabbit wouldn't be enough food for all of them, so she took the opportunity to teach Giovonna how to use the crossbow. Sydona wouldn't be eating the skewered rabbit roasting over the small fire, so she tried to find a place to sleep. The lack of sleep and running for half the morning finally caught up to her, and she asked Silas where she could nap. He had a tent set up, but it looked very lived in.

“I have a bunch of blankets in the bed of my truck. You can sleep there as long as you don't try to steal it...” Silas said with a lighthearted tone. Sydona swore he held back a smile. She felt unsure if her speech would change his mind, but her gut told her otherwise. He missed the company.

She made her way over to the sea of blankets that lined the bed. They weren't clean and smelled of mildew and dust, but they were soft and that's all she cared about. It even felt better than the sleeping bag. Raoul joined her with his full belly. As she lay there looking up into the branches and bright blue sky, she felt the wind blowing gently on her face and listened to the crackle of the fire until she drifted off to sleep.

As she opened her eyes, the blue sky turned into painted white clouds on a blue ceiling. Rubbing her eyes, unsure of how the sky changed, she realized she was back in her bedroom from when she was a little girl. Everything seemed a few seconds behind as she glanced around the room. Everything moved in slow motion, and it made her feel dizzy. Sliding off the side of a small colorful twin bed, she looked down at her feet to see shiny black shoes. The only time she ever wore those shoes was when her family would go to fancy places. She also had on her black frilly dress that she wore once when the dog they had died, and they had a funeral in the backyard for him.

"What's going on?" she asked herself.

She ran over to the mirror that hung over her white dresser and looked at her reflection. The face staring back at her was herself as a nine year old again with short, curled blonde hair. She tried pinching her arms over and over again, and nothing happened. The pain from the pinches lingered but did nothing to wake her up. She suddenly heard a faint calling of her name from behind her bedroom door.

"Mom?" She whipped open her bedroom door and ran down the stairs as fast as her newly small legs could take her. Her mother floated inside from the backdoor with the sunlight shining angelically behind her. Sydona stood in awe, and tears flowed down her fresh young face. Without hesitation, she ran up to her mother and hugged her as tightly as she could.

"Syd? What's this about?" Her mother laughed. The laugh echoed throughout the house as if they were in a tunnel.

"You feeling okay, sweetheart?" a man's voice came faintly from behind her.

It was her father sitting at the table with a coffee cup as usual. She turned her head quickly and ran to him to squeeze him just as tight. She took in everything she possibly could: his scruff, the smell of his coffee, and the cologne he always wore.

He pulled her away with a concerned smile, "Syd, what's going on?"

"I'm just so happy to see you guys," Sydona squeaked. Her father wiped tears off her face that couldn't seem to stop flowing.

As she grabbed her mother's hand, in order to touch them both, she heard the slight sound of helicopter propellers growing louder and louder. Her heart pounded with each whip of the propellers, and she wasn't sure why, but it meant something very bad.

"We need to leave! Now!" She seized her dad's hand, smashing the coffee cup on the floor. The sunlight that once burst through the windows became black, and it looked as if a tornado formed out of thin air. The helicopter landed in their front yard that was covered in dead, yellow grass, and men in white coats poured out by the dozens. Sydona clasped both of her parents' hands even tighter and sprinted to the backyard. Suddenly she felt as if she were on a conveyor belt that was leading to the front yard, right to the helicopter. Tears blurred her vision and the back door seemed to be rotting away and getting further from her reach.

Looking down at her empty hands, she panicked and wondered when her parents had let go of her. She searched for them frantically as the house fell apart. She saw them in the front yard, fighting off the army of men. Soon, the men had caught up to her and tackled her to the ground. She felt every scratch, kick, and grab. Unable to defend herself, she could not stop them from taking her away in the van with her parents. Everything went black.

As darkness took over, she prayed that when she opened her eyes she would be awake. But once her eyes decided it was safe to open, she found herself rolling down a white hallway on a cart with blinding florescent lights on the ceiling. She tilted her head to the side and saw the men in white coats pushing her cart.

She instantly panicked. Struggling to move, she felt her hands and feet strapped down and a bright white sheet covering her body. Her head was the only part of her that could move freely. Doors lined the hallway. Most of the doors were opened wide, and she could see people in the rooms clear as day. She heard every single sound in the strange place: screaming, blood curdling screaming, electric tools, metal things dropping, pounding, thumping, and crying. It all echoed through the hall and into her small ears. She wanted to cover them up, but her hands were still bound. Then, all at once, it stopped. She feared she had gone deaf.

She was rolled into a big white room. They positioned her to where she could see her parents strapped to devices on the the wall. She felt sickened to see all the wires being hooked up to both of them but more traumatized to see them sliced open. Their eyes had been removed, and it bloodied their faces and bodies. There was so much blood; Sydona swore their skins had been turned inside out. They were still conscious according to the machines they were hooked up to, and Sydona wanted to scream, but no sound came out. She then saw another man wearing a sterile white coat walk in, but he seemed different than anyone else she saw so far. He wielded a butcher's knife and smiled menacingly at her.

"Hello, Sydona. This will only hurt a little."

He removed the sheet from her body, and she saw herself in the same state as her parents. She could see her heart pumping as fast as a mouse, and her face turned white. The man with the knife stood over her, aiming the knife right at her eyes, and she began to scream. Her screaming made no sound, but it didn't matter. She screamed until she could hear herself, and her voice slowly came back to her lungs.

"Syd!" Raoul yelled in her face until her eyes forced open.

She sat up quickly with a fast beating heart and sweat dripping down her face. The crying she had done in the dream transformed to real life tears and had soaked the comforter below. Silas stood by the edge of the truck with a worrisome look. Her face flushed with the idea of her screaming randomly in the middle of a forest, scaring the daylights out of Raoul. Silas and Raoul seemed to be the only ones there, so Giovonna and Willow were probably out hunting still. The shadows didn't change very much, and the sun shone brightly. Once again, she lacked sleep.

"Bad dream?" Raoul asked as he stood on the side of the truck bed.

She nodded and took a deep breath, not really wanting to revisit the nightmare. But she spoke up softly and Raoul and Silas leaned in to listen. "I was back home and a kid again. Mom and dad were there and--it felt so real..." She held back tears. "Mom looked like an angel, and dad was same old dad with his coffee. And then--it changed. The sky turned black, and men in white came bursting into the house. It felt like hundreds... They took them away and--took me, too. I..." She stopped to cry. She sobbed harder than she ever had before.

She caught Silas's face in the midst of the tears, and he looked as if he was on the verge of tears, too. Silas caressed her knee and nodded slightly. Revenge. Anger. Remorse. Disbelief. Hate. And now, scared. She understood now. And Silas knew she understood where he came from. Although, this didn't make her feel any better. If anything, it made her feel embarrassed.

"Can I be alone please?" she said.

Raoul didn't move because he knew that she didn't really want to be alone. And he was right, she didn't want him to leave. Mostly, she didn't want Silas to see her so vulnerable. He respected her request and walked away from the truck.

Grabbing a couple blankets to make a softer pillow, Sydona lay back down and wiped her face with another one. Only a minute later she felt the truck bounce as if someone sat down inside it. The middle tiny window opened up between the bed and the front seats.

"Did you know butterflies used to be plump, fat, ugly worms?" Silas asked her after several minutes.

Sydona scoffed. "Silas… please. Not now."

"I mean, they are born, and they are these little fat worms that just crawl around and eat all day long. For months, or I guess years for them, they just eat and eat and eat and try to avoid being eaten. Like, it must really suck to live as a caterpillar."

"What's happening right now?" She furrowed her eyebrows at Raoul who just shrugged back at her.

Silas continued. "But then, something happens. These dumb little worms have this brilliant dream. A dream of making a cocoon bed for themselves. They stay in that bed for days, just thinking what it would be like to not be a dumb little worm who does nothing in the world. And thinks real hard what it would be like to fly. To have wings and go anywhere they want and not be limited to where they can go. To pollinate flowers and make more flowers and make the world a more beautiful place. To wonder what you might look like when you wake up. Are you going to be a purple butterfly or an orange one or yellow? You could be anything."

"Silas..." Sydona said then looked up and saw him upside down, looking at her through the window.

"What? You told me about your dream, so I told you mine," he said with a wink and a grin.

Sydona couldn't hold back a full smile. "Are you saying I'm a butterfly?"

"I'm saying--don't let a silly dream hold you back," he said.

Sydona's heart skipped a beat. Even with his shaggy hair and dirty appearance, she somehow found him attractive. The smile he liked to show off wore on her, and she enjoyed the feeling. As she lay there, staring up at him, he blankly stared at something next to her. She could tell he was deep in thought, and she waited for the next thing that would come out of his mouth.

"I'll go with you." He spoke just above a whisper.

His answer was not what she expected. He didn't seem excited or afraid, just average. Almost like he felt guilty for not going. But he said yes, which meant they had their ride.

"You'll go?" Raoul said excitedly.

Silas nodded at Raoul and hopped out of the car to face Sydona.

"Are you sure?" Sydona asked and sat back up.

"Yeah. You need my big strong male muscles to take this place on. I couldn't deprive you of something so essential." He posed and kissed his arm muscles hiding under his loose jacket.

Sydona gazed into his eyes with seriousness, knowing he only used humor to hide his true feelings. He reminded her a lot of Raoul who always joked in serious moments.

Silas sighed. "You're right. I can't just stay here and do nothing. I would be as useful as this truck here, growing rust."

Sydona smiled. "Thank you."

"Yeah, yeah. We're gonna be spending a lot of time together, and I only ask one thing of you." His voice got louder and more confident. "Don't you go falling in love with me, okay?"

Sydona held back a smile and felt her cheeks grow rosy. "Okay."

"I'll make sure that doesn't happen!" Raoul burst between them and gave Silas the stink eye.

Just then, they heard Giovonna and Willow laughing as they walked back to the camp. Willow carried all the kills:

rabbit, squirrel, and a small fox. Giovonna hardly limped at all as she joined the rest of the group.

"Look what I got, Syd!" She pointed to the animals in Willow's grip as she proudly held them up.

"Great! Will be plenty for you three," Sydona said with slight sarcasm.

"I tried looking for not meat things like mushrooms or berries, but I wasn't sure what would kill you or not," Giovonna said with a shrug.

"I probably could've told you, but that's okay. Silas has enough for me for now," she said and exited the truck.

Willow got busy adding wood to the dying fire and began to skin the animals. Glancing at the sun, Sydona assumed it was about noon. Her mind began to wander back to its original track and getting to Eagle Lake as soon as possible. Just as she was ready to tell the girls the good news, Raoul spat it out.

"Silas is coming with us!"

"Really? That's great!" Giovonna jumped up and hugged Silas, catching him off guard.

"Good! That means we should prolly start headin' out soon, huh?" Willow informed as she put the fox on a metal skewer.

"Yes. I want to leave in the next hour or two. Whenever we're done eating and pack stuff up. Still gonna be a long drive," Sydona said as she grabbed more food from Silas's stash.

"What changed your mind?" Giovonna asked and then took a swig of water.

"Oh ya know… I realized that I need to be a part of something bigger. Instead of bumming out here, eating rodents. Squirrel gets really old after a while," Silas said truthfully.

"Glad you're coming along, Sil. Okay if I call ya Sil?" Willow asked as she devoured more jerky.

"No." Silas laughed.

The group finished eating and talking about life, taking their minds off of the road ahead. Raoul bragged about all the embarrassing stories involving Sydona, and she couldn't make him stop. If she thought crying in front of a stranger was embarrassing, the story about her sleepwalking naked and wandering into the parking lot of a mall was just the tip of the iceberg. Her and Raoul were homeless at the time, and it was the middle of summer. He said her unconscious mind wanted to find a lake to jump in. The fact that he didn't try to wake her up for a while was new information to her and made her slightly upset. Instead of chasing him around the fire like a child, she buried her face in one of her shirts.

The fun soon came to an end, and they began to pack up all of their belongings. They took as much food as they could, and with the extra space in the bin, Silas hid things inside it. Most of the blankets were stored in it to make room for whoever sat in the back. Willow made a point to sit up front with Silas so that she could help navigate since she had more experience. And with Willow upfront, there was no room for anyone in the middle, which meant Giovonna sat in the back with Sydona and Raoul. She kept one of the blankets with her, so she could try to sleep on the way.

Silas slammed the gate of the truck bed shut, making the girls jump. She caught his gaze as he made his way to the front. From the corner of her eye, she could see Giovonna with a big goofy smile.

"What's that about?" Giovonna whispered as she leaned in closer.

"What? Nothing…" Sydona shook her head and made herself comfortable in the corner of the bed.

"Yeah huh. I saw the look you gave him." Giovonna jabbed her knee.

"Stop it. There was no *look*," Sydona mumbled and avoided eye contact.

Raoul and Giovonna burst into laughter as they exchanged nods and eye wiggling.

Sydona rolled her eyes and lay down in the truck to try catching up on her sleep. Silas pulled away from the campsite, and they were finally on their way to Oregon.

Chapter Twelve

The sun was beginning to set when she finally woke up. Most of the ride she could hear Giovonna and Raoul talking away. She was glad that Raoul got along with her. They practically had the same level of maturity, and Giovonna could handle his energy. As she fully awoke, she listened to Giovonna talk about her school friends she missed. She wasn't sure if she would ever see them again. Sydona knew that the few friends she had, like Annie, she wasn't sure she would see again either. Her stomach churned thinking about Annie's son, Joseph, whom she always admired. Every parent wished for a kid as sweet and kind as Joseph. She never realized how much she missed that little kid. She wanted to get their whole plan over with, so she could see him again. The last time she saw Joseph was when they were in Mayfield, and they stopped the bounty hunter. She hoped they were okay. As she wondered how the NFA treated people who interfered with their work, her eyes turned brown. Annie seemed intelligent and most likely drove away once they were out of town.

Her mind drifted back to Eagle Lake as trees whizzed by at sixty miles per hour. Then, she sat up.

"Hey!" Sydona yelled up to Silas through the tiny window. "I think we should stop soon."

"Why? Do you have to pee?" he yelled back.

"Ew, no. We need to talk about stuff," Sydona said and rolled her eyes.

"What kind of stuff?" he asked flamboyantly.

"Oh, just pull over!"

Silas pulled over to the side of the rocky road, kicking up white dust. Willow pulled out the map of Eagle Lake that she got from the train station and flattened it out on the hood of the rusty red truck. The park seemed pretty large according to the streets nearby, but for being a park named after a lake, the lake wasn't really that large. There only seemed to be one entrance with a small booth that was probably for park fees or information. There were big hills on the west side behind a much larger building labeled as the visitors' center.

"What do you suppose they use that building for?" Sydona pointed to the largest building on the map.

"Maybe that's where we're all held?" Giovonna guessed.

"Ya think? Doesn't seem like it would be that big," Willow said.

"Yeah, I'm thinking it's used for the experiments and maybe where the doctors go. Set up like a temporary blood drive," said Sydona.

"Do you think they are using the entire park?" Silas asked.

"I think so. Would be kinda strange to be doing experiments only a few feet from a kid on a swing," Sydona said matter-of-factly.

"Well that would imply that the park is small. Why couldn't they be doing their experiments on this side of the lake only and still have a functioning kids park on the other side?" Silas retorted with the same attitude.

"Yeah, I agree with Sydona," Raoul said, standing on the map and looking at it more intently. "Why would they choose this location if they are using half? I mean, I think they would either use the entire thing or find a more remote location."

Silas shrugged in defeat and then nodded his head.

"Well, all I really care about is where John Malik is. He's in charge of everything," Sydona said more seriously.

"Do ya think he's actually there, though? He may be in charge, but who knows if he will be there when we arrive. If he's smart, he will be operatin' remotely or somethin'," Willow said.

Sydona pondered on this for a moment. Maybe she was right; he might not even be there. It wouldn't make the trip useless because she still hoped to find her parents and end the camp for good. But seeing him and putting him to an end would be the cherry on top.

Willow finally spoke up. "I say we head there after dark, maybe even midnight."

The group nodded in agreement.

"We head for the cabin first; I have a feelin' that's where all the action is. Possibly where Dr. Malik is too," she said.

They nodded again.

"What if there are guards?" Giovonna asked.

"We take them out," Sydona said while putting up her hair in a ponytail.

"What if there's a bunch of them?" Willow asked.

"And it causes a ruckus, and we get caught?" Silas added. Sydona glared at him.

They stood around the truck thinking of what to do in every circumstance.

"I got an idea!" Willow yelled. "Just be yourselves."

"What, fliers?" Giovonna asked.

"Willow, that's suicide," Raoul said.

"Hear me out, y'all. I can act as a hunter and put y'all in the back of Silas's truck and pretend like I'm there to turn ya over. Once we get inside: bam! We catch 'em all off guard and rally everyone up. It's a perfect plan!" Willow waved her arms around and stomped her feet with excitement.

"Will we need to be tied up or something, too?" Giovonna said worriedly.

Willow frowned a bit at Giovonna's reaction. "Yeah, prolly a good ide'r. Gotta make it look legit."

"What about our weapons?" Sydona asked softly.

"You got your knife; you can have that under your shirt. I doubt they will pat ya down if it looks like I captured you. I woulda got rid of all that stuff. I can make your knot looser, so when the time comes, you can break from it and cut Silas and Giovonna free. Their weapons will be under blankets behind them in the truck. The crossbow for Giovonna and, uh, Silas's wit?"

Silas laughed. "I have *stuff*. And even then, that's only four of us against god knows how many? There's no way we can defeat them."

"Well not with that attitude!" Willow punched his arm, causing Silas to rub it.

Willow looked to Sydona for approval. "Whad'ya say, princess?"

Sydona looked around at the group; all eyes were on her. "I actually think it's a valid plan. Is everyone else on board with this?" She mainly asked for Giovonna's sake since she was the youngest and least experienced. She would have to be okay with killing someone if it came to that.

Giovonna nodded with a small smile, almost hiding how she really felt.

Sydona walked closer to her and whispered. "You sure?"

Giovonna lifted her chin and stared at Sydona. "Yeah." She smiled bigger with confidence.

"I think it's a good a time as any to practice usin' that crossbow again." Willow patted Giovonna's back, pushing her forward and making her smile more authentic.

"We should go back into the woods, then, until night. Rest, sleep, practice." Sydona folded up the map and handed it back to Willow.

They all hopped back into the truck, and Silas drove a little further down the road until he found an opening to hide back in the woods. Willow took Giovonna away from the group to practice aiming, breathing, concentrating, and shooting with the bow. Raoul tagged along with the girls since he still wanted to talk to Giovonna more about random things. This gave more alone time to Silas and Sydona as well. Sydona sighed deeply as soon as Willow and Giovonna were out of sight and began get the truck ready for the lake. She left all their supplies in the brush, hidden from people and animals. Figuring out Sydona's plan, Silas began to help her hide their things as he worked up the courage to start talking.

He cleared his throat. "So, uh..." he started, "are you involved at all?"

"What?" Sydona dropped the box of food.

"You know, a boyfriend or girlfriend at home?" Silas asked with caution.

"Seriously?" Sydona placed her hands on her hips and cocked her head sideways.

"Well, I just want to make sure I don't overstep my bounds," he said.

Sydona laughed to herself, unsure of where the conversation stemmed from. "Didn't you just break up with your girlfriend like--no, I'm not having this conversation with you. We need to stay focused on tonight."

"Oh come on. Just trying to lighten the mood. You know, in case we all die tonight," Silas said as he gathered up branches and leaves to hide things.

"Way to stay positive," Sydona spat.

"Well, I'm trying to. But you're like a robot. Focused on one thing and no room for anything else." Silas raised his voice.

Sydona scoffed. "If we're all gonna die, what does it matter if I have a boyfriend? And besides, I just met you. You're giving off a serious creepy vibe." She threw her hands up.

"Oh, I'm creepy now? Wow. You're--just--" Silas shook his head.

"What? What am I? Please tell me because you already know me *so* well," Sydona yelled in his face.

"You're afraid! You're afraid of letting people get close to you. As soon as someone shows any interest you put up your walls and shut people out. And--make them feel stupid." Silas's eyes glowed green.

"That is not true! And don't pretend to know me. You have no idea what I have been through to get where I am today." Sydona's eyes were green underneath her hazel contacts as she stood nose to nose with Silas.

"Oh really? You wanna to go there? Let me take a guess... You had an abusive father who would beat you every time he came home from work because his boss was too hard on him. And almost killed you the day he came home from work early because he had gotten fired? And a mother who was too afraid to face him and let him kick you while sleeping in the middle of the night because he had no other way to get out his aggression. After this happened for six years of your life, you start to blame yourself for his actions and begin to start hurting yourself because you think that it will make it better and he won't hit you as much. But no, it doesn't. Just leaves scars on your wrists and ankles. After you figure out how to survive on your own, you leave home at eleven years old, leaving your baby brother to fend for himself--" Silas paused.

Sydona backed away from him, and her eyes turned normal. Silas put his head down in shame, choking on the last sentence that he never finished. She felt her eyes getting wet as she observed his wrinkled face. He turned to walk away, but Sydona could hear him sniffle.

"I--I had no idea…" Sydona stumbled, wondering if she should follow him.

"It's been thirty years since I've thought about that--Sorry. I didn't mean to vomit all of that on you."

Sydona shook her head, unsure of what to say. Standing alone and messing with her fingernails anxiously, she tried to think of things to say that would make him feel better. Nothing came to mind. He made his way to the truck bed and sat down on the edge. Taking off his jacket that he wore since they met, he revealed his arms covered in tattoos. Not a single space on his skin was naked, and it was beautiful.

Sydona smiled genuinely. "They look really nice."

"I got these to cover up the scars." He rubbed his wrists. "But I can still feel them."

She observed his tattoos of dragons overlapping each other, but they intertwined in a unique way that didn't ruin the image. Symbols and words filled the gaps where images would've been too small. Words like hope, strong, faith, and perseverance.

As she took his arm that he willingly gave her, the simple act of touching his soft warm skin made her tingle. Her fingers made their way down to his wrists where his scars resided. A flinch from his arm as she touched them only made her want to explore more. With just a look, she reassured him that things were okay, and she felt five deep scars just above the skin. Her thumbs caressed both wrists as she admired all of his tattoos that she assumed had stories. The tingling feeling kept increasing the longer she sat there with him in that tender moment. Sadness had a way of bringing people closer and even creating feelings of intimacy for someone you never thought possible. She always found it curious how those two things were connected.

As she stared off thinking about this, Silas lifted her chin to level his eyes with hers. Her entire body flushed with heat as he closed his eyes and leaned into her. There was no way to fight the feeling. As she leaned into him, an annoying high pitched voice came barreling through their faces.

"Who's hungry?" Raoul shouted as he flew right between them.

Giovonna stopped mid step and gawked at the two in the back of the truck. "Were you guys just kissing?!"

"No! No no no." Sydona dropped his arms and jumped out of the truck.

"No, no no. Not at all… what we were… doing…" Silas faded off as he watched Sydona run away.

"Of course they weren't! Sydona isn't that desperate!" Raoul piped up.

Sydona heard this, and her eyes flashed green. "Raoul!"

"What? I'm helping you," Raoul said.

"I wondered what we missed when we left you two alone," Willow said, jabbed Giovonna, and laughed loudly.

"Enough," Sydona boomed, quieting the laughter. "We need to eat, conserve our energy, and sleep. Enough with the mindless banter. We are on a mission and need to keep our minds sharp."

The rest of them hushed and stuck to making the fire and helping with the kills Willow made. They made the fire just behind the truck so Willow could sit inside. Being the older woman that she was, she expressed many times that she had back problems. The best way to cease the complaining was to not have her sit on the ground. Giovonna, Silas, Sydona, and Raoul sat in a circle around the fire as they quietly ate. Silas kept trying to look at Sydona, but she was avoiding eye contact. After Raoul's comment, she felt even worse.

The sun set quicker and quicker with each passing minute. The conversations were brief and to the point--like the skunk was too tough, or is there any fruit left? Raoul kept asking if any fresh fruit was left, but he had eaten it all already. None of the small talk was about Eagle Lake. No one wanted to talk about it, but it was like a giant elephant in the middle of the fire.

Once the stars were beaming bright and the moon became their main light source, it was time to plan. First, they removed their disguises and took out the contacts. As Sydona removed her second lens, she caught Silas's gaze, and he smiled big. It was the first time he had seen her natural purple eyes, and it made her blush.

Next, Willow began to load the truck with their weapons, hiding them under blankets randomly thrown about to make it look like it was just an untidy car. As planned, Willow tied up Giovonna and Silas with a piece of white rope tight enough to where it couldn't slip. Sydona's ties she made a little looser, so she would be able to break free and grab the dagger equipped to her hip. Giovonna lay in the middle while Sydona lay on her right and Silas on her left. Willow then continued to tie up their feet, and the three lay in the truck bed, but as she got ready to pull the tarp over the fliers, she paused.

"Y'all okay?" Willow asked with a genuine soft voice.

They all nodded and looked to the sky, and Willow covered them up before she dared to shed a tear in front of them. The comforting moonlight was gone; there was just blackness. Willow started up the truck, Raoul joined her in the front seat, and off they went.

As they drove to Eagle Lake, the truck and road would make sounds, but one sound didn't sound normal to Sydona, and that was the sniffles coming from her left.

"Gia?" Sydona turned to the side to look at her, even though she still only saw darkness.

"I don't think I can do this…" Giovonna let more tears and sniffling loose. "I've never killed anyone before. Do we really need to kill them?"

It pained Sydona that she couldn't do much, so she pondered her words carefully since they were all she had to comfort Giovonna. Words were never really her strong suit, and part of her wished that Silas would jump in. Even if it didn't come from her, something needed to be said, otherwise Giovonna would blow their cover. Or would she? Tears would be normal in such a situation. Why wouldn't a young flier be crying after being captured for experiments? Sydona thought it might even be a good tactic to make their plan more believable. Then, she realized comforting Giovonna should have been her first priority. She shifted her focus to that.

"You don't need to kill anyone if you don't want to. But if someone is trying to kill you, you can't just stand there and cry. You'll die," Sydona started sweetly but then got too real.

"Oh god!" Giovonna wailed. "I don't wanna die!"

Sydona felt a lump in her throat and was afraid that her words did the opposite of what she wanted.

"Gia, you're not going to die. Trust me. I'll be there. And Willow, Raoul, and Silas. You're not alone. What did Willow teach you out there in the woods?" Sydona pressed.

Scattered squeaks and moans delayed Giovonna's response. "Um--well--she taught me to breathe and focus."

"Good! Yes, you need to breathe and concentrate. Can you do that if you're crying?"

"Noooo…" Giovonna whined.

"Hey, hey. Listen." Sydona tried to comfort her and turned to her left side. "*I* need you."

And as if her fears went mute, Giovonna stopped. "You need me?"

"Mmhmm. And so does Willow and Silas. We all need you. I--I wouldn't even be here if it wasn't for you. Those contacts were pure genius, and your optimism is just incredible."

"Ya think?" said Giovonna, her smile almost big enough to hear.

"Oh, most definitely!" Sydona said in the highest voice she could bear.

Willow opened the tiny window to yell back to the group. "Get ready guys. I see the gate."

"Thank you, Syd," Giovonna said softly, sniffing one last time.

This was it, the moment of truth. With her hands tied down behind her back, the tarp sat on top of her face and made it hard to breathe. At least, she told herself that was why she had trouble breathing, not because of what was about to happen. She noticed a hole in the tarp and positioned herself in a spot that allowed her to get more fresh air. Wiggling closer to the hole, she peeked outside, and it was suddenly as bright as day. There was no way they were in that truck long enough for the sun to come back up.

"Raoul!" Sydona whispered loudly.

Raoul flew to the back immediately and slipped underneath the tarp. His orange glow illuminated the group, so they could see each other's faces. "Why is it so bright outside?" she asked in a panic.

"There are giant security lights surrounding the park. About twenty feet high," Raoul answered.

"Are you serious?" Silas asked concerned.

"What are we going to do?" Giovonna looked more worried than Sydona had pictured. Her face was still wet from tears with no way to wipe them away. Dirt and sweat drenched her tiny face, making Sydona feel extreme guilt. She could feel her pulse pumping through her veins. The confined space became more like a sweat lodge, and the bright lights intensified it by a hundred.

"It'll be fine. We can work around it," Sydona calmly answered even though her heartbeat felt like a hummingbird's.

Willow slowed down to a halt, and Raoul scrambled back up front to hide underneath a blanket. There were two guards at the gate who looked like normal police officers with black uniforms, nightsticks, and handguns. Willow jumped out with her rifle, shuffled to the back of the truck, pulled the gate down, and flung the tarp off of them.

Willow got into her role instantly. "Ai'ght, come on y'all; we ain't got all night!" The three slowly scooted their way out as planned and stood in a row.

One of the guards approached them slowly and looked them up and down, grabbed their faces to look closer in their eyes. They handled them harshly, leaving red marks on Sydona's face. She could see that Giovonna was on the verge of tears again. Then, the guards did what none of them thought they would do; they searched them. The guard patted down Silas's shoulders, stomach, hips, thighs, calves, and shoes. He moved on to Sydona, started with her arms, and then her chest, which he spent the most time on, making her clench her fists until they turned white. Next, the guard felt her abdomen, and her stomach twisted as he felt the dagger in her holster.

"What the shit is this?" he pulled it out, almost cutting Sydona in the process. "Carl, look at this!" He showed it proudly to the other guard.

Carl laughed and looked at Willow. "Why does she have a knife?"

Willow hesitated for what seemed like an eternity. "I have no idea! How the *hell* did ya get that and sneak it past me?!" Willow kicked her shin as lightly, but also as believably, as she could, making Sydona scrunch her face and hop to the side.

The guard finished searching her and moved on to Giovonna. Sydona stared at Willow with wide eyes, and they mouthed things to one another with wiggling eyebrows and bobbing heads. Giovonna started bawling again and made the guard sigh heavily. Once he finished with her shoes, he regrouped his buddy. Carl lazily motioned his head toward the gate. The other guard went into the small booth by the entrance, and Carl stood by the group without saying a word. The guard came back with a white bottle and something else in his closed hand. He presented himself in front of Silas first, opened the bottle, and poured whatever was in it into the towel he held in his other hand.

Silas saw this and knew what it was instantly. Before he could plead, the guard smothered his nose and mouth, and only seconds later, Silas lay back helplessly in the truck like a dead weight.

Giovonna was next, and the tears began to flow like a waterfall. "Please no! Pleeaasee!"

Giovonna wiggled and squirmed with all her might but was eventually poisoned as well and fell into the metal truck like a boulder. Sydona looked back at her, lifeless and alone, and wanted to rip right out of her restraints. *The restraints!* Willow made them purposely loose. All she had to do was get out of them before they smothered her with that stuff, too. She fidgeted with the knot behind her back and did her best to not make much motion or sound.

Willow caught on to what Sydona was doing and clutched her chest with her hand. "My heart!" She fell to the ground on her knees, yelling profanities. Carl looked at her on the ground and did not make one change in his facial expression. The other guard got his towel ready again, and Willow screamed louder. "Ah, I think I need to go to the doctor!"

Carl uncrossed his arms. "Calm down, we have a doctor here. No need to make a scene," He grabbed his radio and called in that they needed a doctor at the arrival. Sydona whipped her head in the direction of the walkie when she heard 'doctor'. Could Dr. Malik be there? She struggled even more to get her ties off, but it seemed to make the knot more difficult and tighter. Her shaking hands and nervousness were not calculated into the plan. The other guard continued doing his job and smothered her with the cloth. She put up a severe struggle, but the guard was much stronger. He forced the cloth on her so hard that she felt her nose bruising. As she looked down at Willow on the ground, still clutching her chest, her vision went blurry. Before she knew it, she fell in the truck like the other two.

Chapter Thirteen

"Ow!" Sydona exclaimed as a sharp electric zap on her left wrist forced her to open her eyes to a brightly sterile, white room. It looked eerily like what she envisioned in her dream. She felt lucky to still have her clothes on and no incisions to speak of. Without seeing the outside of the building, the room did not look like it belonged in a park cabin because it had been completely gutted out and turned into a hospital. A counter sat on the side of the room with a sink and medical instruments laid out on a table to her left side. She saw strange machines as well and couldn't begin to guess what they did.

"What the--?!" She sat up quickly and looked at her wrist to find a rigid, metal bracelet but was almost more surprised to see Raoul standing on the table next to her. "Raoul? What's going on?"

"Oh good, you're awake." Raoul buzzed up to her chest and lay down to squeeze her in his mini-sized hug.

"What's on my arm?" She panicked as she tried to lift up her hands, but they were restrained with plastic ties.

"I don't know. It seems to have electricity running through it. Did you get shocked?" Raoul fluttered back over next to it.

"Well, yeah! It really hurt," Sydona whispered loudly. "Where is everyone?"

"I don't know. I saw you after I slipped out of Willow's jacket, and I climbed on the cart they wheeled you in on. I didn't see any sign of Silas or Gia." He stroked her arm.

At a loss for words, Sydona paused but then asked even softer, "And Willow?"

"I think she left. She was playing along right up until she was taken to this room, and I think she lost it. Heard screaming and yelling toward the front of the cabin where we came in and then a slamming door and her cursing. At least I'm hoping she left. I can't see them hurting a human," Raoul said hesitantly.

Just then, the door creaked open, and Raoul disappeared from sight in a flash. In walked a man in an expensive looking, navy blue suit with a red striped tie and slicked back, shiny black hair. "I am so sorry about this," he said with a hint of an Indian accent. "Hey, Frank! Get these restraints off her. What are you doing?"

Frank came through the door and put his assault rifle behind his back. He undid her restraints as quick as he could, then left the room without a single word.

"Miss. Please allow me to apologize. This is not how we normally operate here." He shook his head and pulled up a rolling chair near Sydona. He examined her wrists. He had well-manicured hands, unlike her own. He glanced up at her and then smiled.

"I'm sorry. Please let me introduce myself. My name is Dr. John Malik. Welcome to Eagle Lake!"

Sydona couldn't figure out how to react. The man she wanted to stop stood before her, but he came across as pleasant and welcoming. She thought back to the article. Was he genuinely excited about this whole thing? She kept her guard up. His act couldn't fool her.

"Oh, and let me also apologize for the act at the front gate. That is uh--new. We have had some run ins with groups that don't exactly agree with what we're doing here. It's just a precaution, but I promise you, it has no long term effects on you. Just puts you to sleep for a little bit," he explained with well articulated speech and constant eye contact.

"Where are my friends?" Sydona spoke while hardly moving her lips.

"Oh, the man and teenager with you? You knew each other? Fascinating… Oh, but they're fine. Already settled in, I imagine." He smiled.

"What's with the metal bracelet?" she asked, sitting more upright.

"Those silly old things? Another precaution. Just lets us keep track of everyone and gives us vitals when we need them in a pinch," he said.

Sydona narrowed her eyes at his calm answer. If it was just a tracking device, why did it shock her when Raoul messed with it?

"Am I a prisoner here?" Her jaw tightened.

He laughed pretentiously. "Oh heavens no! Please don't think of this place as a prison. Think of it as... a temporary vacation while you help the scientific community. What we are doing here is beyond anything you can imagine! The fact that you are here speaks volumes about the contribution you can make with us."

Contribution, she thought to herself. What was that supposed to mean? Sydona decided to stop asking questions because she couldn't tell what was real and what he made up. She just knew she needed to find her friends and figure out their next plan.

After a few silent minutes, the doctor spoke up. "Well, I can see you're still in shock. I am very sorry about that again." He stood up and placed the chair back where he found it. "If you need anything, anything at all, please let me know. It was very nice meeting you, Sydona," he said and left the room.

and you must attend. If you do not show, there will be
nsequences. Any questions?" he asked without looking
rested in her answer. Sydona shook her head after being
lmed with information.

"Good, get in." He opened up the flap further.

She entered hesitantly, and the two guards left right
he tent was even smaller than she had anticipated, and
d came within inches of touching the lowest part of the
A man slept on a cot to her right, and to her left was an
cot with an embarrassingly thin gray blanket and a flat
on the end. On each end of the beds stood the buckets the
talked about, which was probably cause for the bad smell.
ce scrunched up, and she pulled her shirt over her nose. A
makeshift table also sat in between them with a book and
lantern on top. The man was snoring and didn't seem
d by the guard's loud talking or the fact that it looked like
ght with the beaming lights. He was probably used to it.
ily, their tent sat in a spot where a small amount of shade
er side made her cot darker. She lay down on the small one
n bed and pulled the blanket up over herself.

The night grew colder and the crickets--the only sound
could coax her to sleep--began to fade. She felt exhausted,
the smell of the man's bucket overwhelmed her. She
ndered if his time to empty it was soon. Laying there, alone
cold, she couldn't help but to try to figure out how she ended
in this situation. Their plan completely backfired, and she
ldn't fathom the amount of guards they had; it was like a max
son but worse. At least in jail they had actual beds, real toilets,
d showers with running water. She dared not think about the
od they gave them, though she was surprised they fed them at
l. But then again, they would need live subjects for their
periments.

The blanket did squat to protect against the cold that
rept into the tent from a small hole she saw in the corner next

The mentioning of her name made her heart jump. How
did he know it? Her right index finger looked redder than
normal, like it was pricked with something. Did they take blood
samples? That must be how he knew her. She wasn't sure how
to feel about that. And why didn't Silas and Giovonna go
through the same process?

Three men entered as the doctor exited. Two of the men
had guns, and one carried a pile of clothes with a pair of white
tennis shoes on top. He placed them on the table next to Sydona.

"Undress," one of the guards said.

Sydona glanced at him while rubbing her wrists and
scoffed at him.

He pointed his rifle at her. This *was* a prison.

"Does Dr. Malik know you're doing this?" she
challenged, hoping that she might be special and they would
back off.

"Shut up and strip," the same guard yelled and stepped
closer, towering over her.

"Okay, okay." She slid off the metal bed and slowly
started removing her shirt, pants, socks, and shoes. She felt
strange bruises in spots but had no idea how she had gotten them.
Standing there in her undergarments, she reached back for the
pile of blue clothes.

"Nope, keep going," the guard stopped her and pointed
at her with the rifle again.

Sydona stared blankly at them. "You must be joking."

"Do it," he said.

Sydona closed her eyes in embarrassment and did as she
was told.

"*Pick your battles,*" she said to herself, even though she
heard the two dim-witted guards snickering to each other as they
caught glimpses of her exposed skin. Silently, she placed her
hand on the clothes and looked to the guards for confirmation.
They nodded together, and she quickly got dressed. She slipped

on a "one-size-fits-all" flesh colored bra and panties that were at least one size too big. Or maybe she had lost weight from the last few days because her ribs seemed more prominent than normal. These were paired with what looked like a nurse's scrubs. The plain cobalt blue clothing could fit both herself and Giovonna at the same time. Her eyes morphed into auburn as she thought of her and Silas. She wasn't sure if she should take the doctor for his word or not. Until she could physically see them, they could be dead for all she knew.

She slipped on her thin, white shoes and socks as the guards stood behind her, hinting it was time to leave the room. As one guard stood at the door like a wannabe soldier, one walked behind her at a frighteningly close distance. She glanced back to get another look at Raoul under the table, and he held out a thumbs-up. This made her heart smile; Raoul might have a plan.

They led her down a long hallway with many doors on either side like a doctor's office. The whole place screamed hospital with Malik, her scrubs, and the men in white coats. The cabin that once held children's activities and wildlife conservation exhibits was now turned into a full-on working hospital building with guards holding automatics and rifles. It felt as if they had transported her to another country. Once they left the hallway, she saw the front of the cabin still looked normal. The space still had paintings of what the park used to look like, displayed with stuffed animals, park maps and benches for visitors to sit on. Guards populated the area pretty well, but it looked as if the room was used for hanging out. Some were playing cards and chess while others sat by themselves with earphones in, bobbing their heads. She couldn't escape their looks as some stared too long, making her feel hostile again. They opened the door, and though it was still dark out, it looked bright from the towering stadium lights surrounding the place. More shocking than the blinding lights in the middle of the night

was the sea of tents laid out
perfect location to oversee ever

She tried to count the
could see them. She came up wit
they continued down the flight c
of white tarps. As they walked by
moaning from some of them tha
They were some of the most dep
heard, and what was worse was th
all; she had to ignore it and move o
to this and just kept their eyes forw
and behind her with guns in ready p
tent with the number 43 written or
entrance in permanent black marker.
wondered what she would find inside
shelter. Was this the temporary vaca
mentioned? Talk about false advertisin
her way inside, a guard blocked her
making her jump back.

"First rule here: absolutely no ta
guards started. "Second rule: if you talk,
your tongue out because you wouldn't
speak. Third: you have a bucket to relieve
you are to empty it into the stream down
guard escort you, and today is Sunday, er
so Thursday will be your day to empty it. F
meals a day held in a big tent to the north
which groups of tents will be going when.
you do not eat. Fifth: bathing is optional, bu
us off because you smell so bad, you will be
takes place higher up in the stream where we
of soap, and this is done on Sundays. Sixth rule
tests every Monday, and again, we will call up
and you will go to the far field west of the f

The mentioning of her name made her heart jump. How did he know it? Her right index finger looked redder than normal, like it was pricked with something. Did they take blood samples? That must be how he knew her. She wasn't sure how to feel about that. And why didn't Silas and Giovonna go through the same process?

Three men entered as the doctor exited. Two of the men had guns, and one carried a pile of clothes with a pair of white tennis shoes on top. He placed them on the table next to Sydona.

"Undress," one of the guards said.

Sydona glanced at him while rubbing her wrists and scoffed at him.

He pointed his rifle at her. This *was* a prison.

"Does Dr. Malik know you're doing this?" she challenged, hoping that she might be special and they would back off.

"Shut up and strip," the same guard yelled and stepped closer, towering over her.

"Okay, okay." She slid off the metal bed and slowly started removing her shirt, pants, socks, and shoes. She felt strange bruises in spots but had no idea how she had gotten them. Standing there in her undergarments, she reached back for the pile of blue clothes.

"Nope, keep going," the guard stopped her and pointed at her with the rifle again.

Sydona stared blankly at them. "You must be joking."

"Do it," he said.

Sydona closed her eyes in embarrassment and did as she was told.

"*Pick your battles,*" she said to herself, even though she heard the two dim-witted guards snickering to each other as they caught glimpses of her exposed skin. Silently, she placed her hand on the clothes and looked to the guards for confirmation. They nodded together, and she quickly got dressed. She slipped on a "one-size-fits-all" flesh colored bra and panties that were at least one size too big. Or maybe she had lost weight from the last few days because her ribs seemed more prominent than normal. These were paired with what looked like a nurse's scrubs. The plain cobalt blue clothing could fit both herself and Giovonna at the same time. Her eyes morphed into auburn as she thought of her and Silas. She wasn't sure if she should take the doctor for his word or not. Until she could physically see them, they could be dead for all she knew.

She slipped on her thin, white shoes and socks as the guards stood behind her, hinting it was time to leave the room. As one guard stood at the door like a wannabe soldier, one walked behind her at a frighteningly close distance. She glanced back to get another look at Raoul under the table, and he held out a thumbs-up. This made her heart smile; Raoul might have a plan.

They led her down a long hallway with many doors on either side like a doctor's office. The whole place screamed hospital with Malik, her scrubs, and the men in white coats. The cabin that once held children's activities and wildlife conservation exhibits was now turned into a full-on working hospital building with guards holding automatics and rifles. It felt as if they had transported her to another country. Once they left the hallway, she saw the front of the cabin still looked normal. The space still had paintings of what the park used to look like, displayed with stuffed animals, park maps and benches for visitors to sit on. Guards populated the area pretty well, but it looked as if the room was used for hanging out. Some were playing cards and chess while others sat by themselves with earphones in, bobbing their heads. She couldn't escape their looks as some stared too long, making her feel hostile again. They opened the door, and though it was still dark out, it looked bright from the towering stadium lights surrounding the place. More shocking than the blinding lights in the middle of the night was the sea of tents laid out before her. The cabin was in the perfect location to oversee every single white tent.

She tried to count the tidy rows in the short time she could see them. She came up with about twenty by twenty before they continued down the flight of stairs and into the infestation of white tarps. As they walked by she heard bouts of crying and moaning from some of them that put a chill down her spine. They were some of the most depressing sounds she had ever heard, and what was worse was that she couldn't help them at all; she had to ignore it and move on. The guards acted immune to this and just kept their eyes forward as they walked in front and behind her with guns in ready positions. They stopped at a tent with the number **43** written on the side-flap of the tent entrance in permanent black marker. Her throat felt lumpy as she wondered what she would find inside these pathetic excuses for shelter. Was this the temporary vacation that Dr. Malik had mentioned? Talk about false advertising. As she began to make her way inside, a guard blocked her with his massive hand, making her jump back.

"First rule here: absolutely no talking," the burlier of the guards started. "Second rule: if you talk, you'll wish we had cut your tongue out because you wouldn't even be able to try to speak. Third: you have a bucket to relieve yourself. Once a week you are to empty it into the stream downwind. We will have a guard escort you, and today is Sunday, er technically Monday, so Thursday will be your day to empty it. Fourth: there are three meals a day held in a big tent to the north. We will announce which groups of tents will be going when. You must attend, or you do not eat. Fifth: bathing is optional, but if you start to piss us off because you smell so bad, you will be forced to bathe. It takes place higher up in the stream where we will give you a bar of soap, and this is done on Sundays. Sixth rule: we do the flying tests every Monday, and again, we will call up your tent number, and you will go to the far field west of the food tent. This is required, and you must attend. If you do not show, there will be severe consequences. Any questions?" he asked without looking very interested in her answer. Sydona shook her head after being overwhelmed with information.

"Good, get in." He opened up the flap further.

She entered hesitantly, and the two guards left right away. The tent was even smaller than she had anticipated, and her head came within inches of touching the lowest part of the ceiling. A man slept on a cot to her right, and to her left was an empty cot with an embarrassingly thin gray blanket and a flat pillow on the end. On each end of the beds stood the buckets the guard talked about, which was probably cause for the bad smell. Her face scrunched up, and she pulled her shirt over her nose. A small makeshift table also sat in between them with a book and an oil lantern on top. The man was snoring and didn't seem phased by the guard's loud talking or the fact that it looked like daylight with the beaming lights. He was probably used to it. Luckily, their tent sat in a spot where a small amount of shade on her side made her cot darker. She lay down on the small one person bed and pulled the blanket up over herself.

The night grew colder and the crickets--the only sound that could coax her to sleep--began to fade. She felt exhausted, and the smell of the man's bucket overwhelmed her. She wondered if his time to empty it was soon. Laying there, alone and cold, she couldn't help but to try to figure out how she ended up in this situation. Their plan completely backfired, and she couldn't fathom the amount of guards they had; it was like a max prison but worse. At least in jail they had actual beds, real toilets, and showers with running water. She dared not think about the food they gave them, though she was surprised they fed them at all. But then again, they would need live subjects for their experiments.

The blanket did squat to protect against the cold that crept into the tent from a small hole she saw in the corner next to her head. Doing her best, she rested her eyelids, sighed deeply, and tried to think of positive things. She was still alive, and that was good. Raoul was still there, and he might have a plan on what to do next. Flashes of the conversation with Malik crept into her mind. When he mentioned the groups that didn't agree with them, did he mean the Sparrows? Why did Willow leave? Her suspicions about Willow were coming back. Could she have been playing them all along? The act that she put on was eerily convincing, too. She exhausted herself trying to figure out how to answer all the questions in her head at once. She let her eyes droop and tried to get some sleep.

Chapter Fourteen

"Hey! You better wake up if you wanna eat!" She was awoken from a dreamless, short sleep by an older woman shaking her violently.

Sydona threw the blanket off her face and squinted at the woman as if she didn't hear anything she just said.

"What?" Sydona asked groggily.

"Food! You wanna eat, right, newbie?" she repeated.

"I guess?" Sydona shrugged.

"Well come on then!" The lady whipped the blanket off her and grabbed her arm. "They only give us so much time to eat. If you miss it, you don't eat!"

Sydona rubbed her face and eyes before following the woman out of the tent into the madness that took place outside. It was as if cattle were being directed into the slaughterhouse. Some fliers walked, and some ran like the kid who bumped into her from behind and apologized as he disappeared into the crowd. *How old are you?* she thought to herself. He couldn't have been older than ten.

From the corner of her eye she saw Dr. Malik again, and he made his way over to her. He had his hand out while smiling at her. Sydona shook it hesitantly.

"How did you sleep last night, Miss Wilder?" he asked.

Sydona laughed to herself, thinking he couldn't be serious about the question. Afraid of saying the wrong thing, Sydona only shrugged.

He laughed. "Miss Wilder, you don't need to be shy. How was it?"

Sydona had many things she wanted to say about the conditions of her tent and bed, but felt this wasn't the time or place. "Pathetic."

"Really?" He moved his sunglasses to the top of his head. "How so?"

Sydona's heart pounded harder with each word he spoke, afraid he would show his true colors. She took a gulp as she pondered over the right words to say. "The blankets are really thin, and it was cold last night."

His face hardened at her words, and he closed his eyes. Her breathing quickened and her eyes turned brown.

"I am so sorry about the condition of your room," he said with sympathy and compassion. "I will make sure to get an extra blanket sent over right away. Remind me of your number again?"

"43."

"Right." He looked around for a guard. "Hey, you."

A guard promptly walked over and stood at attention for the doctor.

"Give Miss Wilder here an extra blanket for her room. Number 43."

"Yes sir!" The guard hustled inside the cabin.

Dr. Malik turned his attention back to Sydona. "There, you see. We're not all bad. I want to make sure you are comfortable at every moment of your stay with us."

He put his sunglasses back on, patted Sydona on the shoulder, and walked away.

Sydona wasn't sure what to think of the exchange. He didn't seem to show much interest in any other fliers here. Why did he single her out among the other people around?

Sydona slowly flowed back in the direction of the people-herd. She wasn't even all that hungry. They all gathered under two big tents with rows of long wooden tables like a school cafeteria. She found herself standing in line for food, being shoved along the way, and grabbing a tray absentmindedly like she saw the people in front of her do. As she looked around, she noticed that there were probably hundreds of fliers in this tent, and yet, it was almost completely silent. There were the sounds of silverware clanking, feet scuttling, coughing, and throat clearing, but no one seemed to be talking to each other at all, not even whispering.

Next thing she knew, it was her turn for food, and she placed her paper plate on the counter as they scooped up a mess of brown stuff that looked like a liquid meatloaf.

"Is there meat in this?" Sydona leaned in and whispered to the lady with a hair net.

She looked right through her and pushed her plate down the line as she was given more slop in a variety of colors. Grabbing a cup of questionable liquid from a tray at the end of the bar, she searched for someplace to eat. But mainly she tried to find Giovonna or Silas. She scanned the room in search of curly black hair and shaggy black hair, but she saw a sea of people from all walks of life. There were older folks that had so many wrinkles that she guessed they were in their hundreds, and there were kids as young as eight. She saw the kid who bumped into her sitting at a table with a bunch of adults scarfing down the slop. She tried to imagine being a kid in this place, not being able to talk, play, be around other kids, or even go to school. It was so cruel and almost too much for her to handle, but just then, she saw a hand waving in the air from the corner; it was Giovonna. Sydona's face lit up like a child's on Christmas morning and even more when she saw Silas sitting next to her. She practically threw her mush down on the table and squeezed Giovonna harder than she had ever hugged a person before. As she let go, Silas went in to hug her, but Sydona took a step back. It was an awkward ten seconds, but then Sydona stuck her hand out, and they shook hands. Her stomach did flips over the weird exchange, but she shook it off. They were both wearing the same blue uniforms as herself, and Giovonna's clothes swallowed her.

"Are you okay?" Sydona whispered as softly as she could to Giovonna.

Giovonna shook her head. "Syd, I'm scared..." She trembled with tears in her eyes.

Sydona immediately brought her in for another hug, even tighter, hoping it would comfort her. "It'll be okay."

"This is a prison. How is it going to be okay?" Giovonna squeaked, trying to keep her voice down.

She was right. How could Sydona tell her things would get better? She didn't know how things were going to turn out. She held Giovonna even longer while she searched for an answer, but she still came up blank.

"Just trust me, okay?" Sydona pulled her away.

Guards were eyeing them, and afraid of breaking the rules, Sydona finally sat down next to Giovonna. The young girl held her hand tightly, fearing that she would be ripped away from Sydona again. Sydona squeezed her hand back with two pulses to somehow convey to her that she had things under control even though she was clueless.

Despite Giovonna's appropriately terrified feelings, Sydona was still happy to see them alive and well. This was the happiest she had felt since arriving at the camp, and she couldn't stop smiling at the both of them. Eventually she had to look down at her food, and her smile slowly faded. Scooping up the brown stuff, she sniffed it, smelled meat, and plopped it back down. She moved on to the green mush, thinking it had a chance of being something more vegetable like. She daringly let her tongue touch it, and it wasn't as bad as she had anticipated, so she took a mouthful. Her garden called out to her with its crisp green beans, big carrots, plump tomatoes, and giant potatoes; her mouth watered, and then the green mush tasted terrible. The fork dropped to the table with a bang, making the other two jump and stare at her. Sydona stuck her tongue out with a sour face, and they laughed silently.

She gave up on the food, looked down the long crowded table, and from the corner of her eye, caught pieces of paper being passed back and forth across the table. She glanced to the other side of her and witnessed the same thing further down the line. Was this how people were communicating?

"Alright everyone. Breakfast is over. Let's go!" one of the guards shouted and rang an obnoxiously loud bell over the already silent tent. Everyone picked up their trays, dumped leftovers in bins, set the trays on top, and kept walking just like the sheep they had been turned into. As the three gathered in the massive crowd, they grabbed each other's shirts to stay together and took the opportunity to talk as quickly as they could.

"Which tent are you?" Giovonna asked.

"43. You?" Sydona asked.

"We're both in 56," Giovonna said and gestured at Silas.

Sydona looked at her, puzzled, "You're together?"

They both nodded. Sydona wondered how they got put together while she ended up with some random person. As the crowd dispersed into their own tents, Sydona motioned for them to sneak into hers. They finally reached tent 43, and the blanket the doctor told her he would bring was folded nicely on her cot. Dr. Malik actually did something nice, and his action was beginning to sway her opinion of him, just slightly. Sydona moved the blanket and sat on the cot with Giovonna next to her. Silas found a place on the grass and sat with his legs crossed.

"Who's in here with you?" Giovonna asked only above a whisper.

"How should I know?" Sydona answered bluntly.

Silas changed the subject. "Where's Willow?"

"Raoul said she was screaming and yelling on her way out of the cabin. He thinks she left."

"Raoul? You spoke with him?" Giovonna turned toward her.

Sydona flashed a quick grin. "Yeah, he snuck in and was under the table in the hospital."

"Hospital?" Silas asked.

"Yeah, the big cabin was turned into a hospital. You didn't see it when you woke up?"

Silas and Giovonna looked at each other, and Silas answered. "No, Syd. We woke up in our tent with a guard standing over us. Why were you in the cabin?"

"Maybe they know what we're trying to do..." Giovonna said with an even softer voice.

"No. I think it's because I had a knife on me like Willow had brilliantly suggested and then tied my knot too tight." She rolled her eyes thinking of that stressful moment.

"What happened?" Giovonna asked.

Sydona forgot that they were already passed out. "I was trying to untie my knot, and I couldn't, and she faked a heart attack. It was so embarrassing..."

Giovonna smothered her laugh since she knew it wasn't very funny to Sydona.

They sat silent for a moment and listened to the noise of shuffling people quiet down, but then Giovonna spoke up in a whisper. "What do you suppose these bracelets do?" She held out her left arm.

"Dr. Malik said it's a tracking device," Sydona said.

Silas's eyes widened. "Dr. Malik?"

"You met him?" Giovonna asked louder.

"Yeah… I don't think it's true, though. It shocked me when Raoul tried taking it off."

Silas observed his more closely, curious about the shocking aspect.

"What was he like?" Giovonna scooted closer to her.

"Uh--nice…" Sydona said.

"Really?" Giovonna asked.

"Yeah... It was strange. He apologized a lot. For the chloroform at the gate and for restraining me. He was angry when he saw me tied down to the table."

"You were tied down?" Silas said in disbelief.

"Yeah. He called this place a temporary vacation," she said with an eye roll.

"This guy sounds delusional," he mumbled.

"I don't know..." Sydona faded. "He seems… passionate. But obviously doesn't want to harm us. And I think the guns they carry around are for the resistance. Not us."

"Wha--they know about the Sparrows already?" Giovonna said.

"He said that there are groups out there who don't understand what they do. Maybe they don't..."

Suddenly a man in his mid-sixties with gray, balding hair and glasses walked through the flap entrance. "What are you all doing in my tent?!"

The three looked up at him, surprised as he stood in the entrance. They were at a loss of what to say to him. "They better not catch you in here," he grumbled as he went to the cot on the other side. He opened up a tattered book stored under his bed and began to read while still mumbling.

Sydona looked at both Silas and Giovonna, trying to determine if they should just leave. They didn't think about what would happen if they were caught inside another tent. Sitting silently on the one side of the tent, they stared at the man who seemed very disgruntled.

"How long have you been here, sir?" Silas spoke up at a whisper.

"Sonny, I lost count the first week I was here," the man answered while keeping his eyes glued to his book.

"How long ago was that?" Silas pried.

"Years."

Giovonna and Silas exchanged a worried look.

"This has been here for years? Why are we just now hearing about it?" Silas asked.

"Don't be naive, boy. They moved us here." He coughed deeply.

"Moved? Moved from where?"

He turned a page in his book. "Somewhere else, where do you think?"

"Are there a lot of people here like you? I mean, who have been here for years?" Giovonna jumped in.

"Oh yeah. Tons of us. That's what most of us are. Been getting a lot of newbies lately, though. Guessing you are one of them." He looked over at her, peeking over his bifocals.

"What have they done to you?" Giovonna asked sympathetically.

"They treat us like second class citizens. Give us crap food, test us once a week; won't tell us what for. Make us fly with a chain rigged to our feet, sometimes force us to carry heavy things. Hardly let us talk; gotta write things to people all the time. Don't want us to start an uproar or communicate big escape plans, I guess. They put these goddamned bracelets on us to prevent us from flying away." He sat up and put his book down. "But the worst part is the isolation. You start to go crazy here. If they notice you're spending too much time with someone, they will separate you, keep changing tents. I've even seen them beat the living hell out of some guy because he wouldn't stay away from his wife." He paused and frowned as if recalling a terrible memory. "He died."

Silas shook his head in disgust. "We have to get out of here!"

"Ha! Good luck with that! Tell me how that works out for you." The man chuckled with a cough.

Maybe Dr. Malik wasn't as welcoming as she had thought. This would be a real problem for the group. If they planned on overthrowing the place, they had to congregate at some point.

Sydona straightened up. "We will get out of here."

The man laughed louder and shook his head.

"And we'll get you out of here and everyone here. You watch." Sydona's eyes turned green.

They heard the faint voice of a guard in the distance ordering fliers to go back to their own tents and reminding them there was to be no talking.

"You better leave," the man warned.

"They put me here," Sydona said without skipping a beat.

Both Silas and Giovonna said their goodbyes and as soon as the guard had his back turned, they were gone.

Sydona lay flat on her metal and cloth bed and stared up at the ceiling of the tent. It was pure white with one part bleached a bit brighter because of the sun. There was no breeze, no trees, not even any birds she could hear in earshot. She longed for her backyard that was full of so much life: birds, fairies, and the occasional rabbit she would catch munching on her cabbage (that she didn't stop). The squirrels always made it more fun because they were very fond of Raoul's family, and Sydona would catch them playing hide and seek in the trees and bushes. Sighing deeply, she wondered if she would ever see that yard, or house, again.

"Psstt!" came a quiet sound from behind her cot.

Turning onto her stomach, she remembered seeing a hole in the corner big enough for a fairy to fit through, and he did just that. Raoul stood with his hands on his hips.

"Raoul!? How did you find me?" Sydona said, elated.

"I saw them put your file away with a number on it. I had an idea of what the numbers meant. Did you find Gia and Silas?" Raoul jumped up onto her bed and out of site from the man on the cot.

"Yeah, I saw them. They woke up in their tent, though, didn't even know there was a hospital here," Sydona said as her stomach growled ferociously.

Raoul jumped back at the monster vocalizing its anger from inside her body. "Hungry?"

She grabbed her stomach. "Yeah. But this food is garbage. I miss my garden…"

"Me, too. And the mangoes we would get in the city. Oh man, what I would do to get my hands on a mango." Raoul slobbered.

Sydona chuckled, but then had a flash of the fruit stand with Annie and Joseph standing behind it, and her smile quickly faded.

"Ah, mango." The man's voice from the other side made Raoul perk up.

"Who's that?" Raoul peeked over her sideways arm.

"Name's Maverick," he answered.

Sydona pointed her thumb at him. "That's Maverick."

"Oh, Maverick Vandermeade. I saw your file, too." Raoul whispered to Sydona, "He's been in captivity for twenty-two years."

Sydona's stomach dropped, and her monster subsided. Twenty-two years? How long would she be trapped there? Willow mentioned that they moved these camps around all the time. She wondered where they had moved this one from. According to Maverick, they didn't tell them much, or he had moved so many times that he couldn't keep it straight. The story about the man that couldn't stay away from his wife made its way through her head. Could it have been her father? Her parents were always very close, and she could see him fighting to be next to her mom.

She then thought about the guards and the rules. They said no talking, but Maverick didn't seem scared of talking. Was it just a scare tactic? He had been there long enough to know what they could and could not do. The guards seemed dimwitted and more like monkeys with toys. While Dr. Malik wasn't necessarily the ring leader, he was in charge of the organization. Her mind went over the looks on Giovonna's and Silas's faces when she told them she woke up inside the cabin. Why weren't they brought there, too? What made her so different from other fliers there? The bracelets that Maverick mentioned, prevented them from flying. It made sense. But Dr. Malik said they were just tracking devices. His stories were starting to crack. Her nails took the punishment as she pondered over everything.

A speaker phone screeched through the park loud enough to make Sydona cover her ears. "Listen up. Tents one through sixty, report to the northwest quadrant for the weekly flying tests. One through sixty. Report immediately. I repeat…" The announcement repeated three more times.

Maverick closed his book and put it under his bed. "Come on newbie. Better leave your fairy here; they hate them more than us."

Sydona ignored this and opened the big pocket in her oversized blue pants, and Raoul slipped right in without Maverick seeing. They walked out of the tent and into an assembly line of fliers, all walking the same direction in a much more uniform fashion than earlier. This time, they were going to be experimented on, which was the one thing she looked forward to the least. She tried to picture how it would go, but she had been wrong about everything so far, so she just walked in unison with everyone else.

"Name's Sydona, by the way. Not 'newbie'," she whispered to Maverick.

"Nice to meet you." Maverick turned and smiled.

Sydona walked closely behind Maverick, not by choice but because everyone seemed to be crowding each other. The massive group of over one-hundred fliers gathered in a field surrounded by a dozen guards with guns. Everyone made a makeshift line, and a guard tied a small silver chain to the first person's ankle. The chain connected to a circular device that seemed to have extra chain inside of it. A woman in a white lab coat typed things into a laptop with tons of wires coming from it. She took the flier's metal bracelet off after she finished inputting information. She then put a strange headband on his head with the same look and sheen as the bracelet.

The woman said something to the man, and he started running as fast as he could while the chain jerked all over the place. Kicking off the ground to soar into the air, the expression on the flier's face made it seem like it wasn't so bad, like it was a moment of freedom. Do they all look forward to this? The woman in the white coat watched the screen intently and occasionally glanced at the flier up in the air. After several minutes, she blew a whistle that hung around her neck, and like a trained dog, he returned to her and waited for her to take off his metal leash. His face returned back to it's normal mundane look with sunken brown eyes and frown lines.

It felt like hours being out in the hot afternoon sun with no shade and clothes that had no breathing room. She couldn't remember the last time she had sweated that much in her life, and she felt as if she would pass out. If she was this hot, she couldn't imagine how hot Raoul was inside her restrictive cotton pocket. She opened it every five minutes or so, and he popped his soaking wet head up for air. Everyone around her fanned themselves with their hands or used their shirts as a fan, and kids stood behind taller people for more shade. Water was the only thing she could think about, and they weren't offering any at all. It was almost more than she could stand, the inhumanity of treating someone like this, even if they were second class people according to the NFA. As soon as she felt herself get dizzy, she saw that she was next in line. A wave of relief pulsed through her since she would be able to fly and refresh her hot face with some cooler air.

She walked slowly over to the woman in the white coat and noticed her drinking a cold bottle of water with condensation dripping down it. Watching each drip fall off the bottle, her mouth filled with saliva.

"Hot out here, huh?" The woman smiled and laughed.

Sydona glared at her through the sweat in her eyes.

The woman routinely began to put the chain around Sydona's ankle, typed things into the computer, took her bracelet off, and strapped the headband on.

"When you're ready," she said and smiled sincerely, giving Sydona the feeling that maybe not all of the people working for the NFA were bad.

She spun around to see nothing but open, gorgeous grass and flowers. A breeze gently kissed her face, wiping away some of the sweat. She took a deep, long breath and closed her eyes, listening to the birds in the near distance.

"Come on. We don't have all day!" the woman yelled.

She jumped in surprise at how loud she yelled, and her thought of 'some nice guards' went right out the window. She took a step forward and then ran as best she could with the chain whipping around behind her. When she finally took to the skies, the air cooled her off, and she felt at peace. She then understood the look the first flier had. It was nice to feel free for a moment, even in a place filled with guns. Tall trees lined the forest behind the hospital cabin, and colorful flowers grew in front that she wasn't able to see before. This was the perfect opportunity to take a mental image of the entire park. It was bigger than the map she saw, and she could clearly see all of the tents. Turning her head, she caught a nice glimpse of the lake on the other side of the main entrance filled with ducks and swans. She then tried looking for Silas and Giovonna, since they were within the group the announcer called, but was unable to find them. She assumed they were shading themselves behind bigger people.

Looking down farther in the giant line, she noticed an older woman who looked extremely familiar just by the way she stood. She stood very close to an older man who also looked familiar. The woman had blonde hair with streaks of gray, and the gentleman had all grey hair. As she studied them, the woman happened to look up directly at Sydona, and her heart sank. It almost made her fall out of the sky when she realized who the woman was.

"Mom!"

Chapter Fifteen

Sydona screamed at the top of her lungs so loudly that she felt as if her vocal cords would crack. Her mother covered her mouth with shock and jabbed the man next to her. Sydona's hands shook as he looked up at her, too. It was her father.

"Dad!" Sydona's heart trampled her insides.

She changed positions to fly to them as quickly as possible. Her parents were just as excited to see their daughter and ran out of the line to her. Sydona didn't care what the consequences would be; she needed to be with her parents and didn't care how she did it. Then, she heard a booming, deep voice yelling at her parents and whipped her head toward a guard pointing a rifle at them.

"No! Stop!" Sydona flattened her body as much as she could to reach them quicker and then saw another guard adamantly making a circular motion with his arm.

"Oomph!" she cried as the chain yanked her back.

The woman in the lab coat reeled the chain back in so forcefully that Sydona swore they were trying to tear her leg off. But Sydona fought it hard with adrenaline pumping through her veins just as quickly. Grabbing the chain with one arm, she tried taking it off, but it was being held together with some kind of strong magnet. The more she focused on trying to get it off, the lower she sunk to the ground. She was fighting a losing battle, but she would be damned if she gave up so easily. Raoul would be able to help her get back into the air, but she couldn't risk anyone seeing him. Not after Maverick's snide comment in the tent.

"Would you idiots shoot her down already?!" the woman in the lab coat cried out.

She panicked at the woman's words, and her hands became useless, full of sweat. As soon as she decided she should just give up, she felt a sting in her neck. The same feeling from Willow's house. The next thing she knew, she plummeted to the ground like a sack of potatoes.

She woke up with a massive headache and blinded by the bright florescent lighting. It appeared she was back in the same room from her arrival. Without skipping a beat, she opened her mouth and called out for her mother.

"Tsk, tsk, tsk, tsk," a man to her left shamed her as he sat beside her bed. Dr. Malik shook his head with disappointment. His demeanor was drastically different from their last visit, and he seemed less enthusiastic. Once she fully awoke, she noticed her arms were restrained again. She wondered why he didn't have the restraints taken off this time. Was her act during the flying tests going to have serious repercussions? As long as they didn't hurt her parents, she was ready for whatever he threw at her.

"Where are my parents?" Sydona quivered.

"You need not worry about them," he said in a much deeper, more serious tone.

Although she tried to stay strong and not cry, her eyes turned auburn. The doctor smirked at her changing eyes.

"Such an ugly color," he said softly and began to outline her metal bracelet. "One thing about you people I don't care for. Doesn't interest me. But, I'm not here for your eyes."

Sydona's heart raced again as the doctor's body language changed, and he seemed like a completely different person than before. He grabbed a wooden tongue depressor from his coat pocket and used it to trace the bracelet.

"I need to punish you," he continued. "What you did out there… what you did…" he gritted his teeth and inserted the stick underneath the bracelet and twisted to make it shock her.

An extreme jolt of electricity bolted through her body like a lightning strike. Her hairs stood up on end and goosebumps ran all through her skin. Squeezing her eyes shut from the sudden pain, she dared not cry out in agony.

"You could have really screwed things up for me, do you know that?" He kept his jaw tight.

Tears ran down her cheeks without her even realizing it. Her body felt as if it were on fire, and there was no escape. She wriggled from side to side, trying to free herself from the restraints, but it seemed he had all of this planned. After what felt like forever, he finally stopped and removed the wooden stick.

Her entire body experienced tingles left over from the extreme bolts. Nothing she could have done would have prepared her for this kind of torture.

"Do you know why I do this?" Dr. Malik asked.

Sydona tightened her jaw and glared at him with green eyes.

"When I was growing up, I lived in the states with my parents in Southern California. Well one day, I was just outside, minding my own business, playing with toys or something. And I look up and there is this little girl with blonde hair flying around the streets. All I remember was the look on her face of just pure joy. Like nothing else in the world could make you feel that way. That happy and free. From that point on, I have made it my life mission to bring joy like that to the world." His smile faded. "And nothing is going to stop me from making that happen."

He leaned in, standing only an inch from her nose and staring down into her green eyes. "Nothing."

Backing away from her, he returned his chair to the side of the room.

"You're a coward," Sydona said before he reached the door. "You can't make your own happiness, so you have to steal ours. You're pathetic."

She could see both his hands folding into fists. He then reached back in his pocket and revealed the tongue depressor again. He stormed back over to Sydona and leaned into her again as he placed the stick back under the bracelet.

"You're lucky I'm choosing not to kill you instead."

As he twisted it, her whole body seized up again with the electricity pumping at full speed through her. She closed her eyes and arched her back in pain. Through the current that she could hear through her eardrums, she also heard his clanky shoes walk away and through the door. He had left the stick under the bracelet. Unable to hold back the agonizing pain, she cried out as loud as she could. Sweat soaked through her clothes and her throat was dried up from crying so hard. Her entire body shook violently, unable to move much under the tight restraints. She knew she screamed loud enough for guards to hear her, but no one came to help.

Next thing she knew, the shocking stopped. The sound of the wooden stick hit the floor, and it was the sweetest sound she ever heard. Exhausted from the heinous act, her eyes closed, and she wanted to lie there in silence. She didn't care that she was still tied up; her body was too tired to move. Only minutes later, two guards entered the room and took her restraints off. All of her muscles felt dead, and she couldn't take revenge on the guards even if she wanted to. They had to sit her up, and she felt like a complete rag doll with no control over anything that happened. Even her eyelids struggled to stay open, so she kept them closed. The men carried her by her feet and armpits as they walked out of the cabin. She could hear laughter coming from the men as they passed through the cabin.

She thought about what she looked like: a lifeless body made a fool of in front of everyone. Could her actions jeopardize her seeing her parents? It was too hard to think about that. All she wanted was for her body to stop tingling. Soon, the guards dropped her onto her cot carelessly and left her there. Curling up into a ball, she turned away from Maverick, who was staring at her, and let more tears out.

"What did they do to you?" Maverick asked softly.

Sydona heard his question but couldn't bear to speak.

He touched her shoulder, making her jump.

"Are you okay?" he asked as he knelt down beside her cot.

Sydona shook her head. His hand never left her shoulder as he gently caressed it. She found it sweet that he was trying to comfort her. But all she wanted was to see her parents and make sure they were okay. The possibility of them being put through the same torture gave her a headache. Grabbing the thin blanket, she scrunched it up and pressed it close to her to dry her face.

A loud bell rang several times throughout the park, signaling food.

"Lunch. You coming?" asked Maverick, getting back to his feet.

She shook her head again.

As Maverick left the tent, it took her no time at all to fall asleep once the tingling stopped. Her brain was unable to think about anything but resting and recuperating. She feared that with the amount of electricity that pulsed through her, she might have serious long term damage. The thought quickly went to the back of her mind as she slept a dreamless sleep.

A loud, obnoxious snore woke her as it roared across the tent. Crickets came out to play sometime in the night, and the air felt cooler. She assumed she slept for a solid eight hours and felt somewhat refreshed. A grin spread across her face as she looked down by her stomach where Raoul was curled up and sleeping. She stroked his wing that laid across his body and closed her eyes again, dreaming of better things.

The sound of finch and starlings, and the bright rising sun woke her slowly. Raoul still slept next to her, lying partially under the blanket with drool on his mouth. The events of yesterday were still fresh in her mind, but she tried to focus on the upcoming day. She would finally find her parents, and that thought alone made her smile.

"Morning, Syd," Raoul said sleepily.

"Hey, buddy." She smiled down at him.

He sat up. "Are you okay?"

"I'm better." Sydona lay on her back with her knees propped up.

Raoul smiled in response and said, "I have some good news for you..."

"What?"

"I know where Ian and Evey are," he said as he did a little dance on the cot.

"Really? How?" Sydona's eyes lit up.

"I went to go find them once you saw them and made that big commotion. No one saw me."

Sydona smiled briefly as she thought about his words. He flew away, vulnerable to being captured or killed. How could he be so careless? But on the other hand, he was able to find them, and she settled on talking about that instead.

"How are they?" Sydona asked.

"Good! Maybe a little skinnier than they should be, but that could be because of their age, too," Raoul said. "I told them you were coming to breakfast today, that way you could see them. You know, up close."

Sydona laughed. "Yeah. Thanks. I should probably eat something soon anyways, before my stomach devours itself."

A guard yelled a few tents down from their own. "Peterson! We got another one!"

The conversation stopped. They didn't realize how close the guards were. Sydona's heart sped up at the thought of them catching Raoul in the tent with them. They sat silently as they tried to decipher what he was yelling about.

"Name?"

"Uh, Lydia Garrison."

"How'd it happen?"

"Looks like it was a plastic knife, up her wrists."

"How long was she here for?"

"I don't know. Couple years, maybe? Does it matter?"

"Yes, Dr. Malik needs to keep track."

"She makes three this month. *Useless* bi--."

"Hey. Not here."

The guards faded off.

Sydona couldn't help but peek out the opening in the tent entrance. And she wasn't alone. As she looked around, others also looked out to see who the victim was. The guards exited tent 46, carrying a body with the blanket covering up most of her. The blood on Lydia's lifeless arms looked bright against her snow-white skin. The blanket didn't conceal much, and Sydona caught a glimpse of her face. She was pretty and young, maybe in her twenties.

"Back in your tents!" the head guard shouted, carrying her feet.

Sydona did as she was told and went back inside with a heavy heart.

"How'd she do it? With a plastic knife? Idiot. Now they're gonna take them away from us," Maverick scoffed without a trace of empathy in his voice.

"How can you say that? A woman just died…" Sydona whispered angrily.

"The last time someone killed themselves that way, they fed us liquid crap for months. Sometimes don't even give us spoons! Selfish..." Maverick grumbled.

"Selfish? You are a heartless--"

"Look. When you have been here as long as I have, you see a lot of death. Fliers are killing themselves all the time. This isn't anything new. And she's selfish because when she dies, they go out and find someone to replace her. Putting us more at risk. People need to learn to be more positive."

Sydona and Raoul sat flabbergasted by Maverick.

"Don't look at me that way," Maverick said. "You think I'm heartless. I'm realistic. I've stayed around this long, so they don't bring new people in. I can't comment on why they brought you here and others as of late. But I know for a fact, every time someone commits suicide, someone else has to take their place."

Maverick then pulled out his book and flipped to his bookmark in the middle.

The thought of having to witness so much death was hard for Sydona to fathom. She wondered if Maverick had any friends left. Did he fear making new friends with the risk of losing them? It made her depressed to think about, but she could tell he was done talking about it as he had his nose in a book. After several quiet moments and getting past what she just witnessed, she tried changing the subject.

"How many times have you read that book?"

"About twenty times now." Maverick turned a page.

"Do you know every word in it now?" she asked.

"Pretty much. But it's still a great story."

"How did you get it?"

Maverick closed it quickly. "From the guards' break room in the cabin. When you've been here as long as I have, you can get away with getting things as long as you stay quiet."

"The breakroom, huh?" Sydona played with her messy hair, trying to brush it with her fingers.

Maverick made a confirmation sound and buried his nose in his book until the bell rang.

It was the first time Sydona actually felt excited for mealtime, and she thought that maybe she would actually eat, too. As the crowd of hungry fliers piled into the tent, she grabbed her tray and went through the motions of getting her food, which smelled much better than she remembered. When she turned to face the crowd after getting her meal, she instantly began to look for her parents. She spotted a couple with white hair at the table farthest from the entrance. Like a little kid, she ran to them with a smile stretching ear to ear. She threw her tray down on the table they sat at and gave her mom a tight hug, not wanting to ever let go. Then she transitioned over to her father, squeezing him as if he was going to somehow slip out of her grip.

No words were needed; the touch of her long lost parents' hands and staring into their eyes made her feel as warm as the distant sun. Evelyn gently caressed her daughter's cheeks. She studied her mother's features that had changed so much over the years. Her hair was pure white, straight, and came down to her shoulders; she used to look like Sydona. The wrinkles around the curves in her face were soft yet deep. Evelyn used to stand up proud and straight, but she now suffered a slight hunch, making her a tad shorter than Sydona. But her purple eyes were exactly the same, almond-shaped and sparkling.

The three finally sat down with Sydona in the middle. Her cheeks were sore from her uncontrollable smile. Then, she ate. And ate--and ate. Her hunger never seemed so strong, and she didn't care what it tasted like because she was in the presence of her family after fifty heartbreaking years. Evelyn reached into her pocket, looked at the guard to make sure his back was turned, and slipped a scrap of paper over to Sydona. She opened it underneath the table, and it said "We are in tent 5" in her mother's beautiful, familiar handwriting that Sydona always admired.

Glancing around for where the guards were looking, Sydona put the paper in her oversized pocket.

Once it was announced that breakfast was over, the three got up, emptied their trays, and walked together to number five. Raoul already sat waiting in the tent as he peeled apart a small orange. They embraced one another once again. Sydona took a moment to finally absorb everything about her father. He had the same weathered wrinkles as her mother, but his darker skin made them much more defined. His once brown and feathery hair had become thin, gray, and receding. Her father's purple eyes seemed sunken and lackluster. She assumed it was just a part of getting older, but maybe it from being imprisoned for decades.

"I've missed you guys so much!" Sydona cried out, almost choking on her words.

Her mother nodded quickly and played with Sydona's long blonde hair.

"We've missed you too, Syd. We're so happy you're okay," Ian said, lovingly grabbing her shoulder.

"Same here. I still can't believe I'm talking to you right now--" Her voice cracked. "Look, Raoul! It's them! I found them…"

Raoul grinned and flew over to her shoulder. "*We* found them," he whispered.

"You've been okay? They treat you alright?" Sydona asked.

Evelyn shrugged. "Considering. We do what they tell us, for the most part, and they leave us alone. They really don't like when we talk. Luckily, most guards don't care, but some take it very seriously."

Sydona nodded. "What do you know about the breakroom?"

"The breakroom? You mean for the guards?" Ian asked.

"Yeah, my roommate Maverick said that fliers who have been here a long time can get away with certain things. Like getting books from there. Do you guys do that?"

They gave her frightened looks. "No. Never," her mother answered.

"Too risky. You could get caught, and they'll do bad things to you." Ian shook his head and sat on the opposite bed.

Sydona furrowed her brows with confusion. "But Maverick made it seem like he does it all the time, and nothing's happened to him."

"Yeah, he trades books with them. They have a whole library of books I'm sure none of them can read." Raoul laughed.

Her parents were stones. Just then, it occurred to her: had they never done anything? Never tried to escape this place? It was as if they had been broken like wild stallions; they were nothing like the parents she grew up with. The fight they put up when they were captured seemed to have been left in that house in California.

"What happened to you guys?" Sydona changed the subject, almost upset with them.

Her parents both stayed silent and sat together on the cot with Sydona standing over them. They stared at each other and rubbed each other's hands. Evelyn finally confessed.

"A couple years ago, we all knew of a couple here, Devon and Kiara, who had just gotten married a few months before they were brought in. Well, being as most newlyweds are, they were all over each other and would talk a lot in their tent when they first arrived. They were warned time and again to stop talking, and they ignored it. So they were separated into different tents. Well somehow, Devon kept finding out where his wife was and always got caught in her tent, even though it was forbidden for him to be there. Until one day, they went to his tent and saw he was missing again and went to Kiara's tent. Three guards dragged him out and--beat him to death in front of his wife... Later on, I heard they didn't mean to kill him, just teach him a lesson, but it didn't matter anymore."

Evelyn paused. "About a month later, during our baths, Kiara drowned herself in the stream."

The tent went dead silent; Sydona buried her face in her hands.

"That's why we do as they say," Ian said to the ground.

"I don't mean to interrupt, Syd, but we better go," Raoul said as he peeked out of the tent.

They all gave each other one last big hug and a peck on the cheek, and Sydona snuck out of tent five. Hiding behind the rows of tents, she strategically made her way back to her own where Maverick sat in his usual position reading a different book.

"Where you been?" He looked up at her over his rims.

"I found my parents," she grinned, really loving saying the words.

"Oh, good for you." He grinned back.

Sydona slumped down on her cot, and Raoul joined her.

"I have an idea." Sydona messed with her fingernails.

"Oh?" Raoul asked.

"I need to get to that intercom," she said seriously.

"How are you going to do that? There are guards everywhere." Raoul threw his hands up.   Sydona smiled down at him with raised eyebrows.

"No no no no... I'll get caught!" Raoul said angrily.

Sydona shook her head. "You're fast, Raoul. Faster than any other fairies back home."

He blushed and sighed heavily. "What do you need me to do?"

"Just keep track of the guards. See if they run on a schedule, when, and what time. And of course, find out where they make announcements from."

"Yeah, that doesn't seem so bad. I'll just have to stay hidden," Raoul agreed with a surprised face.

"Exactly. And then just come back to me and let me know what you find out. And take your time. I don't need to know right away. Less chance of you getting caught if you study their behavior first."

"Hey!" A guard parted the entrance with a rifle and poked his head in. "This is your first warning. Don't make me come in here again!" he barked, then left.

Sydona panicked and looked for Raoul who disappeared from the bed.

"Raoul!" she whispered and got on her knees to look lower. From the corner of her eye, she saw the flutter of a red wing. Raoul winked at her and she laughed. "Yeah, I'm not worried about you at all."

Getting up from the grass, she sat back on her bed and sighed. "We need to find a way to communicate without talking."

Maverick laughed under his breath.

"What?" Sydona said shortly.

"Nothing. I just admire your drive. I remember when I had that."

Sydona rolled her eyes and lay back down on her bed. She thought she had a pretty good idea, considering she had a secret weapon that no other flier had. Raoul and Sydona went through so much together, and she would trust him with her life just as he trusted her with his. She wondered what Silas and Giovonna were up to. She wanted to tell them her plan, and maybe they would have their own ideas. If she skipped the next meal, she could sneak to their tent in the crowd and be there when they got back.

As the bell rang for the end of lunch, the time came for her to sneak away. Maverick gave her a discerning gaze over the rim of his glasses as she walked out, and she scoffed at his attitude. She slipped into the crowd with Raoul in her giant pocket and right into tent 56. The first thing she noticed was a book sitting on a makeshift cardboard table called *War and Peace*. Was it already there a couple days ago, or did they somehow smuggle it in? Either way, she thought it was an interesting book considering where they were.

As she pondered the book, Silas entered the tent alone and jumped back at her presence. They exchanged a few darted looks and awkward smiles. Sydona sat on one cot while Silas sat on the other, and they waited for Giovonna. It wasn't long before Giovonna entered the tent and squeezed Sydona so hard she let out a noise.

"What are you doing here?" Giovonna whispered, and Raoul flew out of Sydona's pocket. Her face lit up even brighter. "And Raoul is here, too? Just like old times."

"I missed you guys," Sydona took Giovonna's hands and swayed them back and forth. "Aaand I think I have a plan."

"Really?" Silas asked curiously with his arms folded.

"Raoul is going to study the guards' behaviors, schedule, if any, and where the intercom they use for announcements is. I think it could be the most effective way to get everyone together. If we could trick them and get into the building undetected, that might be enough to give everyone the confidence they've been missing."

They nodded, and Giovonna looked at Raoul. "You're good with this?"

Raoul nodded with a smile but then turned his head quickly and shushed the group. He flew over to the entrance and poked his head out to see a guard walking down the aisles, listening for voices. He stuck out his hand as a stop sign and waited for him to walk past before putting his arm down.

"We gotta find a way to talk without talking. And I feel paper is a limited supply." Sydona flopped down on Giovonna's bed. The group started thinking of ways they could effectively communicate when Silas spoke up.

"I know sign language."

"What, really?" Sydona smirked.

"I didn't know that," Giovonna said.

"Well, there's a lot you don't know about me. For example, did you know I can juggle, snowboard; play guitar, trumpet, piano and violin; and I'm considered a doctor in four countries?"

"No you're not," Sydona said smugly.

"Alright, well the last one isn't true, but I do know sign language. My brother is deaf... was deaf," Silas corrected himself.

Silence overcame the tent. She wondered how long it had been since he saw his brother.

"What's his name?" Sydona asked softly.

"Raymond," he answered with hesitance. He couldn't look either one of them in the eyes, reeling over the guilt of leaving him behind.

"What happened to him?" Giovonna asked.

Sydona shook her head at Giovonna, signaling that it was not a good topic of discussion.

"Do you think you could teach us?" Sydona chimed in, changing the subject.

Silas's smiled returned. "Of course."

Chapter Sixteen

The three spent the rest of the afternoon following Silas's hand motions and learning basic things like the alphabet and words they thought would be used the most. Raoul stood by the entrance and shushed them any time he heard a guard walking down the rows. Sydona quickly realized that the guards wouldn't really on check on them if there wasn't noise. This lax policy made her worry that they didn't have a set schedule and would make things trickier for them. She supposed they didn't really care as long as no one tried to escape or speak to one another.

Once dinner was announced, Silas and Giovonna convinced Sydona to eat since she skipped lunch, but she mainly went for the possibility of sitting with her parents. They were all able to sit by each other in the crowded, quiet tent. Sydona sat between her parents, and Silas and Giovonna sat across from them. They decided not to show off any sign language in public to avoid getting caught. She imagined they might cut off fingers or something to prevent it from spreading just like they separated people who got caught talking. It surprised Sydona that they didn't do more to prevent talking.

As she sat across from Silas, she occasionally felt his feet messing with hers. He kept nudging her leg with his foot and looking up at her, waiting for a reaction. In response, Sydona would gently kick back and mouth 'Stop'. He would silently laugh, causing her to suppress a laugh as well. The group, as well as strangers, stared at them during this playfulness. Her face turned red, and she stopped as she realized how many people were staring.

She hated to admit to herself that the food was growing on her since it was the only steady meal that she had since she left her house. Occasionally, she would close her eyes as she guided the fork up to her mouth, picturing eating cake or a big stalk of broccoli. It helped a little bit but was ruined as soon as she had to open her eyes again.

Once dinner ended, they shuffled back into the crowd and then the individual tents, and Sydona decided to go back to her own for practice. She gave everyone big hugs and pecked her mom and dad on their cheeks. Every time she hugged them, her heart felt three sizes bigger, and she had to fight with herself to let them go.

She sighed with relief as she made it back to her tent and found it empty. Maybe she could get a little practice in with Raoul helping her remember certain words. Not long after, Maverick waltzed in and landed on his cot with a squeak, and Sydona dropped her hands into her lap.

"What was that?" Maverick asked bluntly.

"What?"

"What were you doin' with your hands?" Maverick pressed.

"Nothing--just itching them."

"Was that sign language?" he asked with a bounce in his voice.

Sydona immediately shushed him, afraid of a guard overhearing.

"That's incredible! Why have I never thought of that?" Maverick sat up and removed his glasses with a look of pure joy plastered across his face. It was by far the most emotion Sydona had yet to see from him, and it took her back a little bit.

"Well, do you actually know it?" she asked.

"No. Could you teach me?" he pleaded.

"I'm learning from a friend of mine, from tent 56," she said trying not to smile at his behavior.

Maverick nodded and returned his bifocals.

"Once I learn more, I can try to teach you. But you can't do any of it in front of security, okay?" Sydona stuck her hand out.

He shook her hand.

"Lesson one. This is a handshake," she teased.

They all did their best to practice what little they knew from only an hour or so of lessons from Silas and worked up until the frogs in the stream were almost deafening. The night was much warmer than usual, allowing her to ditch the blanket and sleep peacefully while falling asleep to the sounds of nature.

The next day was a trial run for Raoul to do security checks and see what he could find out by visiting the cabin. As soon as he woke up, he stretched, did some lunges, jumping jacks, and stretched his wings out as far as they would go. After a quick hug on her forearm, Raoul gave her a stiff salute and flew out of the hole in the tent. She bit her nails subconsciously as he headed out, nervous about what he would go through.

The announcements rang out once again like clockwork. Going to meals wasn't such a drag anymore because she knew she would see her parents and friends each time. Once breakfast ended, she parted ways with Ian and Evelyn and followed her friends back to tent 56.

Silas reviewed the alphabet, and both girls did well remembering so he moved on to actual words. Such as 'meeting' 'cabin' 'office' 'guards' 'tent' then moved to 'beautiful' 'stunning' 'charming'. Once Sydona got the hint on what he was doing, she blushed and made him stop. Raoul wasn't their lookout this time, so they had to be careful about how much sound they made. If they did take a break to talk, they had to whisper extremely low, and every sound made them cease conversation immediately.

They practiced for several hours, and the tent became hot. For some reason, Silas was growing on Sydona, and she didn't want him to notice her sweating. She craved a hot shower with her waterfall shower head and favorite tropical body wash.

Then, the bell for lunch rang. It surprised her to learn they were at it for almost a solid five hours. They waited until the crowd gathered in front of the tent, so Sydona could sneak out without notice. Lunch came and went, and Sydona decided it would be better to head back to her tent to practice. She considered herself lucky for not being caught after staying and whispering in their tent for so long.

The five got ready to hug and return to their tents when Sydona heard a loud truck. Something about the loudness of this vehicle struck a familiar chord with her, and she searched for it curiously. The truck drove to the front of the main cabin, about thirty feet away from where she, Giovonna, and Silas stood. Both the girls' eyes turned green at the sight of the man who slinked out of the vehicle. Harold. The folks going back to their tents were walking in between them and Harold, but all Sydona could see was his wrinkly, dirty face.

Harold caught Sydona's eye as he exited the truck. "What in the hell are you doin' here?"

Sydona narrowed her eyes at him, remembering the bounty hunters he sent after them.

"Y'all are lucky I found them in time. Peter was in serious pain. And I noticed the arrow stickin' out his shoulder. Willow's. She bring you here?"

Sydona stood her ground and pursed her lips at the mention of Willow.

Harold chuckled as he tried to put things together. Sydona could see the wheels turning in his tiny head. "Lemme get this straight. Y'all injure and tie up my guys for trying to bring you here, but then, here you are... That just don't make sense."

Sydona darted her eyes, surprised at his quick thinking. She justified it by not knowing them, and they could've killed her at any second.

"N-Hey wait a minute," Harold changed the subject as he looked over the group. "Are you--are you Evey's daughter? Sonna bitch. That woulda been good money." He stomped his foot.

Sydona looked over at her mother with confusion. "Evey? And what are you talking about?"

"She does speak!" Harold chuckled. "And what you mean, what am I talkin' about? If I coulda guessed, I would say you dumber than me, and that's sayin' somethin'!"

Silas challenged him by stepping forward, warning Harold with his sparkling green eyes.

"And just who in the hell are you, bub?" Harold puffed his chest out and threatened him by putting his hand on the gun resting at his belt.

Silas stayed quiet but kept a smouldering look.

"Is this your boyfriend or somethin'?" Harold asked and looked at Sydona for some sort of reaction. But all Sydona did was lift her chin up and glare at him with more anger, hoping it would be enough to get him to leave.

"Well, isn't this adorable! Did you meet him here? They must be way more lenient on y'all than I thought." He laughed. The scene attracted a crowd of guards and fliers alike.

"Well, this should teach ya where you stand here." Harold wound up a clenched fist and socked Silas in his jaw, making him fall to the hard ground. Sydona refused to react because she knew that was all he wanted. As much as she wanted to take his gun and pull the trigger right between his ears, she settled with digging her fingernails into her palm. Harold gave a less than satisfied look once Silas hit the ground and saw no reaction from Sydona. Making a huffing noise and a sniff, he shook his hand, stretched it, and shook it again.

"Harold! My good man, come inside, out of this heat!" Dr. Malik walked out onto the porch of the cabin wearing a white polo and black dress pants, oblivious to what just happened.

Harold looked back to him with a grin and a nod, then turned back to Sydona quickly.

"Oh, and by the way. I sent Meg and her group after y'all 'cause her boy needs a heart transplant, and I told her how to find ya. Now, I dunno if he'll live. But congratulations…" He stepped back, spread his arms out wide, and turned his body to look around the camp with a false pride. "I guess you won."

Harold then turned around to Dr. Malik and greeted him like an old friend.

Was he serious? The hunters did mention someone named Nathan, but she had no idea it was a little boy. Her stomach did somersaults thinking of a boy in a hospital bed, looking for his mother. Maybe Harold wasn't as bad of a guy as she originally thought. But did it truly justify hunting them for a bounty?

Once the men left the scene, Sydona immediately joined Silas on the ground. Blood covered his scruffy face. She did her best to help wipe it off before they were jabbed in the back with guns. Wanting to comfort him in some way and thank him for standing up for her, she squeezed his hand as she helped him up. Silas understood as he squeezed back and glanced at her with a smile. The glance made her feel warm inside, and she held his hand as long as she could. She wanted to follow them and help him with his hurt lip, but she knew it was probably in her best interest to go back to her own tent. Ian and Evelyn made their way to their tent as well with nothing but a reassuring smile from Sydona, but they seemed content with that.

Back in her tent, she sat down and massaged her temples.

"What's wrong?" Maverick spoke so softly, he could barely be heard.

"Nothing." She shook her head.

"Where've you been?" he said louder.

"Ran into someone I knew."

"Who?"

She stopped rubbing. "Some guy named Harold."

Maverick's eyes widened. "Harold?"

"Yeah, you know him?" She pulled the blanket up over her legs.

"Know him? Of course. Everyone here knows him. He's Dr. Malik's best recruiter."

"Recruiter? That sounds almost respectable," she said sarcastically.

Maverick chuckled and shrugged his shoulders.

Sydona lay down and tried to clean the blood off her hands, but it was already drying. As she messed with her hands, she noticed something underneath her metal bracelet. Moving it down slightly, she saw a perfect brown line circling her wrist. The electricity from the bracelet burned her skin, but it wasn't scabbing or painful. It reminded her of a tattoo, smooth to the touch and permanent. The sound, the pain, and the feeling of electricity pulsing through her body unyieldingly flashed back into her head. Not wanting to dwell on the memory, she used the palms of her hands to pound the sides of her head over and over again. It was working and giving her a headache to focus on until Maverick interrupted.

"Hey, hey, hey! What's going on?" Maverick grabbed her hands to stop her.

Sydona let him stop her and looked down at her lap with shame.

"They did do something to you, didn't they?" he whispered and looked her in the eyes.

Tears flowed down her hot cheeks, but she quickly dried them, took a deep breath, and lifted her chin. Maverick stared at her with concern as he clasped her hand in his.

Sydona changed the subject. "If I can get Raoul to get a pen, can you do me a favor?"

Maverick frowned but went along with it. "You're in luck. I already have one."

He reached behind the mesh table and grabbed a pen covered in dirt.

"Where'd this come from?" She asked.

"I got it years ago. Forgot I had it actually, until now. Used it to write notes to people, when I had friends… What do you need it for?"

"A message. Mind if I use one of your books?" Sydona asked.

"I suppose." Maverick grabbed his only book from under his cot and handed it to Sydona. Sydona tore out the blankest page she could find and wrote: *Borba i amor bez strah.*

Maverick looked over her shoulder as she folded it up. "What does that mean?"

Sydona smiled. "Hope."

"Am I getting my book back?" he asked.

"Oh. Uh, no…" Sydona said with a head shake.

Maverick sighed.

"I learned more words, if you want to practice," Sydona suggested to get his mind of his stolen book.

"Well, I guess since I have nothing to read now," Maverick said with sarcasm.

They practiced well into the night, even skipping dinner. They quizzed each other to make sure the words really stuck and went over the alphabet, spelling names of people they knew. Maverick taught her his daughters name, Joelle. He was a single father when he was taken from his home with his infant daughter. They had been separated in the chaos, and he had been in captivity and traveling with the NFA for the past sixty years. He told her that he had been looking for Joelle ever since, hoping that she would at least be at the same camp, so he could see her again. He thought that since the NFA knew they were related, they made a point to not have them in the same area.

Sydona assumed the only reason she was in the same place as her parents was because she had been brought there decades later. Thinking back to when she was eight, she was even more grateful that she had gotten away because she may have never had the chance to see her parents again. Then, she wondered why her parents were still together. Maybe his theory wasn't completely true.

As the night sky darkened and filled with stars, she started to worry about Raoul since he had been gone almost the entire day. They decided to stop for the night, and Maverick even formally gave Sydona his book since he had it memorized. It had been days since she read anything, so she was excited to be able to escape into another world and be distracted from reality. She could only read for so long before her eyes strained, and she had to give up and fall asleep.

During the night, Sydona woke to a high pitched cry from a tent in the next row. She didn't move but lay in bed listening to the commotion. A muffled sound escaped every so often as if a hand or pillow blocked the sound. The cries were that of a female, and some of the noises were of a deeper voice with a harsh tone. Grunting and moaning filled the air, and the deeper voice cursed at the woman to shut up. A tear fell down Sydona's face as she realized what was going on, and it made her feel nauseated. She scrunched up the blanket with her hands until they turned white then turned her head to face Maverick.

To her surprise, he was wide awake and lying on his side, unable to block out the noises. He looked just as distraught as she felt. She wondered if this was as common as others committing suicide, but by the look on Maverick's face, she guessed not. After several agonizing minutes, it became quiet again, but the sounds played over and over in Sydona's head all night. It took hours for her to eventually fall asleep, but somehow she did.

The next morning she woke up with heavy lids and painful thoughts. But as soon as she saw Raoul at the foot of her bed, her spirits lifted.

"Hey you," she said sleepily. "How did it go?"

Raoul yawned, stretched like a cat, and pointed to the underside of the bed. She flipped her hair to the side and peered underneath to see a stash of food. Apples, oranges, bags of almonds, chips, snap peas, cups of noodles, and random pieces of candy littered the ground.

"Oh my god, how did you get all of this?" she seized a green apple and started eating it ravenously.

"I have my ways. These guards are idiots!" Raoul giggled and sucked on a hard candy that didn't quite fit in his mouth.

Maverick woke at the sounds of whispering and giggling and asked for an orange. Once they all filled up on snacks, Sydona and Raoul spoke seriously.

"So what did you find out?" Sydona started.

"There are a lot of them. I would gather about fifty guards work per day. I counted about fifteen on average in the cabin at a time, sleeping, eating, talking, and cleaning. It was a challenge to stay hidden because everywhere I turned, there was someone around. I also checked the perimeter, and each guard that stands watch is immediately relieved by someone else. There are at least two guards with the job of walking each row all day long. The guards who watch the meals and the ones who guard the front gate. Oh and there's also a… pretty impressive arsenal, too. Rifles, shotguns, handguns, tranquilizers, assault rifles, and I'm sure others. I wasn't sure what they were called."

"Wow," Sydona mouthed more than said aloud. "Did you find the announcement station?"

"Not yet. Like I said, it's filled with people. Might take me a couple days to find out. Every window I flew into didn't lead to that room, so it must be in the basement or in the center of the cabin. But I was able to sneak in late last night into the kitchen where I saw food and snuck it into the tent!"

Sydona smiled and winked. "Thanks, buddy. I'm sure you've been starving."

Raoul nodded his head and licked his arm and hand that were sticky from the candy. The announcement came on for breakfast, and Sydona planned on stopping by her parents' tent, since it had been a couple of days. She wanted to tell them what she was planning on doing and hoped that they would be more okay with the sign language plan since it was silent. Maverick's book poked out of her pocket slightly; she wanted to give it to them.

Once again, the crowd led her into tent five. It was barren of books and everything else, making her a little depressed. She wondered how they hadn't gone crazy yet from sitting quietly without books or conversation. As a wrinkly hand with a gold band on the ring finger tucked the flap back, she stood up, ready to hug them. Ian and Evelyn came in holding hands, and both gave her a soft hug with a peck on her cheek.

"Hello, sweetheart. Are you hungry? You missed breakfast," her mother asked and touched Sydona's stomach.

"No, I'm okay. I already ate," Sydona said. "Raoul got me some food."

"He did? How?" Ian spoke up quietly.

"The cabin. He's been scoping it out for me." Sydona could not keep the excitement from her face.

"What?!" Evelyn exclaimed.

"Sh, no, it's fine. We have a plan," Sydona explained quickly. "He's going to find where they make announcements, and I'm going to break in and try to talk to everyone. Silas and Giovonna are going to help, too."

"No. Absolutely not, Syd," Ian said in a deep, fatherly voice and furrowed his bushy eyebrows.

"But it's--"

"I agree with Ian; that is stupid and dangerous. We won't allow it." Evelyn shook her head.

Sydona stepped back in shock. "Won't allow it?"

She took a few long moments to avoid yelling in case a guard stood nearby.

"In case you guys haven't noticed, I am not eight years old anymore. I am sixty-two now and have been on my own since you were taken away. Please don't treat me like I don't know what I'm doing. I had to survive for over fifty years without you. I think I deserve to be treated like an adult since I had to grow up after you left me!" Sydona stopped, and her heart sank.

Everything she felt from the minute the NFA stole them from her life built up to this exact moment. She knew it wasn't their fault they were taken, but a part of her felt as if they could have fought harder to get away. Or at least be running the place by now. The parents she once knew when growing up seemed to be completely different people, and it was beginning to crawl under her skin. The years of looking up to her mother and father and putting them on a high pedestal crumbled like wet sand.

"I don't know what to say." Evelyn grabbed her daughter's hand and was on the verge of tears.

"I'm sorry. It's just--I have waited my entire life to see you again, and all the memories I had were of your strong will and strong family values. And now, I see you, and you've given up. You have no interest in leaving this place and have accepted your fate. That's not the mother I knew," she said while trying to hold back her emotions.

"Here. Maybe this will help you remember who you were." Sydona handed the small book to her mother with the message inside.

Evelyn looked at her daughter and the book, perplexed. Sydona felt overwhelmed with the range of emotions pulsing through her and didn't want to lash out at them anymore. The words she shouted at them rang through her mind with guilt. She had to leave before she did any more damage to their already fragmented spirits. Lifting the tent flap, she wiped her face and left without so much as a goodbye.

Chapter Seventeen

Sydona left her parents with blurry eyes and shaky hands and headed back to her tent. A wave of mixed emotions flowed through her like a monsoon, and she wasn't sure which one she should be more focused on. With all of the confusion in her head, she was completely oblivious to the fact she was out in the open with guards walking around.

It all happened in a flash. As Sydona heard a guard yelling at her to stop, she turned to see the guard being distracted by a glowing orange light. The man waved the gun around, trying to hit Raoul down and missing terribly. Then, Raoul flew in the opposite direction of Sydona, and the guard ran after him. This was her chance to run back to her tent and hope that the guard didn't see her face or recognize her at all. Her heart felt as if it was going to pop out of her chest, and it made her emotions all the worse. Now, she had to worry about Raoul who put himself at risk because of her.

Luckily, she made it back without anyone else seeing her. Diving back into her bed, she threw the covers over her as if she had been sleeping the whole time. She thought she saw Maverick on his side from the corner of her eye and prayed that he didn't try to talk to her. After several minutes passed, nothing happened, and she could finally breathe again. Her heart began beating normally.

Raoul risked a lot to get her to safety, and she knew she wouldn't be able to sleep until she knew that he was okay.

What was he thinking?! she thought to herself. After the encounter with her parents, this was almost too much for her to handle. Her leg shook uncontrollably, she bit her nails raw, and she stroked the ends of her hair so much, she swore it was falling out. The one thing she really needed at that moment was someone with her, anyone. Even Willow the Widowed would do. The nickname Giovonna gave her made Sydona smirk.

She then thought about Willow, where she could be, and how it felt like forever since she saw her. Could she be getting backup? Willow was part of the Sparrows and was in the military, so Sydona knew she wouldn't give up easily. She thought her mother had that trait once, too. If it was lost, maybe Sydona could help her rekindle the flame just enough to ignite again.

Several hours passed, and she had not moved an inch, but her eyes were still red and sore. To her surprise, she felt someone touch her hair. She instinctively swung her fist as hard as she could in a backwards motion, hitting the person behind her.

"Son of a--!" the person yelled quickly and grabbed his head in agony.

"Silas?" Sydona sat straight up in bed. "What are you doing here?"

He rubbed the side of his face and plopped down on her cot. His face was still bloodied from earlier, and her punch looked like it reopened the wound.

Sydona sat next to him and grabbed his face gently to assess the damage. "I'm so sorry... And I mean for earlier, too."

"That guy was a douche. Don't even worry about it," Silas said softly and tried smiling at her, but his lip was still split. As he gazed at her longer, his face changed as if he were looking at a ghost.

"What?" Sydona asked curiously.

"Your eyes!"

"What about them?" She darted her eyes, seeing if she could somehow feel what was wrong.

"They're... turning blue..." he said with wonderment.

"What?!" Sydona exclaimed and looked around the tent for something reflective.

"Well, not totally blue. More like a purply-blue." Silas couldn't take his eyes off hers.

Grabbing the lantern, she rotated it around to find something she could see herself in. The glass was turning black, but in one little section, she was able to see her eyes. Silas was right, her eyes were much more blue than normal.

"Are you wearing some weird version of Gia's contacts?" Silas asked.

"No..." Sydona frowned. Then, it hit her.

It had to be the bracelet and the shocks that went through her body. Somehow the effect of it changed her eye color. Why would it affect that part of her body though? She thought the amount of electricity that went through her was enough to kill her. In everything she knew from reading books and her basic knowledge of science, nothing could explain it.

Sydona kept a hold of the lantern, blinking her eyes several times and waiting for it to go away. She wiped off the surface of the glass, but it didn't do anything to make the reflection clearer. After a few minutes, her eyes slowly changed back to a normal purple shade, and she relaxed a little.

"Oh, they changed back!" Silas smiled.

Sydona returned to her bed and sat next to Silas.

"How did that happen, do you think?" he asked and scratched his scruffy face.

With everything going on, Sydona didn't want to worry him, or Giovonna, over what she went through. Although it could be the flint for the fire they needed to start a revolution, her wounds were still healing. Especially from her parents. She couldn't imagine what they would do if they found out what *he* did to their only daughter. Probably nothing. But she would rather wait to tell them. For the time being, the pain of Raoul's actions slapped her in the face. The guilt of worrying about herself instead of Raoul hurt her stomach.

Silas seemed to catch on to the fact that Sydona didn't want to talk about it, but she had a feeling that he knew she was hiding something.

"Where's Raoul?" he changed the subject.

She shook her head, and her stomach twisted even more. "I think he was captured," she whispered.

"Oh no..." he breathed. Then, he hesitantly turned his body, so he could touch her back and rub it.

His worry was comforting to her. Raoul was the one she would turn to in the past when she felt down or depressed. He may have been small, but his familiarity was all she needed sometimes to feel better. But Silas was with her now, and she needed someone to lean on, someone to hold her and tell her everything was going to be okay. The big gentle circles he made on her back were working, and it somehow made her want to be closer to him.

"Can you just lay here with me for a little bit?" She spoke softly with cracks in her voice.

Silas lifted his hand off her and asked, "You sure?"

Sydona nodded and lay down on the cot. Silas took a few minutes to join her, and she assumed he was nervous about it. They had to lay extremely close to one another, but they both hung halfway off the bed still. Silas wiggled around to get comfortable and laid his arm around her body. His warmth soothed her, and she could even feel his breath on her neck. This gave her goosebumps that she hoped he couldn't see. It had been several years since she had been so close with a man, and it was a little exciting for her. His presence helped her forget the events from the last couple days if only temporarily. Her heart beat harder the tighter he held her. Sydona could tell he enjoyed being next to her because his fingers gently caressed her arms. Feeling like a caterpillar inside of its cocoon, she soon fell asleep in Silas's arms.

Another several hours passed, and she opened her eyes to see Silas still lying next to her, and she smiled. Turning over to face him, Sydona waited for Silas to wake up. Her heart leaped as he opened his eyes and returned her smile.

She looked over to the other side of the tent and saw Maverick reading his usual book in the glow of the stadium lights that never died out. Sydona peeked over Silas to address him.

"Maverick," Sydona whispered. "This is Silas, the guy who knows--you know what."

Maverick glanced up at them and slammed his book shut, ready to learn.

Silas sat up sluggishly and rubbed his eyes. "Alright, let's do this." Silas taught Maverick the words he requested to know, also benefiting Sydona greatly. They spent the rest of the lantern's life learning sign language.

Three days came and went with the same old routines and sneaking around to learn sign language. Sydona hadn't visited her parents since their last conversation. Even at mealtimes, they constantly wore guilty faces and could barely look their daughter in the eye. They still hugged and everything, but tension lingered in the air, which made the meals with the whole group awkward. Sydona eventually told Silas and Giovonna what happened with the bracelet and how she felt about the whole thing, causing Giovonna to hug her any chance she had.

Blue still crept into her purple eyes, but the color never fully changed to blue. Giovonna described it as flecks of blue or a mixture of paint in water. She wasn't sure what it meant either. Even though she took advanced science classes and was intelligent compared to most teenagers, none of it sounded familiar. If there was a library around, she would have looked up more information. Sydona had no other visible changes other than the mark under her bracelet. It didn't seem to be fading away   either.

Learning the new language also kept her from thinking about Raoul, who still had not shown up. She thought the faster she learned it, the faster they could come up with a plan to break into the place to look for him and find the announcement station. She tried to remember everything Raoul had told her about the guards from one day of watching: how many there were, where they were posted, and the schedules he noticed. She wished that he had found out where Dr. Malik worked, though. He was the one person that could put a stop to it all if he was dead. And although she knew the arsenal existed and what was in it, she wasn't sure at all where it was.

Sunday finally came, which meant bath time, and Sydona was on pins and needles waiting until she could wash herself. It had been well over a week since she had any soap on her body or hair, and she was surprised anyone wanted to be around her. An announcement came roaring across the park letting everyone know that it was bathing day, and everyone would be called by groups of tents to go down by the stream after breakfast. They were also to clean their clothes at the same time, and of course, there could be no talking or funny business and the area would be heavily guarded. As if this was news.

Once breakfast ended, she went back to her own tent, and they called the same amount of tents that they called for the flying tests. The crowd of fliers began to grow, and Sydona looked for Giovonna and Silas by stealthily weaving in and out of people. They all went down to the stream together, and the crowd turned into a single file line. The guards were carrying giant plastic bins full of soap bars that they handed out to each person. As they grabbed their soap, they shuffled down to the edge of the water where people began undressing and stepping in with shoes still on.

Normally, so much exposed skin would make her extremely nervous, but she felt so covered in filth, she didn't feel completely naked. Following everyone's lead, she peeled her clothes off: pants, then shirt, then undergarments. As she looked around, she noticed everyone kept to themselves and avoided looking at anyone else as they stepped into the water, dipped the soap and scrubbed like hell. She tried to focus on washing herself and scrubbed her skin like never before, turning parts of her red. It was nothing like her shower or bath at home. The water was freezing, things brushed against her legs a couple times, and of course, she was with dozens of other naked people. She felt so degraded, like she was only seen as a body, a dirty body that was only good for flying. The fact they made them clean themselves, she thought, was only to benefit the guards and doctors because everyone smelled pretty rank.

As the announcer said, the stream was heavily guarded with twice as much security as normal. She could faintly hear guards laughing and talking. The way some guards looked at them made her feel inhuman.

She dunked her hair in the water and tried to lather the soap up enough to wash her long hair. Giovonna waded through the water and helped Sydona wash her hair. This made Sydona blush at the thought of Giovonna, the girl she thought of like a daughter, seeing her like this. She then grabbed her clothes, dunked them in the water, and watched as the veterans did it. They cleaned their clothes with the same soap bar, which was extremely difficult to do. Everything was all so strange, like one of her dreams, and she hoped that she would be waking up soon with Raoul at her side.

About half an hour and almost an entire soap bar later, they shooed everyone out of the stream one by one. The guards threw thin white towels into the crowd while people jumped to grab them and dry off quickly. The air made her even colder, forcing her to cover herself with her shivering hands. A towel then came raining down right on top of her, and she grabbed it before someone else rubbed their body parts on it. For only a minute, she had it, and then Silas whipped it out of her hands, making her punch him in the arm. Looking over to the guards throwing towels, she saw a huge mesh metal bin full of towels, maybe even enough for everyone to get one. Another one was thrown her way, and she dried her damp, long hair as best she could before wrapping it around her body. Even though the stream wasn't the cleanest, the warm sun on her skin was the best she had felt in days.

She and everyone else were laying their clothes in the grass next to them, relying on the sun to dry them. Silas and Giovonna sat side by side on the field, and she eventually lay down. The guards let everyone lay out instead of trying to herd them back to the tents. She guessed they had *some* empathy. Sydona folded her arms under her head with her hair stretched out to air dry and closed her eyes. It was so quiet; it felt like everyone had fallen asleep aside from the guards talking amongst themselves in the distance. Birds sang in the May sun, chatting about their days and what they were going to eat for dinner. *'Even the birds get to talk here'*, thought Sydona. Not even five minutes later, she drifted off to sleep and dreamed.

Seven year old Sydona jumped out of her blue and pink covers and ran downstairs, through the kitchen, the back porch, and all the way to the biggest tree in their backyard. Peering inside the center hole in the tree, she saw a big crowd of fairies gathered around one female fairy with a rounded tummy. She lay on top of a block of carved wood with flowers blanketing it. Sydona grinned as she rested her chin on her folded hands over the wooden hole.

"Is it happening already?" her mother's voice asked softly behind her.

Sydona nodded her head excitedly. "I hope it's a boy!"

The pregnant fairy took notice of Sydona and smiled through her labor pains.

"Why do you want it to be a boy?" Evelyn squatted down next to her, and they took turns witnessing the miracle.

"Because I already have a name picked out!" Sydona said.

Evelyn laughed. "Sweetie, I think Cherish would like to name her own baby." She caressed Sydona's short blonde hair.

Just then, everyone gathered even closer to Cherish. Several minutes later, the midwife with white and indigo wings swaddled a tiny baby in a soft blue cloth that looked as if it was made from a scrap of Sydona's baby blanket. It wasn't any bigger than her thumbnail.

Sydona could barely sit still in her anticipation. "Well?"

Cherish was handed the baby and answered, "He's a boy."

"I knew it!" Sydona hugged her mom.

The crowd parted in order to give Sydona a good look at him.

"He's so small…" she whispered in awe.

"And he's yours once you turn eight," Evelyn said.

"I can't wait!" She focused on the tiny fairy baby with a full head of brown hair and tiny red wings that popped over the blue blanket. "We're going to have the bestest adventures ever, Raoul!"

A gentle shake of her shoulder interrupted her dream, forcing a tear to roll down her face, and she rolled over towards Silas. He mouthed 'You okay?' while helping her up, and Sydona closed her eyes with no response.

The group of fliers were all being commanded to get up, return to their tents, and grab their clothes that were just dry enough to wear. Silas, Sydona, and Giovonna walked together until they got to their tents, embraced quickly, and parted ways. With her clothes folded over one arm and shoes in the other hand, she reached her tent. Still sporting her towel, she threw her clothes down at the end of her bed and curled up into herself. Maverick soon entered wearing his towel, which barely covered the important parts. He started to remove it and then noticed Sydona facing him, staring at nothing. He made a circle with his finger, hinting at her to face the other way, and she did so without hesitation.

She lay motionless in the cot and experienced a feeling like nothing she had ever felt: complete emptiness. It was as if she didn't know who she was or what to do without Raoul by her side. She even depended on his birth because she knew she was promised him by his mother before he was even born. Her parents told her that Cherish was expecting and had always loved Sydona, so she agreed that her first born would be Sydona's fairy for life. This was traditional in their culture, but it was unusual for an unborn fairy to be promised to a flier. He was special to her since his first moments in life, and now he just disappeared... because of her. How could he be so reckless? As hard as it was for her to imagine what they could be doing to him, or had already done, it was all she could think about, and it enraged her more every day.

"It's gotta be tonight," Sydona clenched her jaw and whispered to herself. Her eyes burned green. She sat up, calculating in her head as fast as the adrenaline rushed through her veins on how to get to the cabin and kill Dr. Malik. She felt as sporadic as a grasshopper, unable to sit still even if she tried. She paced the tent back and forth with clenched fists and jaw, mumbling things to herself while holding up her towel. She slammed one hand into another and then quickly caught the towel before it fell down. Maverick watched her nervously on his side; then, a guard suddenly came through the tent. Sydona turned to him and, without thinking, she lunged at him and wrapped her hands around his thick, bearded neck, taking him down to the ground.

The guard's eyes bulged, and he struggled to call out to anyone. Sydona knocked the gun out of reach and grabbed it. She then pulled the large guard inside the tent, out of sight.

"What are you doing?!" Maverick stood up in shock.

She held the gun to the guard's chest and looked into his wide, frightened eyes.

"Not so tough without a gun are you," she said in a monotone voice with her eyes glowing fiercely green.

The guard was frozen and defenseless on his back. He looked young, too, maybe only twenty years old, and it was just a job for him. He had never done anything to her personally, but she couldn't risk anything. As she stood over him, her feet on either side of his body and gun steady as a boulder, she tried thinking of what she should do with him. It had to be quick because Maverick's yelling had probably already alerted other guards.

"What are you gonna do to me?" he trembled. The corners of Sydona's lips curved upwards, and she answered.

"Depends. What did you to do to that fairy?"

"Fairy? There's a fairy here?" he asked.

"Don't--play dumb with me." She edged the gun closer to his chin.

"Oh yes, that fairy. Well I may have heard that someone got one, but I haven't seen it. It's in Dr. Malik's office; no one's allowed in there." He sweat and gulped audibly.

Sydona glanced over at Maverick with a bigger smile on her face. "Dr. Malik's office, huh?" Maverick did not reciprocate her emotion but sat still in fear as he gazed into her piercing green eyes.

"Take me." Sydona hit his chin with the end of the rifle as he scrambled to stand up.

"Syd," Maverick whispered. Sydona looked back at him with annoyance. "Your clothes."

Sydona was oblivious to fact that she was still completely naked, and she rolled her eyes.

"Here." She handed Maverick the rifle and forced the guard to the back of the tent while she dressed. As she kept one eye on them, they both stood staring at her, truly afraid of what she was going to do next. Once she slipped on her last shoe, she snatched the gun from Maverick's hand and grabbed the surprisingly compliant guard. As she got ready to leave the tent with her hostage, she looked back to Maverick whose eyes had turned brown. She motioned her head to come with, and he slowly shook his head. Sydona signed "Joelle" with her free hand and held a steady look on her face, hoping that was all he needed to come around.

"My baby…" Maverick stood with his chin up and eyes no longer brown with fear. He joined her, grabbed the nightstick out of the guard's holster, and nodded at her. They headed out of the tent on either side of the guard. Sydona angled the pistol at his head and took a hold of his arm. Maverick did the same with his other arm.

She whispered in the guard's ear, "Straight to the Doctor's office."

The guard stayed silent and slowly walked through the tents while Sydona peered between each one they passed, hoping to avoid as much security as possible. The announcement suddenly came on to gather the next group of fliers for bathing time, and people started to exit their tents. Sydona's heart fluttered even faster, but almost in an excited way, because they too would have to see her with a guard as a hostage.

As they made their way to the enormous cabin, fliers and guards alike gaped at the sight, and guards pointed their guns at her and Maverick. She also noticed guards running into the cabin with purpose; she hoped it was to bring out Dr. Malik.

"Tell them put their guns down, or I *will* shoot you," Sydona whispered in his ear again.

The guard stuttered. "Cool it everyone, she's not messing around."

A huge crowd of fliers in blue scrubs and guards surrounded the area. Guards began to gather in the front of the stairs as well, waiting for someone to come out of the grand doors to the cabin.

"Dr. Malik!" Sydona bellowed over everyone and into the cabin.

The area fell silent, and not even the guards tried anything. Sydona could hear her heartbeat out of her chest as she looked over the crowd and had an overwhelming feeling of accomplishment. This was it. This was how it happened. History was about to be made. Everyone was going to revolt and fight for their freedom. As she glanced over the crowd again, she saw her mother and father with looks of complete shock and disappointment. What were they doing there? They weren't called out with the announcement; they should be back in their tents. Or had she drawn so much attention that everyone came out?

"What the bloody hell is going on here?" Dr. Malik strutted out of the cabin with his hands up in the air.

"Where is he?" Sydona demanded.

"Where is who, Miss Wilder?" Dr. Malik asked nonchalantly.

"*You* know who," Sydona yelled.

Dr. Malik chuckled and put his hands in his pockets. "Why are you doing this? You're fighting a losing battle, you know…"

Sydona tightened the grip on the gun and put a dent from the barrel on the guard's temple.

"Tell me where my goddamn fairy is, or I will blow his head off!" Sydona threatened.

He walked down the stairs, looking more closely at the hostage and narrowing his eyes through his glasses. "Wait. Do I know you?"

"Name's Doug," the guard said.

"Why don't I know you, Doug? I've never seen you before." He inched closer, making Sydona more nervous.

"I'm new, sir," he squeaked.

"Ooh, you're new… that would explain it." He smiled and turned his attention to Sydona. "You can kill him then. I'll find someone else."

Sydona paused and looked at Doug who she swore wet his pants with the look on his face. She tried to think of what to do next. She found it difficult to kill an innocent guard, especially one who wasn't worth anything to the Doctor. People were disposable to him. But Dr. Malik was right in front of her, walking away. He was the one who needed to die, not Doug. She removed the gun from Doug's head and aimed at Dr. John Malik's back.

And pulled the trigger.

Chapter Eighteen

The most gut wrenching sound flooded her ears. The gun was empty, and her stomach suddenly felt like an anchor. Dr. Malik turned back around at the sound of the empty gun. He looked down at the pistol that Sydona still wielded and then back up at her. She tried to assassinate the leader of the group and failed. All guns and eyes were pointed directly at her, and she found it difficult to swallow. She lowered her gun while still keeping her eyes on the doctor. Surprisingly, he turned his attention to her hostage

"Tsk, tsk, tsk. Oh, Doug... " He shook his head with disappointment. "Rookie mistake, son. Did you miss training? You know, where you learn to load your guns? The only thing standing between us and them? But... in this scenario, it did save my life. Otherwise, she would have blown my head off!" Dr. Malik burst out laughing, making Doug chuckle nervously.

Sydona stood on the side, watching the interaction between the two men. Why was Dr. Malik unconcerned about what she just tried to do? She thought that maybe he knew the gun was unloaded, which would explain why he turned his back on her. By the way he looked at Doug, she knew that he was in some deep trouble. While the heat was not on her, she took the opportunity to glance around the crowd. Giovonna and Silas stood in the front row, watching the show like everyone else.

Silas signed 'Raoul' to Sydona as low as he could. Sydona slyly signed back 'Doctor's office'. He nodded and grabbed Giovonna's hand, and they both sank back into the massive crowd toward the outside of the cabin.

Sydona slowly started listening to the conversation again between the doctor and Doug. "...and I'll make sure this mistake never happens again."

Dr. Malik grabbed a nearby guard's gun and aimed it at Doug's temple. Doug pleaded with him, tears streaming down his young face.

Suddenly a gunshot went off but not from Dr. Malik. His expression was just as shocked as Sydona's. Doug fell to the side and onto the ground with a thud, and everyone paused. A sound of distant cries echoed in the otherwise silent park. They soon got louder and louder, faster and faster. Looking around to see where the shot came from, she stared off into the distance, past the stream. Dozens of fliers flew their way, bearing bows and shouting out war cries. It was the Sparrows, and they came just in time. Her breathing intensified at the sight, and adrenaline pumped through her even more.

The crowd went absolutely crazy as the fliers from above began to dive bomb guards and used their own guns against them. Her first reaction was to find her parents, but they disappeared into the crowd, much like Dr. Malik. Unsure of where they could be, her true feelings told her to find Raoul first. She knew where he was, and she needed to rescue him from whatever he was enduring.

Soon, humans from the Sparrows joined the fliers in battle, running from far off fields and wielding weapons of every sort. As Sydona edged to the side of the cabin, she stopped to look for Willow, thinking she would be right in the front lines. A woman with blazing red hair and camouflage face paint came running through the stream beside her fellow rebels. Willow noticed Sydona immediately and flashed a great big smile. She took out a couple guards running at Sydona before joining her and embracing her with a crushing hug.

"Willow the Widowed... you came back." Sydona grinned.

"Well of course I did, princess! Couldn't leave Gia behind!" Willow punched her shoulder and stuck her tongue out.

"Come on, let's go," Sydona said.

"Where we goin'?" Willow gladly followed her as if she had a new commander.

"Getting Raoul back." Sydona sneaked around looking for guards.

"Raoul? What happened? Oh, and here, take this." Willow handed her a spare pistol hiding in her boot.

"Thanks... It's a long story. He's up in Dr. Malik's office."

"That's the prick I was trying to shoot! Can't believe I missed..." Willow shook her head.

Sydona looked back at her. "That was you."

"You betcha sweet patootie! I'll get him next time."

"Actually, I would like to take care of him if you don't mind," Sydona said, and Willow laughed.

"He's all yours, princess." Willow followed her through a door in the back.

The cabin was a ghost town; it seemed everyone was outside. There were a few people running in and out: fliers, Sparrows, and guards alike. Sydona shot the one guard that came in without hesitation, and he broke a chair as he collapsed to the ground.

"Hey, up here!" Giovonna's voice rang from the top of the stairs.

Willow's face lit up, and she ran up the stairs like a herd of cows to pummel Giovonna into a hug. Silas popped his head around the corner and smiled at Sydona. She felt relieved to see both Giovonna and Silas unharmed. Giovonna hugged Sydona as soon as she let go of Willow, and Willow and Silas only nodded at each other.

"He's over here." Silas cleared his throat, standing alone and waiting for everyone to stop hugging.

The upstairs looked more cabin-like with rustic décor. They walked past a few doors, but those led to either bathrooms or small rooms with bunk beds. Dr. Malik's office sat at the very end with the door ajar and light shining through it. Sydona gripped her pistol firmly out in front of her, ready to use it at any second. The group slowly followed her down the hallway as their footsteps creaked against the wood boards. The door squeaked as they stepped into the office, and she put her pistol and guard down. An enormous mahogany desk sat in the center of the egotistical doctor's office. Books lined the walls of the office, only lit by a dim lamp in each corner. On the opposite side of the room stood a red leather couch and cigars on a table next to it. And finally, on the same side of the room as the door sat a metal table with a bird cage in the center. The table was bolted to the floor just as the cage was bolted to the table. It seemed more like a decoration than a cage for a living creature. Raoul lay on the bottom of it and seemed to be unconscious. Sydona tried opening the tiny door in front but was unsuccessful.

"We think it's made of titanium. We've been looking for a key but can't find it anywhere," Giovonna said desperately as she watched Sydona looking frantically through the desk and cabinet drawers.

"He has it," Sydona stopped searching and whispered to herself. "Of course he has it…"

"He couldn't have gotten far. I got people patrolling the area," Willow said while she guarded the door.

Sydona popped all ten knuckles forcefully as she made her way back to the cage.

"Raoul? It's me. You're gonna be fine… You just--gotta hang in there, okay?" Sydona whispered while holding back her tears. Her shaking hands felt around the cage. Grabbing the top of the cage and interlocking her fingers through the holes, she pulled as hard as she could. "Someone help me, please!"

"It's no use, Syd… We tried. It's not coming off…" Silas said with sorrow in his voice.

"Not with that attitude!" Sydona grunted as she kept pulling. "Come on!"

Silas and Giovonna took either side of the cage while Willow put her hands on the table and used her body weight to hold it down. The three wriggled and shook it as much as they could. Raoul still lay on the bottom, not phased at all by what was going on. With all their force and several attempts, the cage finally broke loose and Raoul was free--kind of. Sydona held the cage up to her face, so her eyes were level with Raoul. "I'm gonna get you out of there… don't you give up."

As the group got ready to leave the room and look for the key, a familiar face appeared in the doorway. Blood splattered his face and tattered white shirt.

"I knew you were part of this..." said Harold, who only seemed to notice Willow in the back of the group.

"Well ain't this nice." Willow spat on the wood floor. "I'll catch up with y'all."

"You gonna be okay?" Sydona asked as her eyes turned green and fists curled up.

"Yeah. You go on ahead," Willow said, keeping her eyes on Harold.

They shuffled past him, and Silas snarled on his way out. Sydona cradled the cage underneath her arm and led the group back downstairs.

"I also found this in his office." Giovonna stopped Sydona and handed her the dagger she always used to have with her. She smiled in gratitude and then a light went off in her head.

"I need to find my parents." She sprinted out of the cabin and into the battle happening out front. Knowing her parents were involved in such a brutal scene made her insides twist like a wet rag. Red and blue lights caught her eye at the entrance of the park. This war was far from over. Dr. Malik needed to be found and killed for what he did. His death might not stop the battle, but it could put an end to the war. Her head swirled with who she needed to deal with first: getting Raoul out and safe, finding her parents, or killing the doctor. They all seemed equally important to her, but she was only one woman. As she planned on what do next, she noticed she was alone. Both Silas and Giovonna were pulled into battle and fighting off guards.

She took a few steps toward her friends but was suddenly knocked to the ground. Raoul's cage went flying so far away from her that she couldn't tell where he landed. She only got one good look at her attacker's face; it was the woman who ran the flying tests a few days before. She had a bloody face and tangled hair that wrapped around her raging eyes. Sydona could only worry about Raoul even as the woman pummeled her like dough.

Just as she began to process everything, a gun shot rang out and the woman's blood splattered onto her scrubs. The guard rolled off of her as she looked toward her rescuer.

"Mom?" she said with disbelief.

"Sydona! Come on!" Evelyn shouted and ran toward her to help her up.

"Mom!" Sydona looked back at the woman. "You-- killed her."

"Yep. And saved your life, too, if you didn't notice." She grinned and began to run behind the cabin, out of the chaos.

She took a second to search for the cage but didn't spot anything resembling it. Being out in the open was too dangerous, so she followed her mom. Sydona was flabbergasted to see her mother out in the middle of everything and fighting. The familiar spark in her mother's eyes was back; the one she longed to see again. They took a moment to breathe in the shadows of the cabin.

"You saw my note," Sydona said, unable to take her eyes off this newfound spirit.

"I did. And you were right. I did give up. We both did… and I'm so sorry, sweetie," confessed Evelyn, and she gave Sydona a tight hug.

The hug was filled with more love than she felt since she first saw her mother again. She was back. It was like an evil curse had been broken. Evelyn was going to help put a stop to this and kill the doctor. She then wondered about her father and what he was doing in the mess. If he was okay.

"Where's dad?" she asked.

"Your father is fine. He agreed to stay back in case you went looking for us in the tent. He's armored." Evelyn winked.

Words were hard to form because Sydona's cheeks felt sore from smiling. "It's so good to see you again. Oh and look--"

Sydona pulled out her dagger with the inscriptions still as fresh as the day she got it.

"Oh my. You still have this?" Evelyn asked with tears forming.

"Of course I do. This is why I came out here. This blade, this motto--gave me hope."

Evelyn wrapped her soft hand around Sydona's. The connection Sydona felt with her mother in that exact moment was more genuine than any she had encountered so far. It was a moment that Sydona consciously told herself to burn into her memory so that she would never forgot the feeling.

Sydona wiped a tear from Evelyn's red cheeked, wrinkled face. "We should go. I need to find Raoul. He was knocked out of my arms."

The women headed out of the shadows and back into the chaos to look for Raoul. Just then, Giovonna ran in front of them with Raoul safe and sound in the cage.

"Oh, thank god." Sydona smiled with relief.

"Let's go to our tent, number 5. Ian will be waiting in there. Just make sure to say the secret password in order to get in. Otherwise, he'll shoot you," Evelyn stated calmly while Sydona and Giovonna exchanged worried looks.

"It's tater tots." Her mother smirked, making Sydona and Giovonna laugh.

Another gunshot rang out but much closer than the ones she had been hearing for the last hour. It was too close to home. As Sydona turned to her mother, Evelyn was already on her knees, and her scrubs were soaked in crimson. A second shot hit her, throwing her to the ground, and she cried out in pain.

Sydona trembled helplessly as she watched her mother writhe in pain. She knew she had to kill the shooter before they killed her, too. Sydona picked up her mother's pistol and aimed it right back at the assailant before he could do more harm. But killing him did no good in reversing the damage he already inflicted.

"No. No no no no..." Sydona cried, letting out a deluge of tears.

Evelyn was in such shock from the pain and blood loss that she was unable to form words. Sydona took her mother's hands as they slowly lost color and warmth. Soon, Giovonna ran over with Raoul to find out what happened.

"Oh my god!" Giovonna cried as she saw the blood soaking the grass.

Sydona's hands and body shook uncontrollably, as her heart beat against her rib cage.

"Mom. Please. Don't leave me!" Sydona said as she pushed her mother's hair back from her eyes.

Evelyn used all of her strength to look her daughter in the eye and open her mouth.

"Fight--Love. Without--fear. My sweet--baby... Girl…" Evelyn gasped her last breath as her body laid to rest.

"No! No! Mom! Wait--you--you can't do this to me! Please!" Sydona screamed.

Giovonna grabbed Sydona's shoulder, yelling at her to move. But her words were muted and slow. The battle happening around her didn't seem real anymore. It was as if she was watching an old movie filled with guns, fire, and death. The seriousness of what she caused weighed heavy on her shoulders. Sydona wiggled her way out of Giovonna's grip and went back to her mother. There was no way she could leave her there alone. Sydona scooped her up with both arms to take her back to her parents tent. The girls dodged and weaved through the battle as bullets and people whizzed by them. The tent wasn't far, and when they finally arrived, Giovonna yelled the password. Ian responded, letting them know it was safe to enter.

The look on her father's face as Sydona entered the tent was too much for her to watch. His smile faded as he saw his lifeless wife's body in his daughter's arms. Ian threw his shotgun onto the cot and grabbed Evelyn's hand.

"Evey?" Ian blubbered. His eyes turned bloodshot red, and he almost fainted from the sight.

Sydona's heart was in her throat as she placed her mother down softly on the empty cot. Her father embraced her tightly, and his muffled cries soaked into her clothes. Giovonna placed Raoul's cage down with him facing the other way in case he woke up.

"I'm so sorry, Syd," Giovonna said. She hugged both Sydona and Ian tightly as they cried together.

Sydona squeezed her eyes tightly to clear them of tears, but every time she closed them too long, a vision of her mother dying flashed in the darkness. Opening her eyes, she took a long deep breath and pulled away from them.

"Borba i amor bez strah. Fight and love without fear," Sydona said calmly. "Stay here. I'm ending this. Now."

Sydona gave her dad a peck on his sweaty forehead, squeezed Giovonna's arm, and nodded. "Take care of them, please. I'm counting on you." She smiled, making Giovonna lift her chin with confidence.

As she left the tent, she lost her composure for a split second and broke down crying. Why did this have to happen now? In the middle of everything? Why her mother? What did she do to deserve this? These questions would never be answered. After everything Sydona did to find her again, she was gone within mere seconds.

Wiping her face of tears, she stood up and took big strides back to the cabin to look for the doctor. Doing her best to avoid anyone, she slumped around in the shadows and kept an eye out for guards. She took the gun her mother used and kept it close to her chest. As she peered around the corner of the cabin, she felt a tapping on her shoulder that made her jump. She spun around with gun aimed at the last person she expected. Silas held his hands up in surrender. His hair was messier than usual, and he suffered a few scratches on his face.

"Hey. You okay?" he asked.

"Scared the crap out of me!" Sydona flared.

"Sorry. Where are you headed?" he asked while he helped her keep a lookout.

"To stop this. I can't have anyone else die," Sydona said.

"Who died?"

Sydona couldn't bring herself to say it. "Doesn't matter. I'm going after Malik. He's not getting away with this. Not while I'm still breathing."

"Want me to back you up?" Silas asked with concern.

"No. Help Giovonna and my father look for Raoul's key. They are in tent five. I have to do this alone."

Sydona looked both ways to catch an opening and take off running. Just before she took a step, Silas grabbed her hand to stop her. Sydona turned around to face him. He guided her hand up to his lips and kissed it softly.

"Please be careful."

Sydona quickly smirked, and Silas let her go. She sprinted off into shadows of the forest.

Chapter Nineteen

Even though the sun was low and beaming brightly, the sky became darker by the minute and made it difficult to see anything. Soon the stars would be out and sky black; she needed to hurry. Staying low and in the shadows, Sydona did her best to listen to any kind of movement. The forest was eerily quiet in the wake of battle; not even the birds sang. She stepped lightly on the forest floor, avoiding branches and dead leaves. Occasionally, she heard a rustle, and then some creature would take off running. But the sound was so small she assumed it was a squirrel or a rabbit. Her dagger was out, and she kept her eyes opened wide.

She heard a new noise, and she listened eagerly as something big grew closer and closer. Unable to place the sound, she headed back toward the edges of the forest to search for it. Wind came from nowhere, in all directions, and rapidly like a tornado. She then noticed someone about half a mile from her running out of the woods toward a helicopter that hovered just beyond the tree line. Her heart leaped, and she sprinted after him. The dagger was infused to her hand, and her pulse pumped so hard that she could feel every muscle in her body move as she ran. Revenge made her move faster than ever, maybe even faster than when she flew.

As she gained on the coward, she noticed a rope ladder being rolled down in order for him to jump. Before he could make it to the ladder, she tackled the doctor to the ground like a linebacker and turned him around to face her. She pressed the dagger tightly against his hairy, sweaty neck, drawing a sliver of blood. Her blonde hair whipped around in the wind from the helicopter blades as Dr. Malik burst out into laughter. He lay limp on the ground as she straddled him, but she didn't need to use much force because it felt as if he had given up.

"I had so much hope for you, Miss Wilder," he managed to say between laughs.

Sydona's eyebrows furrowed in confusion at his reaction and his words.

"What do you mean?" She bared her teeth.

He laughed again like Sydona wasn't getting the obvious joke. Itching to wipe the grin off his face, she punched him in the jaw, turning his teeth red as he laughed again.

"I didn't need anyone else. I mean--it's important to have them here, too, but you're the only one I really needed." He gazed into her eyes inquisitively.

A man from the helicopter kept shouting the doctor's name, but he ignored it. As Sydona glanced up to the helicopter, she noticed a man standing in the door holding a large gun. She pressed the knife closer to Dr. Malik, making it obvious she had his life in her hands.

She knew she would regret asking, but her curiosity was overbearing and nagging. "Why me?"

He coughed through his bellowing. "You don't know, do you?"

"Know--what?!" Sydona cut his arm, forcing the doctor to cry out in pain.

"Your parents never told you?" he asked more seriously.

"What do my parents have to do with anything?" she yelled, getting fed up with him beating around the bush.

"You're part human, Miss Wilder. You're the first one of your species I've come across that was only half, but you hold all the same abilities as a full fledged flier. You hold the key to so many possibilities..." He grinned as he looked even deeper into her eyes. "And your eyes... changing from green to blue... proves that your parents were right."

A pitter patter from her heart rang in her ears.

"You're lying!" Sydona cried out and raised her arms up with knife in hand, ready to stab him in the chest.

Suddenly, a loud gun pop came from the helicopter, and Sydona went flying backwards, off of Dr. Malik. As she grasped her burning and bloodied shoulder, she glanced up to see the doctor find his feet and take off running to the ladder.

It wasn't so much the gunshot wound that hindered her from getting up but the breaking news he told her. It was impossible. He had to be lying; she *knew* he was lying just to distract her. In the crucial seconds that she used to process this, he made it out of reach and reached for the rope ladder hanging from the copter. Her adrenaline had never pumped so hard, causing her to rise to her feet and run after him again. Tufts of grass sparked from underneath her muddied tennis shoes, and she gripped her blade tightly, thirsty for blood.

Another bullet buzzed past her as she ducked sideways; then, another almost hit her foot. She could hear Dr. Malik shouting at the gunman to ceasefire while waving his arms, and the bullets stopped. Finally jumping to the rope, Dr. Malik began to climb, but Sydona caught up and grabbed a hold of his slippery, black shoe. With the blade in her right hand, Sydona took the opportunity to kill him once and for all. His upper thigh was as high as she could reach, and she sliced his leg. And as he bent down to grab it, she impaled her knife into his side. Crying out in agony, the doctor lashed out and kicked Sydona in the face, causing her to fall twenty feet back down to earth. As she fell, she gazed upon the bloodied man being pulled up by the gunman and holding his ribs. The doctor was safe and flew away from Eagle Lake.

The ferocious tumble made her gunshot wound intensify by a hundred. Still, she rolled onto her back to watch the helicopter fade farther and farther from sight. Her entire body ached from the fall, and shooting pains creeped up her back, forcing her to arch her body like a cat. The ground was not forgiving to her bones, and she swore something broke. Maybe it was just the feeling of all her body parts bruising at the same time. Whatever pain she was experiencing, the thought of what Dr. Malik said was all she could focus on. The last words he uttered lingered in her mind as she laid frozen on the grass. The blue showing through her natural eye color must have had something to do with her being part human. But why would it just now be appearing that way? Sydona wished she could see a mirror to see how much the blue showed through. Did the extreme torture of electrocuting her somehow change her biologically?

Doing her best to roll over and get up, she felt a hard metal piece in the grass. It was a small silver key, possibly for Raoul's cage. She assumed it fell out of the doctor's pocket when he ran. Suddenly, she heard her name being carried through the wind by a woman.

"Syd! Heavens woman, you okay?!" Willow asked as she finally reached her and kneeled down next to her.

"Look." Sydona flashed the key at Willow.

Willow nodded, helped Sydona off the ground, and asked again, "You gonna make it?"

"I'll be fine--" Sydona grunted.

"You get shot?" Willow asked.

"No big deal." Sydona put her good arm around Willow and changed the subject. "What about Harold?"

Willow smirked. "Don't worry 'bout him. Did ya kill Malik?"

Sydona paused, trying to figure out if she should lie and say she did, so everyone could rest easily. Or say that she did her best and hope for the best. It suddenly felt simple to answer.

"He's dead."

"Good riddance," Willow said.

They finally made it to the camp, and Sydona felt relieved. The fall made her entire body feel like a bruise, especially her back and tailbone. The walk was excruciating, but she couldn't vocalize her pain to Willow. Besides, there were pressing matters to deal with other than her wounds. Sparrows walked around the camp, checking the bodies on the ground. The bodies of dead fliers in blue uniforms covered most of the grounds. The ones still breathing were rushed inside the cabin by several able Sparrows. Sydona looked over the horrific scene, and the first person she recognized was Maverick, lying face down next to a woman Sparrow. She looked more closely at a tattoo on the woman's arm. It read 'J.V' making Sydona's heart ache and eyes turn brown. Sydona guessed the initials stood for 'Joelle Vandermead", Maverick's daughter. A smile then creased her face as she thought of Maverick finally seeing his little girl after years of her status being unknown.

"*Amor bez strah...*" Sydona whispered to herself. "*...love without fear.*"

"What's that?" Willow asked.

"Nothing..." Sydona answered. "Are we close to Raoul?"

"Oh, I dunno. Hey, Oscar! Come help me with her!" Willow shouted, making Sydona flinch.

From across the way, Oscar ran over to the women, and Willow transferred Sydona over to him. As he walked her up to the cabin, Giovonna, Silas, and Ian interrupted. The sight of her father made her feel uneasy. He looked completely drained and stared off into nothingness. It wasn't until he saw Sydona's face that he brightened up a little. The news of her being part human trickled its way into her mind. She wasn't sure how to feel, yet. She was still devastated over her mother but had many questions she wanted to ask about who she really was. It was hard to assess when a good time would be to ask her father anything.

"Syd! Are you okay?!" Giovonna asked frantically, touching Sydona's face and wiping off sweat, blood, and mud.

All she could do was nod in assurance. "I need to see Raoul," she said as she noticed Silas carrying the cage. She caught Silas's eye as she reached for it, and he gave her a worried look. Looking away from his gaze, she took the key out of her pocket and opened the door.

Raoul slowly stepped on the metal bar where the door once held him back and took a deep breath.

"You alright?" Sydona asked.

"Don't worry about me. Are you?" Raoul asked softly.

"I've been better." She smiled slightly.

"What about the doctor?"

Sydona hesitated and noticed everyone looking at her, even random fliers who had gathered around.

"Killed him!" Willow announced proudly to the surrounding onlookers.

The crowd cheered loudly, hugged, and high-fived each other. But all Sydona could do was try to swallow the rock in her throat.

"Come on, let's get you patched up, killer," Silas gently brushed hair out of her face.

Oscar helped her onto a bed in the same room she arrived in when she first got to the camp but with a much different atmosphere. The room looked somewhat intact, although there was another table with a Sparrow lying on it as a couple of others helped her. From what Sydona heard, she had a gunshot wound on her leg and was bleeding out quickly. Oscar and another woman began to work on Sydona, starting with cleaning her face and wounds. Then, they moved on to examining the gunshot wound in her shoulder. She was lucky enough to have the bullet go all the way through, but she needed a sling and was told she could not use her arm for a while. Oscar gave her strong pain pills to help her relax and sleep off the pain.

Silas found a few extra blankets, laid them on top of her, and gave her another pillow to elevate her back. Everyone eventually left the room to let her rest, except for Raoul. The Sparrow next to her was fast asleep while Raoul ate like he hadn't eaten in months. As she lay there watching him engorge himself, she felt like she was in her own bed again. She even swore she could look out the window to her right and see her backyard. But then again, maybe it was the pain pills.

"Feeling better?" she asked once Raoul slowed down.

He gulped a bite of apple. "Yeah, a million dollars better."

Sydona stared at him, glad to see him be himself again. Even though his wings were torn and his hair was a mess, which she dared not say anything about, she was happy he was still alive.

"What did he do to you?" Sydona asked in barely a whisper.

Raoul paused. "I don't wanna talk about it."

Sydona lay still, noticing the trauma plastered to his face. "'kay--" She hesitated. "I'm so sorry for what happened."

"It's really fine," Raoul answered shortly.

"It's not, though. I was being stupid and selfish," Sydona argued.

"Syd. It's done. Leave it alone," Raoul said.

A knife felt like it had been stabbed through her chest. No amount of pain pills could help the guilt. There was nothing she could do to turn back time and change the outcome. But imagining what he went through ate at her like a piranha. She understood how he felt, but she still wanted him to open up just a tad.

"Raoul--" Sydona started, and then, a soft knock rattled the door.

"Hey." Willow entered without an answer. "I wanted to give ya an update on what's happenin' from here on out. If you wanna know."

Sydona sighed as she looked at Raoul who still stared off with his arms tightly crossed. With no hope of getting him to talk, she answered Willow.

"Yeah, what's up?"

Willow pulled up a metal chair and placed it next to her bed. "'Kay, so first thing's first: gettin' these metal bracelets off y'all. Silas showed Giovonna the thing in the basement, and she thinks she can figure it out. Plus some of the Sparrows are good with that stuff, so we have a whole team workin' on gettin' them removed. Once that's done, I'll get in contact with a group on a private island that we just discovered a couple months ago, and we think it could be a fresh start for a lot of you.".

"An island?" Sydona asked.

"Yep. It's non-inhabited. Only wildlife and the sort. I think as long as you okay with bugs and not showerin', it's paradise," Willow laughed.

"So, you're asking us to go?" Sydona looked at Raoul who met her gaze.

"I think you'll be the safest there." Willow examined a clipboard she brought in with her.

"Safe?" Raoul interjected. "Safe from what? Dr. Malik is gone. There's nothing else to worry about."

The knife turned sideways in Sydona's body, and she closed her eyes in agony.

"Just 'cause he's gone, buddy, doesn't mean there ain't other threats out there. Until we know that they shuttin' the experiments down for good, y'all need to lay low," Willow said, trying to sooth his temper.

"But he was the leader... of the entire thing! Why would it still continue?" Raoul asked furiously.

"Raoul," Willow said calmly, "we don't have any details yet. They may replace him and get it up and runnin' with a new director. We can't be sure."

With that answer, Raoul huffed and flew clumsily out of the room with his torn wings.

Willow shook her head with a heavy sigh. "Poor fella…"

Sydona anxiously picked at her nails under the blankets, feeling overwhelmed with feelings and information. "Thanks, Willow. I'll think about it. But I wanna try to sleep for a bit first."

"Course. Rest up, princess." Willow grinned and left Sydona to herself.

As Willow closed the door, a million thoughts rushed through her head. She had the chance to start over on a new piece of land untouched by people, and she could finally live in peace and quiet. She could grow her own food, hunt if she ever ate meat again, and maybe even build her own home. These were all things she really enjoyed doing for the past forty years, but now it was more a form of survival, which intrigued her. She also thought about Raoul and wondered if he would ever be the same. When he ate, he sure seemed alright, but deep down, there was something seriously wrong, and she wondered if she would ever be able to help him. The guilt she felt about it grew stronger every minute.

Guilt was becoming the theme at Eagle Lake. She wondered if asking her father about her being part human would fill him with remorse. Humans were the one thing she hated most in the world; they took her parents, tortured her friend, and murdered her own mother. They were the one thing she ran and hid from her entire life, afraid they would hurt her or alienate her for being different.

A gentle knock at the door made her thoughts pause, and her father walked in with a slight smile. He couldn't fool Sydona, though; she knew what her mother's death meant to him. The strong emotions Sydona felt couldn't compare to the way her father felt. The one woman who stood by him for all those years slipped away from him.

"How ya feeling, baby?" Ian asked as he caressed her forehead.

"Can't complain." Sydona smiled, trying to lighten the mood.

"You did a brave thing, sweetie," said Ian. "Your mother would be proud."

Sydona smiled and changed the subject as her stomach twisted. "What's it looking like out there?"

Ian shook his head. "It's a graveyard... But good thing is, we won. No one died in vain."

This made Sydona want to curl up and shrivel away, but she could only nod her head.

"Everything okay?" Ian asked, confused.

Nothing was okay. Nothing. Her mother was gone, never to be seen again. A part of her was human, and she wasn't sure why she heard it from Malik and not her own parents. And he could come back. He might still be alive. The curiosity was too much to handle, and she had to know before anymore precious time passed.

"Am I part human?"

Ian stared at her, wide eyed. She could hear him gulp, and he took a step back.

"I am. This--this is--I can't..."

All of Sydona's breath escaped her at once.

"Syd, I can explain..." Ian said as he took her hand.

She turned her head away from him, ashamed to even look at him.

Her father let go of her hand and pulled up a chair to sit beside her. She heard a deep sigh echo through the room.

"Dad. You don't have--"

"No, it's alright. You deserve an explanation," Ian began and cleared his throat. "Back before you were born, your--mother--and I were friends with a man named Carter. She and Carter fell in love--even though he was a human. And, long story short, she got pregnant--with you. But not long after she found out, Carter was diagnosed with cancer and passed away only a few months later. Not being able to leave your mother alone with a baby, I wanted to help her raise you. We ended up--falling in love a few years later--and got married."

His voice faded off, and Sydona noticed tears running down his worn, sunken skin. She took his hand, and he happily grabbed it back, trembling slightly. The room went silent. Sydona found it hard to make him continue, but she was still unsure how the doctor knew.

She asked him softly, "How did Malik find out about me, then?"

Once Ian let out enough tears, he was ready to talk again.

"Your--mother… She, uh, spoke up. The doctor just went crazy one day. All of his results were coming up inconclusive, and he was unable to make any headway for months, and then he threatened to kill us. Everyone. Even lined us all up on our knees with guns pointed at our heads because we were of no more use to him. A waste of his time, a waste of space. He said he couldn't let us all go because we would go after him in his sleep. And so he tried killing us.

They were about to kill a little boy that was next to her--and that was when she told him. She told them she had a daughter and that she had a human father but could fly like a flier. This gave him hope and stopped the mass killing. But it caused us to move to a bigger area and advertise in order to bring in more fliers. She told him we hadn't seen you in forty years, so we weren't sure where you were… She did tell him you had blonde hair, but that was all. We never thought he would be able to find you. We were just praying that you were in another country--that you left this place…"

Sydona sat wide eyed in disbelief. "What would have happened if I never came on my own?"

"We tried not to think about that." Ian shook his head.

As Sydona lay in bed, trying to understand everything, she couldn't help but think of how difficult it must have been for her mother to tell the doctor about her only daughter. To risk speaking up to someone holding a gun to her head, unsure of whether or not he would use it. She severely underestimated the bravery her mother and father both had. They just stored it down deep so that they wouldn't draw anymore attention from the doctor than they already did. They stayed quiet and stopped taking risks to stay alive.

Her father stood up and looked down at Sydona. "I want to have a funeral for Evey."

Sydona smiled. "That sounds nice, daddy."

Ian took a deep breath and smiled at Sydona before he walked out of her room.

"Hey dad?" Sydona blurted before he shut the door. "By chance, do you know if Carter had blue eyes?"

"Ah… yes, I believe he did. Why?" Ian answered.

"Just curious…" She gave a quick smile.

After her father left the room, no one came in for several hours, and Sydona fell asleep.

The next day, Sydona heard about the funeral service planned for the afternoon. Willow, Giovonna, Raoul, and even Silas were helping to set it up. She felt so helpless lying in bed with a sling and nothing to do but wait for people to give her updates. The thin mattress felt like a cloud, though, so she didn't mind too much.

Finally, Raoul came buzzing through the open door to her hospital room and told her it was time. As she tried to move her body, she felt every muscle in her legs, arms, and torso.

"Can you do your--thing, please?" Sydona grunted.

Raoul laughed and dusted Sydona with his fairy dust, making her feel light as air. She still felt her muscles ache, but it wasn't nearly as bad.

"How does she look?" Sydona asked as she shuffled slowly out of her room.

"Peaceful," Raoul said and landed on Sydona's shoulder. He dusted her every minute or so as she walked down the long hallway to the outdoors.

"Are you feeling better?" asked Sydona.

"I am. Are you?" Raoul asked in return.

"Yep," she grunted. "I'm glad you stayed with me, Raoul. You're my best friend, and I don't know where I'd be right now if you weren't here. And I'm sorry again, for everything I put you through… I don't deserve you."

Raoul chuckled. "Thanks, Syd. Where's this all coming from?"

"Don't laugh. I'm being serious," Sydona said.

"...You're my best friend, too," Raoul agreed with a quiet voice.

The sunlight burst into her eyes, illuminating the park ahead. The grounds were covered in white sheets where the fallen lay. As Sydona made her way down the stairs grudgingly, she noticed some sheets had yellow daisies on top. She assumed they were meant for the fliers more than the guards, and it was a nice gesture. Over to her right stood a huge gathering of people. Almost all of the survivors surrounded a single person, Evelyn Wilder.

The crowd began to part like a sea, and she was the trident. In the middle stood her friends and family: Willow, Giovonna, Silas, and her father, Ian. They were all waiting for her. Giovonna was the first to hug her, then her father, then Silas. Willow stood resilient but then gave in and squeezed her like a teddy bear. The site looked gorgeous with red and white flowers blanketing the space around her mother, including a bouquet someone placed in her hands. Evelyn looked different than Sydona remembered. She looked like an angel beneath the white sheet. The blood had been washed away and she had absolutely no imperfections. Evelyn's hair was combed and feather-like as it spread over the pillow her head rested on.

No one could hold back their tears. It warmed Sydona's heart to know how truly loved her mother was and how much she would be missed. Silas gripped Sydona's free hand while Ian put his arm around her waist. As everyone gathered closely around Evelyn, Raoul began to dust her from head to toe while fliers sang a tribal song known by fliers and fairies alike. The dust would help Evelyn's body adjust to the afterlife and keep away the bad spirits that may sway her. A couple of people standing near her head pulled the sheet up over Evelyn's face, and the dusting was completed.

Sydona held her friends and father close as she said her final goodbyes. As she finished, she looked up toward the sky to see a single finch singing a happy song. Her blue eyes followed him as he flew around the group, and she hoped that somehow it was her mother watching over her.

The End of Book One

More about the Author

Laura Mae is a Tucson, Arizona resident and lives with her sister, who helps take care of her four pets. This is Laura's debut novel and has been in the making for 8 years. Writing will always be a passion of hers, but she also loves to hike, play video games and drink the occasional bottle of wine.

If you are interested in following her, she is on Twitter, Facebook, Instagram, and of course her website at www.lauramaeauthor.com. Her website also includes fun interviews of the main characters in this book!

And of course, thank YOU for reading and I hope you enjoyed reading this as much as I enjoyed writing it. A great way to help me is to review *Fliers* on Amazon or Goodreads and share with everyone how much you loved it!

Thank you for supporting indie authors!

Coming Soon in 2019!

9 781645 162230